W9-BMZ-377

A CLASH OF
INNOCENTS

SUE GUINEY

Ward Wood Publishing
www.wardwoodpublishing.co.uk

Published by Ward Wood Publishing
6 The Drive
Golders Green
London NW11 9SR
www.wardwoodpublishing.co.uk

'An everywhere of fields,spattered with animals,pricked with beings' is reprinted from EIMI by E.E. Cummings, by permission of W.W. Norton & Company. Copyright © 1933, 1961 by the E.E. Cummings Trust. Copyright © 2007 by Liveright Publishing Corporation

British Library Cataloguing in Publication Data. A CIP record for this book can be obtained from the British Library

Designed and typeset in Garamond by Ward Wood Publishing. Cover design by Mike Fortune-Wood from an original photograph courtesy of Elizabeth Lowey. Printed and bound in Great Britain by MPG Biddles Ltd, King's Lynn, Norfolk.

To my mother and father, Marcia and Bill
To my sisters, Linda and Karen

An everywhere of fields, spattered with animals, pricked with beings.

EIMI, E.E. Cummings

FEBRUARY

Welcome to Cambodia! We are so glad you are here to learn about our glorious past and experience our remarkable culture. Come see the beauty of our traditional dancers. The comfortable temperature of February is a pleasant time to visit our many temples and our modern capital city. Please let our happy Khmer smiles be your guide.
Cambodia From Us to You: A Touristic Handbook, p. 8

You live here long enough and you stop taking things for granted. Where I grew up, in suburban Ohio, I could assume one day led to another, one season to the next: you reap in autumn what you sow in spring. People were who they said they were, generally speaking, and if they weren't you could pretty much avoid them and surround yourself instead with people you could trust.

But in Cambodia, you can't trust anything or anyone. The rice you plant in May won't necessarily be there in November to harvest. And if it is, it won't necessarily be yours. A child who's been put to bed by the caring hands of his mother might never feel that touch again. Actually, it's not so much that you don't know who to trust, it's more that you don't know what the word trust means. But after all these years in Phnom Penh, I had gotten kind of used to that. Trust. Friend. Murder. Victim. All ideas more like science fiction shape-shifters than real words. You think you have a hold of them, then suddenly they change. It makes for an interesting and challenging life, I'll tell you that. And after so much time, I can't really imagine myself living anywhere else.

I suppose the Phnom Penh of 2007 is about as far removed from the Ohio of my youth as anything can be. America of the 1950s and '60s was a place where everything looked simple and happy on the outside, a make-believe land where every child had two parents, home-cooked meals and a black-and-white TV set. The houses in our town were large and clean with small, well-tended lawns, a car and a few bicycles in the garage. It was normal, nice. The only special thing about our town was that the local university where our best and brightest went was just down the road. You could see its chapel spire from the cemetery where my reckless brother used to drink on Saturday nights. For most of my life, we were proud to be the town just down the highway from such an important centre of higher learning. But of course all that changed when our idyllic Kent State became synonymous with anti-war protests and the murdering of innocent students. Living in the shadow of a place notorious enough to have a Vietnam protest song written about it became too much, for me at least. But what does that have to do with this new Cambodia I was now living in at the start of a new century? Nothing. Everything.

Cambodia is not supposed to be cold in February. The nights might be a bit chilly, but by February you'd think you would start feeling the onslaught of those months of intense, dry heat where the only moisture in the air is the sweat that's pouring down the front of your blouse. But not this year. This year, February saw a cold snap like we had never even imagined. People on the streets were making socks out of plastic bags and towels. Old women walked around wearing every stitch of clothing they owned, one piece layered right on top of the other, and still complained about the cold. I thought it was great for a change. Fresh, crisp clean air. If it had just been me, I would have taken myself for long, bundled walks by the river. But, when you're in charge of a home full of forty orphans, it can never be just about you. Although the sudden cold air might have been good for my lungs, all the kids got sick. Every last one of them. At least seventeen had colds with streaming eyes, uncontrollable sneezing and coughing, chills and headaches. Another twelve actually had high fevers and flu. And the toddlers? Poop everywhere. I thought I would go out of my mind. Thank God for Sam. No matter how rotten she felt, she never stopped cleaning and feeding and warming and cooling and doing whatever else needed to be done. Between her resilient eighteen-year-old body and my stubborn sixty-year-old-lady's brain, we were somehow managing. But what an ordeal.

Keeping to a routine helped. My greatest weapon against the chaotic world around me has always been to set up strict rules, boundaries, timetables. The illusion of control is what I'm after and, although I know it is only an illusion, the myth saves me from being overwhelmed by the insanity that is often lurking just outside my door. My goal is to have each day start off the same. I'm already awake and dressed when I hear the alarm clocks ringing in the kids' bedrooms. Breakfast is boxes of cereal and bowls of fruit, a communal affair where the older kids help the younger ones who help the younger still. When it's time for school one of the older girls leads the way as I stand by the door, smiling, waving, giving hugs and pats on the back, watching them troop out the building 'in two straight lines'. Sometimes I feel like I've stepped into some Khmer version of that guy Bemelmans' book *Madeline*. Next I do a quick check on the smallest ones, the helpers, the cleaners, all the people who have come together over the past ten years to make this Home into a home. Then, and only then, do I sneak off to the room in the back that I call my office for the most important morning ritual of all, namely my ciggie and cup o' joe, as they say. Of course, I know not to smoke. I'm a trained nurse, after all. And I pretend that I can do without it. But God help those around me if I don't get it. Caffeine and nicotine. The revving up and calming down that begins with store-bought chemicals but which becomes a part of your own built-in chemistry, as much a part of you as the oxygen in your lungs and the blood in your veins. Addictions, to be sure. Yet in my world it's almost medicinal. I decided a long time ago that when you live amidst so much poverty and sickness of heart, when everyone you love has a story more horrific than any normal civilized person could ever imagine, then you have to allow yourself one sweet indulgence. In Phnom Penh, if that indulgence is a single measly cigarette a day, then you're nearly a saint.

There was one day that February, though, when nothing went to plan. The weekly job roster showed that it was Nary's turn to lead the kids to school. And although it's only a ten minute walk, my little Nary – so much the small bird that her name describes – was just too sick to go.

'Sam. Samnang?' I called out. 'Line up the ones who are healthy enough for school, will you please? I'll have to take them today.'

'Okay. But I think there are only twelve of them. Sothy's cough is still bad, though he looks happy.'

I had to laugh. Six-year-old Sothy looks happy, she had said. Of course he looks happy. The whole country looks happy, if you don't look too closely. So much is hidden behind those famous Khmer smiles, though. Even the gentle grin of my adopted daughter, Sam. I know all too well what her smile hides. Samnang's her full name and it means luck. It's a common name for a Cambodian child, but for me it couldn't possibly be any truer. Sam really has been my most precious piece of luck from the start.

'Yes, I'm sure he's happy enough,' I agreed, reaching up to give her a morning hug. She's now nearly taller than I am, though she's barely a third my size. But that's my fault. Too much sticky rice. 'Okay. We'll keep Sothy home, too. He can be your helper today. I'll be back soon.'

10

'Dress warm, Mother. It is so cold.' Sam handed me a sweater, a coat and a scarf and stood guard until she saw me put them all on.

'Jesus, Sam. It's not like it's snowing out there.' Snow— that was something I hadn't seen in a very long time. Sam had never seen it. When I opened the door and felt that cold air on my face, I swear I could almost taste that clean sweetness of newly formed snowflake melting on my tongue. 'Okay, kids. Let's go,' I said turning towards the little troupe of intrepid souls amassing behind me. Each one looked at me as if I were about to lead them on a trek through the Himalayas. I made sure everyone's coat was buttoned and each had some sort of hat on his or her head. It was quite a sight. There were two Red Sox baseball caps left over from a shipment of clothes donated by a Catholic school in Boston. Srey, our sixteen-year-old fashionista, wore a pink-and-purple-striped wool beanie she had dug up from who-knows-where. The ever-practical Thom had simply wound his red-and-white-checked *krama* around his head as if he were going out for a day of working in the fields. 'Kiri, where's your hat?' He looked at me with determination, eight-year-old eyes opened so wide they seemed to add a foot to his skinny frame.

'I am not afraid of the cold,' he protested, glaring at me, challenging me, and I was in too much of a rush to argue. I love all my kids and I do love Kiri, but I have to say that of all of them he can be the biggest pain in my ass. Just then I couldn't help thinking, 'Fine, let him freeze. That'll teach him.'

So I grabbed his hand and off we all went into our version of the 'Arctic silence', which really meant a city street full of honking *motos*, blaring radios and the occasional gust of wintry air. It couldn't have been much colder than 40 degrees Fahrenheit. Admittedly, that's pretty cold for Cambodia, but to me as I headed down the road it

11

felt like one of my own childhood walks to school, when the leaves were just starting to turn and fall from the trees and a hint of my breath was made visible in the air. I felt strangely nostalgic for home, for America, and that's something which almost never happens to me. Even when the electricity goes out for days on end or the house floods in an especially bad rainy season, I rarely long for the country I left behind: that country that I still believe betrayed me nearly forty years ago.

I suppose that's what I was thinking as I walked back home after dropping off the kids and unmummifying each from their cold-weather gear, doling out hugs and kisses like spoonfuls of cough syrup. I certainly wasn't paying much attention to what was around me, and I now understand that that solitary act of inattention changed the course of the months to come. There's an insipid expression people used to say back in the '70s: 'Today is the first day of the rest of your life'. Well yes. I suppose. But more to the point, I think, is that it's possible to wake up on any given day – this one was a Tuesday – and find that your world has started to drift onto another orbit. It's bound to be subtle, barely even perceptible, but if you're aware you can sense it and know that your life is now, again, about to change. I do try to be that mindful. It's a Buddhist concept I've attempted to adopt from my adopted country. The acceptance of now and the understanding that everything passes in time, with time. But on that morning I was rushing home, back from the school drop to a house filled with flowing snot and echoing sneezes. So, mindful awareness? Not that day.

I was vaguely aware, though, of someone behind me; someone who was not a regular player in the street scene of my little corner of Phnom Penh. Not one of the mine victims. Not one of the massage girls. I could sense that she was a girl, a young woman, but she was nobody I had

12

ever seen before. Probably British, or maybe American, with an enormous backpack and a pair of flip-flops. 'Oh God, a tourist,' I thought. 'Not today. Not now. Don't ask me for directions to the Killing Fields.' As I reached my door I knew I'd have to turn and there she'd be. Maybe I could find her a *tuk tuk* and let him drive her to some more touristy part of town. What was she doing here, anyway?

'I'm sorry, but are you Deborah Young?' she blurted out. 'Is this the Home for Blessed Khmer Children?' She was fumbling with her backpack straps and pushing her black hair away from her eyes. She looked worried, and in her t-shirt and cut-off shorts, she was freezing, too.

'Deborah Youngman. Yes. And this is the Khmer Home for Blessed Children. And you are?'

'Oh. I'm so glad. I've been walking everywhere.' Relief poured off her like monsoon waters. She reached out her hand. 'My name's Amanda. I'm here to help.'

I looked her up and down, maybe even nodded my head, and said nothing. I certainly didn't shake the hand she was offering me. I immediately assumed some Western Embassy had sent her to me and I hate it when they do that, when they think they can just dump any old do-gooder on me without warning as if I run some bottomless hole of good will here. So I was not grateful for her sudden appearance, *deus ex machina*, into our little Petri dish of germs. I was not nice to her. I was too busy to be nice, to show her what to do, to think of some meaningful job for her. I know volunteers like her mean well but honestly, they're often more bother than they're worth. And besides, I know it's not good for the kids. You can't just come into a child's life, try to get attached, and then leave. It's not good for any kid and it's especially bad for mine. My kids have already had their hearts broken. I can't take the memory of that pain away from them, but I do my damnedest to make sure it doesn't all happen again. So I was angry, and no, I wasn't very nice to this Amanda, whoever she was. And besides, I now knew I'd never get away for that morning cigarette.

I motioned to a corner where she could drop her bag, and went off to check on the kids. I let her stand there and watch, ignored. There were so many noses to blow and foreheads to kiss that I nearly forgot about our uninvited guest. I was legitimately surprised when Sam came looking for me an hour later, only to find me sitting at my deck desperately trying to write some grant proposal or other. She peeked her head through the door and asked, 'Mother, who is that woman in the library?'

'In the library? Who? Oh, Jesus,' I muttered and hurried out the door. Four-year-old Arun was tagging behind, and I scooped him up onto my hip and together we all rushed down the stairs, around through the kitchen into a backroom that is now our library. A while ago, after years of amassing stacks of books in both Khmer and English, I asked some friends from Singapore to come and help me convert this old storage area. Now there are bookshelves, carpeting, small plastic chairs and tables, beanbag pillows. We all love it. Usually, it's quiet, peaceful and calm. As we approached the room that day, though, we heard a medley of sneezes, coughs and giggles. In the middle, surrounded by two of the older girls and three of the younger ones, was Amanda. She sat on a beanbag, a book in one hand, a child in the other, and was reading aloud. My impulse was to barge in, guns blazing, and pull her out of there and away from my kids. But they all looked so content. I tried to be quiet as I stood in the doorway and listened. Her back was turned toward me, and I could see the kids' faces. They all looked sleepy, happy. Soon Arun started to kick his legs. 'Down, Mama,' he cried and rushed off to be with the others. At that, Amanda turned around to see Sam and I standing in the doorway, staring, dumbfounded.

14

'Oh, I'm sorry,' she said, startled. 'But this little guy here saw me standing near the door and took me by the hand. I thought it might be a good idea to read to some of them, you know, keep them occupied? I could see how busy you were. So I just…But, hey, do they really all speak English?'

'No, not all of them. Not the youngest ones yet, but they all will by the time they're nine or ten,' I explained.

'Well, they all seem to like Babar. I hope you don't mind. It was always one of my favorites. Oh, and this one here was coughing so hard she threw up a little. We cleaned it up, right?' she said, turning towards Nary and smiling.

'Yes,' Nary said, smiling back. 'I am okay now, Mom.'

I reached out towards Nary who came over to me and, as usual, threw her arms around my waist. Her small hands came nowhere near meeting – one landed on my stomach, the other on my back. I held on tight. She's so fragile: I've always worried about her. 'Well, let's just get you some cough medicine anyway, shall we?' I said. 'And, well - Amanda is it? I guess you can carry on then. Thanks. If you need anything, one of the older girls can help you. Or me. Or Sam, here.' Sam was still standing in the doorway, smiling somewhat enigmatically.

'Mother, if A-man-da stays with them here for now, should I go help with lunch?'

'Sure. That makes sense. And Sothy? Where is he?'

'Here I am,' he said, popping out from behind a bookcase. 'I go help Sam now?'

'Yes. You go help Sam.'

And so, I had to admit, calm was restored to our house. Everyone was doing their job, taking care of themselves and each other, just as usual, despite the strange cold and this warm stranger.

Mid-morning the next day, I was walking past the front door, reading a newsletter from a local relief agency, when I

15

thought I heard a knock. I stopped and waited. Maybe whoever it was would go away. Then there it was again, only louder. I think if it had been a doorbell that had grabbed my attention I would have automatically responded. There's something about a knock, though. A knock is more personal, somehow, maybe even more dangerous. The postman rings the bell. But a knock usually comes from someone unknown, distant, either very timid or very threatening. So I didn't answer right away. I just stood there and waited until I heard a quiet, 'Hello? Anybody home?' It was Amanda, back again, neither timid nor aggressive, but worrying nonetheless.

'Oh Amanda. Hello.' I was surprised and I showed it.

'Hi. I said I'd be back and here I am. Can I come in? It's still pretty cold out here today. How're the kids? Any more go back to school? Where should I put my coat? Is here okay?' She was talking a blue streak and walked right in as if she owned the place. There was no stopping her energy, her seeming goodwill, her unnerving cheeriness. It took me a minute to react. I suppose the kids have trained me to act first, make amends later. Life happens too quickly around here to do otherwise, and besides, after sixty years on this earth I'm pretty confident about my first judgments. But Amanda had caught me off-guard, again, so by the time I reacted to this, her second coming, she was already back in the kitchen, cleaning up after breakfast. The kitchen was Nita's domain. For years she had been coming to us, frequently, sporadically. She was the one volunteer I allowed myself to depend on. But she spoke very little, and when she did it was almost never in English. Now suddenly there was this chirpy chatterbox whirling all around her. Poor woman, she didn't know what had hit her.

'Mother, was someone at the door?' Sam found me standing in the hallway like a bemused statue, lips slightly parted about to speak, palms facing heavenwards in bafflement.

'Amanda. She's back.'

'Good. She said she would return. Remember?'

'Sure, but people say a lot of things.'

'Yes, but it is helpful. And in good time. I have to go to class now.'

'Yes, of course you do. See you later.' But as I was giving her a goodbye kiss there was another knock, this time with an additional doorbell ring. 'What the hell?' I said, then Sam opened the door to let some new person in before she went out. She waited just long enough to make sure this new face, which belonged to an unknown older Khmer man, was nothing to worry about.

'Miss Deborah?' he asked, handing me a package. 'A box for you. From Kyle.'

'From Kyle? Oh, how nice,' Sam said, giving me a return kiss in the doorway. 'But I am sorry. I must go now. I am late.'

'Yes, of course. Go. Go. We're fine here.' I took hold of the box with one hand and waved goodbye with the other. As I turned to walk back down the hallway, Amanda was standing right beside me.

'The dishes are all done. That woman in there said I could go, so I thought I'd come see what else I can do.' She looked at the box and looked at me. 'Kyle? Who's Kyle?'

I still hadn't said a word to her other than that initial surprised hello, but I took her and the box back into the library where Sam had just left the remaining few kids still too sniffly to go to school. I found them scattered around the room, lying on beanbags, listlessly turning pages of books.

'Mother, what is the box?' asked Sothy between coughs. Soon all the kids, suddenly full of energy, were gathered around me and the mysterious carton. 'A gift for us?'

17

'Well, let's see,' I said. 'Could be. It's from Kyle.' Some of the kids started to clap.

'So who is this Kyle?' Amanda asked again.

'He is our friend,' explained Nary.

'He comes from...' Sothy was searching for the word as he pointed to the giant map taped to the wall. '...Australia!'

'But he lives here now. Not in Australia,' Nary explained. Then they were all talking: 'Yes, he helps people.' 'He *saves* people.' 'He is our friend.' 'He's funny.'

'Gee, how come you've all got so much energy now? I thought you guys were sick,' I said, putting on my big scolding mother voice. Nobody was fooled. Everyone was too busy tearing open the box and peering in. 'Look, here's a note,' I said. 'It reads, "Dear Everyone. Bundle up. It's cold outside. Love, Kyle." It's scarves and hats. Lots of them.' As if it was a costume box, the kids dove in and pulled everything out, dressing each other and themselves in a hodge-podge of knitted, crocheted, handmade and store-bought winter-wear.

'Wow, look at all this stuff. Where did he get it?' Amanda looked on in amazement.

'Where? Who knows where he gets the stuff he gets, how he does the stuff he does. He gets things done, that's all I know. Better not to ask.' I laughed. I was about to say, 'You'll see,' but I stopped myself and Amanda noticed.

'What?' she asked. 'What were you going to say?'

I just shook my head. Kyle Mackenzie was too big a topic to introduce to Amanda now. In my heart I probably would have preferred not introducing him at all. Everyone knew Kyle; everyone who needed to. As far as I was concerned you had to deserve to know him. To me he was that special. And I didn't yet know what this Amanda person did or didn't deserve. All I knew was that I didn't need anything from her. Over ten years a lot of people have walked through these doors. They come, they help, but they always leave. To rely on any one of them would be madness. I appreciate whatever help they give, and if they give money, even better. I don't allow myself to need anything from any of them, not even from Kyle. Gratitude without expectation. That's my motto. So I didn't say anything about who Kyle was, what he did or how he did it. Out of the blue he sends a box. A bunch of sick kids start to feel better. I'm grateful and that's enough.

As February slid towards March, Amanda slid herself into our routine. Every evening I shook her hand, thanked her and said goodbye as if we would never see her again. Then, the next morning, she'd be back just like the rest of us, doing whatever needed to be done. She was great with the kids, and she happily got her hands dirty, washing dishes, making beds, brushing teeth. I rarely asked her to do anything specific. I never gave her any responsibility. Nonetheless, after a couple of weeks, we got used to having her here. Sam went from saying 'If Amanda comes, maybe she can take the kids out to play' to 'When Amanda comes, I can help Thom with his homework'. *If* to *when*. A slippery slope.

Amanda gave me no reason not to trust her, but nonetheless, I didn't. I knew nothing about her and she offered no information. Any question I asked about her past was always answered, but in the shortest way possible. After two weeks, this is what I knew: she was American (I could tell by her accent she was probably from the northeast); she had been 'traveling' for 'a pretty long time'; she liked fried bananas. The rest I guessed at. She looked to me like she was in her late twenties. She must have been well-educated, because she always had a book with her and it was usually a novel by some old heavyweight – Kafka or Hardy – no trashy paperbacks for her. But here was the thing that made me most suspicious of all. She was once, but now no longer, married. Around the ring finger of her left hand was the fading shadow of a wedding band. I noticed it during a dance lesson a few weeks after she arrived.

I have always made sure that the kids have a weekly lesson in traditional Khmer dance, both the boys and girls. They love it. It's important, I think. Of course, they have to study English and math. Even more importantly, they need vocational training so they can make a living when they leave this place. But they also have to learn about their past. Their past, their long ago distant past, is glorious and beautiful and full of magic. And nothing, in my experience, brings that more to life than traditional Khmer dance. First of all, there's the beauty of the poses. Yes, poses rather than steps – almost like yoga poses. Slow, still, with legs bent just so. Arms held just so. Fingers, long and slender, trained over years to bend back over themselves, as if completing a circle out from the brain and back towards the heart. More like moving incarnations of temple sculptures, the dancers tell stories from Buddhist scripture of love and loss and sacrifice. The music – despite the worn-out tapes and the hand-me-down boom box – fills the room with ringing gongs, tinkling finger-cymbals, and the unmistakable nasal reediness of the *sralai*, the traditional Khmer oboe. I think I like the costumes most of all, though. At first I thought it was a silly expense to make the kids dress up in wrap-around trousers, gold embroidered silk tops and fringed belts. But the teacher insisted, and she was right. You take twenty street kids, strip them of their Western shorts and t-shirts and adorn them with silk and gold, and suddenly you have something completely new – seriousness of purpose and a proud link to an ancient shared past. Beautiful.

These lessons happen here every Thursday afternoon. They are the one unmovable fixture in our weekly schedule.

The smallest kids are always a bit frightened the first few times they have lessons with 'Madame.' She can seem very stern and serious. And besides, this isn't some sort of Eastern gym class. These dance lessons are not about exercise. The kids get plenty of that. No, these lessons are about discipline, stamina, poise and history. Each gesture must be correct. Each foot lifted at just the right angle, held for just the right amount of time, just as it has all been done for centuries. There's a reason why Madame seems so stern at first. Yet, over time, each of the kids learns to respect her, and then love her.

So, you can imagine what a jolt it was to the system when, after a couple of weeks sitting in a chair against the wall quietly watching, Amanda jumped up and said, 'Can I try?' Immediately, the kids started to giggle. I heard Madame clap her hands three times, ordering silence. I peeked my head into the room just in time to see her gesture to Amanda. 'Shoes off,' she said, trying to hide a smile. 'Now stand.'

I took Amanda's chair and sat by the door. Sam and I shot glances at each other as she corralled the kids off to the side. Madame pressed the play button on the boom box and started. Slowly, with firm hands, she placed each of Amanda's body parts exactly where she wanted them: right arm held up, crooked at the elbow; wrist bent back, fingers splayed as if in the act of divine bestowal; head tilted slightly to the left with eyes up to heaven. Amanda was smiling. 'No smiling, Lady. Serious face, like me.' That made the kids giggle even more. There was no way Amanda could suppress her smile, though she tried.

'Now, left leg up,' Madame insisted. 'More. Toes point to floor. Stay. Stay.' I watched the sweat form on Amanda's face. Although the ceiling fans were on, the room was still hot and the pose difficult. I know I would have dropped my leg in a minute. We all held our breath to see if she

21

would fall. But Amanda didn't fall. The determination behind her smile was intense, almost worrying. What was she trying to prove? And to whom?

'Very good,' Madame eventually said. 'And now, hop.' Amanda hopped. 'Again.' She hopped again. 'Hop and turn slowly, like the goddess turning to see what is behind.' And didn't you know but she did exactly what she was told to do. Shakily, but still strong, she hopped in a circle, on one foot, all around, ending up exactly where she started. Her arms rigid, her left leg raised, her smile, planted. When she reached her original position, Madame took her by the shoulders to support her weight. 'Good. Very good.' We all clapped as Amanda tumbled to the ground, laughing, exhausted, sweating but proud. 'Next week, more. Yes?' I heard Madame whisper.

'Yes. Next week more.'

I admit, I was impressed. I gave her back her chair and a glass of water while Madame then went on with her class.

'My legs are so shaky, I can't believe it,' Amanda whispered.

'I gotta hand it to you. That was something.'

'That was fun,' she said between sips and deep breaths. 'Thank you.'

She handed me back the cup, and that's when I first saw the shadow of her wedding band. She didn't notice me noticing it. She was too busy watching Samnang, Srey and three other teenage girls easily doing the moves she had just struggled so hard to accomplish. But when I gently patted her back and felt what could only be the hard, bumpy ridge of a long, deep scar behind her shoulder blade, she gave an unconscious, involuntary twitch.

Later that evening, long after dinner, I sat in my office reading the paper. The house was calm and quiet. The little ones were asleep. The older kids were doing homework or talking. Usually at that time of the day I go around from room to room checking up on everyone. Sometimes I help with homework (as long as it isn't math). Sometimes I get trapped into a game of checkers (which I usually win). But that night I was distracted, caught between thinking too much and trying not to think at all. The feel of that scar on Amanda's back still seemed to tingle in my hand. So, although I was trying to read the paper, mostly I was just staring at it. I couldn't bear to read the latest nonsense about the Khmer Rouge Tribunal, who refused to sit next to whom, whose bowl of rice was slightly bigger than the other's. I never used to read the newspaper or watch the television at all. It just always seemed wisest to keep my head down and be as non-political as possible, pasting a Khmer smile on my otherwise gruff exterior. That had worked fine for years. During the violence of the '97 demonstrations, I just shoved the kids into the house and shut the door. The 2003 elections, I did the same. I've come to realize that all my stubborn perseverance was made possible by one simple, though horrifying, fact. In Cambodia, there is no hope. It may sound horrible, but here in this tiny, useless, captivating country, the less hope you have, the better you can get on with living every day. And believe me, in a place like this *alive* is, in itself, an incredible accomplishment.

In a strange, perverted way, we all thrived in our state of hopelessness. We woke up each day expecting little and went to sleep each night happy to have gotten it. But, when the West decided to introduce us all to this new concept of justice, things began to change. The UN came to hold their Khmer Rouge Tribunals and, before I could stop it from happening, somewhere around January 2005, I began to feel bit by bit what I can only describe as a little shiver of hope: hope that we hadn't been forgotten, that right and goodness did exist, and that they would prevail for all of us.

23

It was a cruel joke and I should have known better. I couldn't stop myself, though, and now I read the English language papers every day. I formed opinions. I got excited. And everything, *everything*, looked different.

That evening, after Amanda's dance lesson, I just couldn't bear to read any of it. I was already agitated enough. Sam somehow sensed my mood – she always does – and soon she was sitting next to me as I pretended not to be worried. I remember trying to sound cheerful.

'Everyone's still talking about that "jungle woman",' I said laughing, pointing to an article I hadn't really read. 'Can you believe it? With all that's going on in the world, people are obsessed with this woman who walks out of the jungle and suddenly appears on her family's doorstep.'

'Yes, it is strange,' Sam agreed. 'Wasn't she lost for years and years, ever since she was a little girl? So long she even forgot how to speak, how to dress? Just imagine how her family feels.'

'I suppose. If it really is their daughter. Some people say the family's making it all up, just to get money. They say they're all getting free medical check-ups now.'

'Well, even so. She must be somebody.'

Before I could comment any more on this story that I didn't really care about, there was a knock on the door. In walked Amanda. 'Amanda, I'm sorry,' I said, startled. 'I thought you'd left for the day. You shouldn't stay so late.'

'I was just about to go. Can I come in?' She leaned against the doorway, but Sam jumped up and offered her the chair.

'Here, you sit,' Sam insisted. 'Are your legs still tired from the dance lesson?'

'Yes. I can't believe it. I think I'm pretty fit, but that was something else.'

'It is hard at first. You do get used to being still, the more you practice,' Sam explained. I studied her face as she spoke. It was untroubled and content. Clearly, she didn't share my agitation.

'Standing so still for so long and moving so slowly – I could probably run a marathon more easily!' Amanda said, laughing. 'But you. You make it look so simple. So graceful.'

At that Sam grew quiet and lowered her eyes to the floor. After all these years of being loved and valued, she still has difficulty accepting a compliment. They all do. Soon Amanda and Sam were chatting again and I found myself studying them. They were both friendly towards each other. Perhaps Amanda was a bit more outgoing, but that was to be expected. And, of course, she wasn't Khmer. But Samnang was definitely at ease as well. There were no raised antennae there, and there usually were with Sam. She had been skeptical about Amanda from the start. Maybe even more than I was. Now, just as I was becoming even more wary, Sam was becoming less so. It was all getting a little too comfortable, and I knew I had to do something. I started to speak, even before I knew what I wanted to say.

'Really, Amanda, you've been doing so much for us. You don't need to stay so late. You should go home,' I insisted.

'Oh, it's my pleasure. Really. And I am going now. Back to my little bed in the dorm of the Youth Hostel.'

'So that's where you're staying. I did wonder. You never said.'

'Oh, didn't I? Well, it's cheap and it's safe. But after a few weeks they want you to move on, make room for new people. You're really not supposed to stay longer than two weeks. They've let me, but I'm beginning to try their patience, I think.' Amanda gave an awkward laugh.

'Will you be leaving us then?' Straight out, Sam asked the question and I was sure I heard disappointment in her voice. Yes, Sam was disappointed at the thought of Amanda leaving. She had grown attached to this stranger, and now she was going to be left behind. Again. I could feel the blood rising in my cheeks. This was exactly why I didn't like these outsiders coming and staying so long. The hostel is right. If you're a traveler, then travel. Move on. Find somebody else's face to look back on in your holiday snapshots. Not ours. I took a deep breath and looked down at the newspaper pretending to read, but I couldn't stay quiet.

'Of course, you've been here quite a while. Longer than volunteers usually stay. And you've been a great help to us all …'

'I'm so glad to hear you say that,' Amanda interrupted. 'I wanted to help. I like helping. And I like it here. That's why I was wondering – could I borrow your newspaper? I mean, are there real estate ads in the back?'

'Real estate ads?' I asked.

'Yes, like apartments to rent. You see, I'd like to stay.'

'Stay? Here? In Phnom Penh?'

'Yes. Here. In Phnom Penh,' she said, clearly not understanding why I could be so incredulous.

'And do what?'

'Work here. With you. And Sam and Nita. Like I have been.'

Suddenly, I was on my feet, pacing around the floor, dodging boxes of files and bags of clothes. Now, I like to think of myself as pretty imperturbable. I've seen a lot in my sixty-odd years and not much surprises me anymore. But this did. This, I had never imagined, although looking back on it all now I can't really see why not. You feed a stray cat and it does tend to come back for more. I looked at Sam, and she looked as surprised as I felt. Soon she smiled and nodded, with eyes wide open as if to say 'Yes!' Now I started to act on instinct.

I went over to Sam and gave her a hug. 'Oh, look at the time,' I improvised. 'Sam, would you mind getting the girls

26

ready for bed?' She left silently, of course, and immediately, without any further meaningful glances or hopeful looks. I sat back down again, clutching the newspaper like a life preserver.

'You want to work here? How would that be possible?' I asked, sounding like some Embassy bureaucrat.

'Well, I thought I had been helping. Why couldn't I just continue? Is it a visa problem?'

'A visa problem? No. I hadn't even thought about that yet. But Amanda, I can't pay you. We have no extra money for staff.'

'Oh, that!' She now laughed, relieved. 'Money isn't a problem. You don't have to pay me.   I have money.'

'You do?'

'Sure.'

'Well, I know it's none of my business, but where does this money come from? How can you live without paid work? Phnom Penh isn't so cheap anymore. Not even for an American.'

'I have family money. Believe me, money's not a problem.' I was silent for a while and Amanda was getting worried. 'Deborah, is there something else?'

What could I say? How could I make an obviously wealthy young American woman understand that not everything is as easy as she seemed to think it was? She had money. She had the desire. What more was there? Well, there's a lot more, but how could I teach her that, right there in my office, in a two-minute conversation?

'Amanda, please listen to me. You're a very nice young woman. Don't think I'm being ungrateful for all you've done. Clearly, you like it here. And everyone here likes you. Even me. But you must understand the position I'm in, the responsibility I have. Amanda – who are you?'

Now she was standing and I was sitting. Her voice got quieter, and I think she was holding on to the back of the

27

chair to stop her hands from shaking. That only made me feel worse. I felt like a prosecutor. I sounded like one, too. Suddenly, she seemed less of a threat and more like the threatened. I don't know. I was still suspicious and protective of my own, but that damned maternal instinct in me was kindled somehow too, and I began to feel sorry for her.

Quietly, but firmly, she asked, 'What do you want to know?'

'How about your full name, for one?'

'Amanda Rosen.'

'And you grew up …'

'…in Boston. An only child. My parents are still there. My father is a banker.'

'And they know where you are? Of course, I realize that you're not a child, not some eighteen-year-old on a gap year, but still …'

'Yes, they know where I am. Actually, I saw them just before I came here.'

'They were in Cambodia?'

'No. In Thailand. At the Aman resort in Phuket.' That answer did make sense to me. I started to get a picture of who she might have been, if not who she actually was. But that wasn't enough.

'Ok,' I continued. 'Again, it's not that I want to pry. Your personal life is your own. I've got to be careful, though. For the sake of the children. You must understand that.'

'Of course.'

'Okay, then. Your ring finger. It seems to be missing something that was once there.' Instinctively, she covered her left hand with her right, took a deep breath and stared off into space. But I couldn't let this go. I had to know. 'You were married?' I asked.

'Yes.'

'Are you running away from him?'

'No,' she said, without missing a beat, as if she was anyone saying any old statement about any old thing. 'He's dead.'

And then, right before my eyes, she turned to stone. There were no tears, no sign of a lump in her throat. Nothing but her standing there in space, as motionless as a piece of sculpture turned flesh. Like a Khmer dancer. No more questions would be answered that night, I realized. The source of that scar on her back – that huge question would have to wait.

'Oh. I see,' I said, lying, and handed her the newspaper.

MARCH

Cradled in the arms of four great waterways, Phnom Penh is the gateway to an exotic land. The air is filled with alluring smells. The evening glows with colorful lights. Phnom Penh is a showcase for our beautiful Royal Palace and the sparkling domes of our holy wats. But it is also our capital: a busy, modern city. Walking down our streets you see businessmen side by side with monks. Always will this city of contrasts seduce you.

A Touristic Handbook, p. 9

I'm a snob. I don't mean to be, but sometimes I can't help it. This impulse to judge doesn't show up all that often anymore, but every now and again something will catapult me into an elevated sea of superiority. Phnom Penh itself is often the trigger.

It is very easy, and I must admit understandable, to have a negative view of this place. Many people come here and only see the corrupted remains of a traumatic past. Yes, there is often garbage in the streets. There are rats living with riverside views that would make a wealthy Parisian envious. The pavements are so full of ramshackle shops you can barely squeeze past – auto parts, household supplies, black market pharmaceuticals, trays and trays of ripped off sunglasses and t-shirts. It can drive you crazy. And that's without even talking about the traffic. Many people come to Phnom Penh and see only these things, and those are the ones I can't help but feel sorry for.

But there are others – visitors and residents alike – who walk these streets and see them the way I do. First, we see the colors. I never knew so many colors could coexist before I came here. Each store has umbrellas sparked with blues, whites, reds. Their windows, if they have them, are lined with goods arranged for symmetry of hue. Greens are stacked together next to yellows next to pinks. If there are tables outside the door, they're covered with azure cloth nestled within an embrace of painted red chairs. Even the secondhand car transmissions piled up for sale gleam with silver and chrome. The streets are filled with colors, as are the people, as is their clothing, as are the emerald trees and opaline flowers. Monks in saffron robes rustle like whispers against yellow-orange walls. Temples gleaming white with golden roofs and red awnings hide around corners, waiting to jolt you into the memory that you are part of everything. You reflect the colors. You inhabit the aromas of jasmine, incense, tamarind. Whose eyes and hearts can be so closed that they don't feel embraced, engulfed and reborn by this living place? By this Phnom Penh? Those poor blind souls who don't feel it, I feel sorry for. But the ones who do feel it all, who see it beyond their eyes, beyond their hearts? They automatically become a part of me.

As Amanda walked the streets, looking at neighborhoods and places to live, she fell in love with Phnom Penh too. I saw it in the flush of her cheeks after each rushed viewing of an apartment. Okay, maybe there wasn't a working shower. Maybe the bedroom would be wall-to-wall bed. But always she would also have noticed that an unknown species of tree with cup-like yellow flowers stood just outside the kitchen window, leading to a view of a distant temple. Or, even if the front door was falling off its hinges, she saw the statue of a gold lion with inlaid ruby eyes standing guard just outside. Each uninhabitable place seemed to bring the discovery of some new desirable neighborhood. Often Sam and I would listen to her stories and laugh. 'Yes, that's near the British School, isn't it? With those high walls and painted doors?' Or 'I know that street. It leads down to the market with the huge glass jars of teas and spices.' As the days went on, I got sucked in, living her discovery of my city with her, urging her on to new areas, new aspects. It gave me energy.

One day, Amanda arrived at the Home with a newspaper clutched under her arm, which was usually the case now. But this time, she had a funny look on her face.

'Good morning,' I said, not bothering to hide the cigarette I had just finished inhaling. 'Something up?'

'Oh, sorry. I'm lost in thought here,' she answered leaning inside the doorway. I opened the window to let out the remains of my morning smoke and invited her in, but she didn't move.

'Problem?' I asked.

'No. No problem. I was just wondering...' and she handed me the newspaper. She had circled a classified ad on the back: 'One br, full bath, nr Tuol Sleng.'

'It's pretty out there,' I said. 'Very villagey. Not too far away.'

'Yes, but isn't that near the Killing Fields?'

'Probably. And the museum. Could be right around the corner. A bit crowded during tourist season maybe.' I didn't think much more about it than that. Funny how time can make even the presence of a torture chamber like Tuol Sleng seem normal.

'Yes. It's more that I was wondering if I'd feel weird overlooking that place every day. I've seen photos of it, of course. The cinder blocks and barbed wire. And those skulls still stacked behind the walls. You'd know they were there.' Amanda shivered and rubbed her upper arms. 'But I do still think I should check it out. What do you think?'

'Sure. Of course you should. The price certainly looks right. You could go now if you want.'

'That's the thing. I'd like to take someone with me. I have this idea that if I went with a Cambodian – you know, not just as any old tourist – I might get a different feel for the place, for what it would be like actually living out there, near all that…you know…horrible history. It *is* a good price.'

'Well, a lot of people do live there, you know.'

'I know. That's what I mean. It seems weird that anyone would want to live so close to those old torture chambers, but lots of people do. Maybe it wouldn't be weird. Maybe it's a good thing. I don't know. Do you think Sam would come with me?' An interesting question. My first impulse was to say no, leave her alone. It's hot enough outside. Why should she also have to endure a hot bus ride and an upsetting reminder of her country's past? She doesn't need to be any more uncomfortable than she already is. 'Any reason why I couldn't ask her?' Amanda continued.

Sometimes a flea can trip you up more than an elephant, if you know what I mean. Was there any reason why Amanda couldn't ask Sam to accompany her to the Killing Fields Museum? Yes. Ten million reasons that I could think of right off the bat. How about the tables heaped with rusty torture devices, for one? Or those glass *stupas* filled to the brim with skulls stacked ten deep, their anguished and hollow eye sockets staring out into the world? Sam knew about all that. Everyone knew that for four years in the 1970's Pol Pot oversaw the genocide of his own people, the systematic destruction of his country's collective will. But that didn't mean Sam needed to ruin an otherwise beautiful afternoon staring at it. Sam's family history was riddled with enough horror stories of its own. When I first found her she was nearly mute. She was a robot, a tiny little robot, shuffling around taking care of everything and everyone, but in silence. Why should she, my daughter, have to revisit all of that now? I wanted her to leave all that horror in the past and only look forward to a better future, which is, I guess, what all Cambodians are trying to do. I wanted to put a big, billowy arm around her and make sure every day was better than the last. But I had to be honest. Samnang was not a kid anymore. When I thought through the day's schedule and realized she had already walked the younger kids to school, was helping teach one of the English lessons later that morning, would then be heading across town to her computer class that afternoon, I suddenly realized she had grown up. At eighteen she was more responsible, more mature, than many forty-year-olds I knew. Should I stop someone from asking her a question? Could I, even if I wanted to?

'Deborah? Is it okay?' Amanda's simple question was turning out to be the most difficult one I had had to answer in a long time.

'I suppose it's up to her,' I finally replied. 'She can make her own decision.' I picked up the mail in my in-tray and pretended to work.

'Okay. Thanks. I'll go check on the kids.'

'Yeah. And will you close the door behind you?' Once I was alone I just sat there staring at nothing. I was motionless and blank, as if all time had stopped, or rather as if time had moved on but left me behind. My daughter was eighteen years old. She was no longer a frightened, damaged little girl and hadn't been for a very long time. That was the good news. Suddenly it struck me that I had to stop protecting her, that that part of my job really was over. It had all happened much too quickly, though. I was nowhere near prepared for the change. Motherhood. Shit.

That evening, for a couple of hours before dinner, Sam and Amanda did go to Tuol Sleng. I was in the room when Amanda asked her and, much to my surprise, Sam was agreeing even before she looked to me for permission. 'Just be back to help with dinner, okay?' I tried to sound as nonchalant as I could.

'Of course, Mother. And you will be fine here?'

'Yes, I'll be fine.'

'Can I go, too?' asked Srey. It was becoming all too obvious that sixteen-year-old Srey was now completely star-struck by Amanda. She followed her around everywhere, asking endless questions about America, movies, clothes. She used to hang around Sam that same way, but her allegiance had clearly shifted. It was hard to tell whether Sam noticed or not.

'No, Srey,' Sam said, not even bothering to wait for my answer. 'You stay here and help Mother. I do not think this will be a fun trip.' And it wasn't, as it turned out.

By the time Sam and Amanda returned, the house was full of noise and activity. My rambunctious Kiri was playing football in the front courtyard with some of the other boys, and no matter how I scolded them, that ball would always end up right in front of my feet.

'Sorry, Mom.'

'Keep it outside, Kiri.'

'I'm trying, Mom, but Sothy kicked it in.'

'I did not. Not me.'

'That's enough. Just do what I say, please.' The usual Kiri nonsense. At the same time, rice was steaming in the kitchen and plates were being put on the table. Srey was washing the little kids' hands and bossing twelve-year-old Netra around.

'Put the babies in the high chairs now. Don't forget to tie them in. Not too tight. You know, like this.' Netra, of course, did what she was told, the ever-obedient younger sister.

Into the middle of all this domesticity walked Sam and Amanda. 'So, how did it go?' I asked. Sam looked fine, but I wasn't sure about Amanda. 'How was the apartment?'

'Very nice, Mother. You should see all the space, and the views from the bedroom. A little noisy, though.' Sam came to give me a hug, and when she did she whispered in my ear, '…But not good for Amanda. Too hard.' Sam was

35

right. Amanda's face was clouded and dark, and when little Arun ran over to her, raising his arms to be picked up, she just patted his head and rushed off towards the kitchen. I wanted to follow her, but Sam stopped me. 'No, Mother. Let her be.'

'What happened there?' I asked.

'Everything was fine. The apartment was two floors up. Lots of sun in the morning, I think. But it did look down over the buildings of Tuol Sleng. You could see the dirt and the barbed wire. When Amanda saw that she got very quiet and walked away quickly. She has been quiet since.'

At first, opening Tuol Sleng to the public had been extremely controversial. For too long, the government had tried to deny the fact that forty thousand people had been killed nearby and buried in mass graves. They just wanted to ignore the fourteen thousand alleged enemies who had been tortured there, beaten and shackled in rows of tiny concrete rooms. Of course they wanted to deny it. Many of the people running the government now had been in the Khmer Rouge back then. For a long time I felt the same way. The past is over: let's get on with today. But lately, Cambodia and its people were changing. The West had brought a Tribunal to our country, and every day more news arrived about steps forward and backward in our progress towards being healed. I think all of us were beginning to believe that confronting the past was better than hiding from it. And although there seem to be no answers as to how something like this could have happened, how a country could have turned on itself in such a vicious, horrifying way, I now believe it has to be faced.

Cambodians know this. For them, even without understanding there can still be acceptance. So they can live in the village surrounding the mass graves of the Killing Fields. They can send their children to school in buildings beside the old schoolhouse which had been used as an Interrogation Centre during all those years of their earthly hell. Cambodians themselves can do this, but most Westerners can't. Certainly, Amanda could not.

I watched her sit quietly at the table as we ate. I didn't need to talk to her. Her face said it all. Her eyes were not sad or filled with horror. There were no lines of anger around the corners of her mouth. Instead, her gaze kept darting between the tables full of children, laughing and teasing each other over plates of rice and chicken as if they were real brothers and sisters. She looked overwhelmed by a profound and convulsive confusion. She looked as if she wanted to shout, 'Where the hell am I?' I did feel sorry for her and a large part of me hoped that this would now put an end to the nonsense about her remaining here. Although we were all getting used to her help, all starting to feel as if she was our friend, I was still a tangle of worries about letting her get too close. But I kept my tongue to myself. I didn't allow myself to say what I knew I really wanted to say, which was simply: 'Welcome to Cambodia.'

Smack in the middle of the month, a package came from my sister, Pat. One of the kids brought it to me. 'From America, Mother. I think will make happy.' And it did make happy. I felt the weight of it in my hands, the texture of the bundled papers bound with cardboard. It remained unopened on my desk for the rest of the day, waiting for me and a bit of secluded time.

By ten o'clock that night, everything was quiet enough for me to grab the package and walk across the courtyard to my rooms. Right next to the Home's main building, within earshot of anything important, these four rooms provide my refuge. There was plenty wrong with this place when I took it over from the nuns about a decade ago, but this was one thing those old girls did right. They looked after themselves and created a luxurious, by Cambodian standards, suite of rooms for the Mother Superior. I have a large bedroom, as she did, with windows looking onto a park, my own bathroom with a freestanding tub, and a small sitting area with an old *Barcalounger* shipped over from my mother's house. From the minute I saw them I knew these rooms would be perfect. I even left the Mother Superior sign over the door.

So there I was in my pajamas, in bed, a cup of tea at my side, by ten-fifteen. Slowly, I opened the package on my lap, as I always did – one flap at a time, smoothing the wrinkles as I went, waiting as long as I could to unveil the wonders that lay in store for me. I wasn't disappointed. There they were, about thirty or forty newspaper clippings from the most outrageous tabloids in America, all set with big bold typefaces and exclamation points between every phrase. Plus, resting on top, were two sheets of watermarked stationery with my sister's handwriting. Now this was something special. Usually, Pat just packed up a batch of papers and scribbled a note on a yellow stickie. But a couple of times a year she actually wrote a proper letter. Sure, we exchanged emails pretty regularly, as I did with my other sister and used to do with my brother. But there's something remarkable about a letter; something quite touching about seeing the actual hand-made markings of someone you love, markings with a slant and a curvature belonging only to them. For me, such a letter feels like a gift of time. Everyone is always rushing somewhere to do something. But if a person actually takes the time to sit in a chair, collect their thoughts and carefully put them down on a special piece of paper made just for that purpose – well, that really is a gift.

And so it didn't matter to me that, actually, Pat had nothing very interesting to say. It may sound terrible, but honestly, she can be pretty boring. She tends to get caught in a narrative loop about the trivial when she speaks. Whole sentences are devoted to what she made for lunch, paragraphs to deciding whether to drive to the mall before or after the kids' baseball game. It can be torture. So I admit to skimming the letter, assuming there was nothing really important in it, and going straight to the tabloids. I can't remember for the life of me why we got started doing this. But every few months Pat sends me a package full of these little published nuggets of idiocy, and I love it when she does. In this job, it's great to be able to laugh about something stupid from time to time. As I recall, this batch of clippings was an especially good one. I can remember a few of them now:

My Mother Came Back as a Chicken
French Toast Leads to Disaster!
and the heart-warming:

Man Without Arms Weds Woman Without Legs
I laughed so hard I began to cough. Reaching for the tissue box, I knocked over my cup of tea. Sam had been on her way to give me my goodnight hug when she heard the crash and came running into the room. She found me sitting on the floor, mopping up the tea with the hem of my nightgown, and giggling.

'Oh, Mother. Look at you,' she said.

'Take it easy. I'm fine. Look. A package from Aunt Pat.'

Sam helped me back onto bed as if I was some babbling moron. 'At least nothing is broken, Mother. Would you like more tea?'

'No, no. But just look at some of these.' I knew Sam wouldn't be all that interested. I'm not sure the humour translates all that well into her life experience. 'And there's a proper letter…'

That, she did want to see. 'May I?' She took the pages and read them slowly and carefully. 'She misses us. And says it has been five years since we visited. That is true.'

I knew it was. I remembered all too well. Although we used to go over every year when Sam was small, our last visit was for my mother's funeral when Sam was just thirteen, and five years had already passed since then. Now somehow, it didn't seem quite so crucial to make the long, expensive trip, not to mention figuring out the logistics of finding people to take care of the kids left behind. That was always a nightmare. The younger ones cried and cried, certain I would never return. In some ways it's good for them to learn I can go away and still come back again. But it is exhausting. Five years was too long, though. Pat was right.

'So, what else does she say?' I asked.

'Oh, nothing really.' Sam was already putting the letter away but something on her face convinced me I shouldn't believe her.

'Oh? Nothing?' I took the letter back out of the envelope and started to read for myself. It was true. There wasn't much in it, mostly details about the weather, the amount of snow, the new car they had just bought for my nephew. But there was one remark Sam had obviously hoped to ignore. 'Did you see this? She says all the applications for next year's class at the university are now in. It seems they have more than ever.' I began to read out loud:

But tell Sam not to worry. I have a good feeling about this.

'Well, fingers crossed,' I added. 'It won't be long now 'til we find out if you're in.'

Sam stood up to go, then turned around again as if a cord was pulling her back and forth between both sides of the open door. 'Oh, Mother, maybe we should just tell Aunt Pat to forget the whole thing. I have already forgotten about it. Really, it is just too silly.'

I took off my reading glasses and stared at her hard. To be honest, I had tried to forget about it myself, although I knew it was just my own selfishness that was trying, unsuccessfully, to push the idea out of my head. Pat had been working in the admissions office of Kent State for years and she was right to urge Sam to apply. Where else could Sam try for? For good or bad, generations of us had gone there, and if anyone knew whether it would be possible for a girl like Sam to be admitted, it was my sister, Pat. Sam's life experience was about as far removed from the rest of the suburban Ohio kids applying as Phnom Penh is from Cleveland. But Pat thought it could be done and Sam was much too obedient to refuse to fill out the form. 'You know I filled out the application just to make Aunt Pat happy,' Sam reminded me. 'I would not want to disappoint her by not even trying. Really, even if they do accept me, I do not think I will go. How could I? It is silly. But maybe you should go to America this summer. For a holiday.'

'What? Go to the States? Without you?'

'Yes. I could stay here and look after everyone. I am old enough now to do that. Then you wouldn't worry.'

Sam did look old enough, for anything. She certainly looked more mature than any college freshman I had ever seen. Right then, she probably looked more mature than me. There she stood, erect, poised, calm and capable. And there I sat in a bed strewn with papers, my wet and dirty nightgown hitched up above my knees. I was too tired to think, but as I looked at her I could feel heat and pressure rising up to the base of my throat. My eyes teared.

'Mother, are you alright?'

'Of course. Just a little heartburn,' I lied. 'But this discussion is too big to have right now. Let's wait and see, okay? I can't imagine them rejecting you. I can't imagine anyone rejecting you for anything. Let's just wait. Right now, we should both get some sleep.' Sam came around to the side of the bed, tucked me in and kissed my forehead. I hugged her, perhaps, a little too tightly and spoke the words we had said to each other every night since she was four years old. 'In the morning. I promise.'

It wasn't long after Amanda's trip to Tuol Sleng that she actually did find a place to live. Looking out the window of that spacious, well-lighted apartment to see the barbed wire of the old Security Office was like a slap across her face. It didn't cause her to give up the idea of staying on, but it did somehow jolt her back into the memory of who she was, whoever that was, and what she could and could not do. Within days, she narrowed her search to a wealthier part of town, down along the waterfront where the Bassac River meets the Mekong, an area full of joggers during the day and tourists at night.

'I found it,' she announced one morning, shoving a classified ad into my hand. 'Read this. I'll walk the kids to school, and when I get back I'll tell you all about it.' She was like Kiri's football, bouncing every which way off the flagstones, full of energy. 'Come on, troops. Let's go,' she said, marching them out the door, counting each head with a tickle or a poke.

I took a deep breath and picked up Chak, our newest addition. Though five years old, he felt like a shadow in my arms. 'Come on, kiddo,' I said. 'Let's get Mother another cup of coffee. She thinks she's going to need it today.'

I hardly had time for my first sip when Amanda was back. 'So?' she asked, as if in mid conversation. I wiped Chak's runny nose and kissed his forehead. 'You okay, little man? Want to go help in the kitchen? Play with water?' I mimed turning on the tap and splashing. He didn't bite. 'No? Okay, then. You stay with us. Amanda is going to tell us a story.' I put out my hand and he took hold of it, smiling at me as he did. He was beginning to understand. I've found that if you just keep talking to kids, eventually

42

they talk back. It never ceases to amaze me. Chak, who had been living on a rubbish heap and could barely speak Khmer just three months earlier, now clearly understood lots of what was said around him, whether in Khmer or English. And sometimes he even answered. It's almost enough to make you believe in God.

'Here, I'll read it to you,' Amanda said. 'Are we going to your office?' Before I could answer, 'Yes – to my office – you take the kid while I have a smoke,' she was off and running. 'Okay. So it says "New to market. 1 bedroom, 1 bath, all new plumbing. Eat-in kitchen, living room. River view." I saw it last night and it's perfect. Available in about a week. I think it's the one.'

'Great. What floor is it on?'

'Second. A walk-up, but the staircase is wide with new lighting.'

'Who lives below?'

'The landlord, Mr Chea. And that's the great part. It's just the landlord and his family below and me up upstairs. I think he owns one of the restaurants across from the river.'

I was skeptical. Sure, some Cambodians had managed, one way or another, to make some money, buy some property over the past ten years. And sure, it was sometimes legit. But I was long past assuming anything about anyone here in Cambodia.

'I think I want to take it, but I have to act fast. Could you come with me and look at it, just to be certain?'

I was uncharacteristically unsure of what to do. Part of me didn't want to encourage her too strongly, didn't want to get any more involved. But that was ridiculous. I was already involved with this woman, who I still knew almost nothing about, whether I wanted to be or not. So then I started to think that maybe this was a way to find out more about her. I could help her find a place, discover what she liked, what she needed, maybe discover a few stories from

43

her past, memories of other places she had lived. I convinced myself to go. 'Okay. I need some more light bulbs and molly screws anyway. We can go right after lunch.'

'Terrific,' she said, and rushed out the door to take on whatever twenty tasks could consume her morning's energy. She was back in a nanosecond. 'Oh, here. Sorry,' she said and thrust Chak back at me. He sneezed and laughed as he fell into my arms.

'Funny,' he said.

'Yes, she is,' I had to agree.

The *tuk tuk* ride down towards the river was pure joy. There aren't many places to escape the intense heat and humidity of March in Phnom Penh. But when a *tuk tuk* gets going up to speed, a good strong breeze can whip through the sides, front and back, and create a comfortable little microclimate in there under the metal awning. Amanda was surprisingly quiet as we sped past the Royal Palace and down towards the waterfront. I can remember how still she looked sitting there, her long black hair tied back tightly with a simple elastic band. She seemed to be memorizing every shop, every landmark we passed. I guess she was trying to create a picture of her new neighborhood in her head. Suddenly, the driver stopped.

'This is here,' he said. 'I wait?' Amanda looked at me for approval.

'Yes, wait,' I said.

'Will he?' she asked as he slowly pulled to the side of the street.

'We'll see.'

The building looked good, I had to admit. Freshly-painted orange walls with two white cement pillars in the front and a huge potted palm set next to one. Clean tiles leading to the door. I was glad to see it wasn't one of those accordion-gated affairs with a tin awning above it, like so many of the new quick constructions sprouting up everywhere. The building looked sturdy, like it had been around for a while and wasn't going anywhere any time soon. The door was painted green. Mr Chea, I supposed, came immediately to the door. We eyed each other suspiciously.

'Miss Amanda, you have returned?'

'Yes. I said I would. I brought a friend to look with me.'

It was hard to tell whether he cared or not, but he opened the door and led us upstairs. The staircase was wide and well lit, as Amanda had said. And the apartment itself was, actually, quite lovely. Absolutely adequate, by Western standards. Downright palatial, by Cambodian. This was clearly expensive and I was, admittedly, impressed. So there was one question – where did all her money come from? From Daddy the Banker? And if so…well, my brain was already jumping to the idea that maybe Amanda could convince him to generously shuffle some of that money our way. Amanda's eyes locked on me. I couldn't hide how impressed I was. Mr Chea could see it too and became a lot more friendly and helpful.

'Yes, Mr Chea. I will take it,' Amanda suddenly declared.

'Very good, Madame. One month in advance?'

'Yes. As we said.'

'And one year lease?'

Whoa, I thought. Wait a minute. 'Uh, Amanda, may I have a word with you first?' I pulled her over to the window which, I couldn't help but notice, had a fabulous view of both the river and the gardens of the Royal Palace.

'It's perfect, isn't it?' she whispered.

'Yes, it's fantastic,' I conceded. 'But one year?'

'Well, that's what he's offering.'

'But one year? In Phnom Penh that's a very long time.'

'I know, but I'm not going anywhere soon. If I have to break the lease I'll figure something out.' And off she went, back to Mr Chea and the Khmer-English document he was now pulling out of his back pocket.

It took all my self-control not to barge in and try to renegotiate. Amanda had asked my opinion, but it no longer seemed like she really wanted it. Her mind was made up, despite me. Despite any of us.

I stared out the window. The view of the river really was beautiful. The streets were full of people, buying, selling, laughing, arm in arm, men and women all together. An entire world. The wind whipped the flags flying high above the promenade. The grass beside it was full and green. Despite the heat, the city looked alive and moving, full of energy and purpose and I realized I couldn't do anything to stop any of it. It then felt like a switch inside me had suddenly, quietly, turned itself off. Right there and then I began to let go of the illusion of control I had been so tightly clinging to. I had surrendered part of the fight. I turned around to see Amanda shaking her new landlord's hand. Both were smiling, laughing and bowing to each other. As we walked out the door, Mr Chea was reeling off a long list of reasons why 'Miss Amanda' would be so happy living there. 'And, you know,' he said, 'right around the corner is the famous restaurant for foreign newspapermen. Many Westerners go there. Very good drinks, good food. Also,' he added with a slightly creepy wink, 'many Western men.'

And so it was done. Just like that, with a handshake and a wink, Amanda was now a permanent part of The Khmer Home for Blessed Children. Who she was, why she was here, I still didn't know. But with each passing week it all seemed to matter less and less, and I guess that was the most surprising thing of all to me. Over ten years there have been many people who have walked through my door, all meaning well, all wanting to help. Never before had I let any of them stay. I may have been like Cerberus guarding the gates of the Underworld, but that was my way of protecting these children who had stumbled into my care. And they were the ones I did care about, not the volunteers, not the gap year travelers, not even the potential donors who have begun to discover us now that the Tribunal has brought Cambodia back to the world's attention. And yet, here was this Amanda, young, energetic, with a good heart, a disarming smile and a troubled past, staying and staying and staying. Oh yes, something was changing all right. And it did scare me.

Back in Ohio, there was this ritual my mother used to call spring cleaning. I dreaded it. She never warned us that this horrible event was about to happen. Just one day when we all got home from school and the sun was shining and we didn't have much homework and all we wanted to do was go outside and play, she would meet us at the door with some old-fashioned scarf wrapped around her head and say, 'Everyone, grab a quick snack and then it's time to work.' It was torture. Each of the four of us, no matter how young we were, was given a job – dusting, washing, airing out, the list was endless. I can smell that yellow disinfectant even now. The weird thing, though, is that not only do I do the same thing myself, but I look forward to it just like my mother seemed to do. It has to do with renewal, I guess. And closure. Getting rid of all the old dirt and daring to start again even though you know there's even more dirt to come. Here at the Home I've taken to performing this ritual in the weeks leading up to Khmer New Year. Sure, it's the height of the hot season and not technically spring. Sure, it's uncomfortable and exhausting. But that's what ritual and religion is all about, isn't it? Sacrifice and hardship?

Nobody was spared. But I wasn't quite as heartless about it as my mother had been. I did give some warning. I made the same little speech every year. 'Quiet everyone, please,' I'd say when we were all together at dinner. The smallest kids would look curious. Others, worried – especially the older ones who knew from experience what was coming. 'As most of you know, in a few weeks it will be New Year, with lots of fun and celebrations. But we all need to get ready. To prepare. And there are lots of ways that we can do that. What are some ways that we can prepare for New Year?' I liked to believe that I was actually trying to teach the kids something here, but I had to admit that a mischievous streak in me also loved dragging this thing out. I tried to find at least a glimmer of bravery on some face or other before calling on someone. This year was Sothy's turn. Poor kid. He was always so good and so helpful, I really shouldn't have taken advantage of him. But I knew he wouldn't let me down.

'We pray?' he whispered.

'Yes. Good. And what do we pray for?'

'Our ancestors?' came one tiny little-girl voice.

'Yes. Very good.'

'Our families?' came another voice, slightly bolder.

'Yes, our family here,' I said quickly motioning to us all around the table. 'All of your brothers and sisters sitting around you. All of us here at the Home. Anything else?'

'Yes, Mother,' Srey said with such an exasperated teenager's voice I could barely keep a straight face. 'We do spring cleaning.' The tiniest groan escaped from their throats. Not even these docile Cambodian kids could hold back their disappointment.

'Exactly,' I said, clapping my hands and trying to sound excited. 'So, tomorrow after breakfast we make a start. Everyone will have a job.' I sat down and leaned over towards Amanda. 'That means you, too,' I whispered, unable to control a sardonic snigger.

That next morning, we were all up early eager to get going, eager to get it over with. Six hours into the siege we were slowing down. The bedroom walls had been wiped. All the floors were washed. The tops of the bookcases and the books themselves were dusted. I had enlisted Samnang, Amanda and our gentle giant, Thom, to move the refrigerator from the wall so I could get at the year's-worth of dirt behind. That was a bad job, but Thom had been waiting for it all day. Right after breakfast he came over to me and asked, 'When do I move the refrigerator, Mother?'

'After lunch,' I said. Then after lunch, he found me doing laundry and said, 'It is time now, I think.' He couldn't wait to show me how strong he had become. Thom may have been the oldest boy, but he wasn't the biggest, by any means. But now that he was seventeen, I think he was determined to stake his claim as the man of the house.

'Okay,' I said. 'Sam, Amanda? Could you help us in the kitchen, please?'

'I do not need help,' Thom corrected me, quite sternly.

'I know that,' I whispered. 'I just want them to watch you do it.' He smiled. Thom led the way to the kitchen and showed us where to stand.

'Not too close,' he warned us. 'May be dangerous.' Then he took his position by the right rear corner refrigerator. He bent his knees and took a deep breath.

'Jesus, what have I done?' I thought to myself. 'The kid's going to kill himself.' But then I heard a scraping sound. And then another one. The refrigerator moved an inch. Thom went around to the other side and did it again. Bend, sharp inhale, push. Another inch or more. Two more times on each side in silence he pushed and we watched until the huge machine was a clear six inches away from the wall.

49

Amazing. 'Bravo, Thom,' we all applauded. 'You did it. Look at that.' I thought he was going to cry he was so proud of himself. 'Now, you deserve a rest. Have a glass of water and sit down.'

As we watched Thom strut out of the room, I turned to Amanda and said, 'Congratulations – you just witnessed a miracle.'

'Yes,' Sam explained. 'When Thom was young, his father had beaten him so badly he could not walk.'

'I found him crawling on the pavement, begging,' I recalled. Amanda looked at us both with disbelief. 'It's true.' I nodded. 'So let's do him proud,' I said, handing them each a sponge and a bucket of water.

About an hour later, we were done. Actually, they were done. I had already sat myself under the ceiling fan with a glass of water. Amanda dropped down next to me, wrapping a wet towel around her neck. 'And we're doing this now, why?' she asked.

'To prepare for *Chaul Chnam*,' Sam reminded her and handed her a drink.

'None for you?' Amanda asked.

'Maybe later.'

'Sam, go get yourself a glass, too. Then we'll go around and bring some to all the others.' Sam always insists on helping everyone else first before she helps herself. I have to fight her all the time about that.

'Yes, Mother.'

'*Chaul Chnam*? That's how you say New Year?' Amanda asked.

'Yes, it's an important part of the ritual, cleaning the house before New Year,' I explained. 'I just do it a little early because I know if I don't do it now, it will never happen. This place can get crazy around the holiday. You'll see.'

'Crazy? What kind of crazy? Oh, I heard about this. You throw water at each other, right?'

'That's one part of it. Water mixed with talcum powder – a cleansing ritual gone haywire.'

'It is very funny,' Sam then added. 'You must be ready, walking the streets. Everyone gets wet. And we also go to the *wat*. We dance. Paint the children's faces. Many celebrations.'

'Can't wait. Sounds great.'

'It is,' I agreed. 'But we have to be careful, too. You see, New Year is a time to spend with family. People, even the poorest ones, travel all across the country just to be with their relatives.'

'And that's bad?' Amanda asked.

'Well, the men sometimes use the children to show how successful they are. Without children, you look like nothing. Sometimes fathers and grandfathers come here wanting to take their kids back.'

'What? These kids? They have parents?'

'Some of them, yes.' Amanda looked shocked. I was surprised to see her reaction. 'Come on, Amanda,' I said, trying not to lose my patience. 'You can't be that naive. You know *orphan* can mean a lot of different things here. Some of my kids have living parents, even though those parents have given them up. Sometimes they've even taken money for them.' Amanda's eyes were still dark and suspicious. 'Look, I may not know much about you, but you did tell me you've lived in this part of the world for a while, right? You know what goes on here. Of course, I try not to get involved in that sort of thing but sometimes I can't help it. Sometimes it's me or the sex trade. And it's never a problem, unless one of the fathers decides he wants the kid back. Not forever. God, never forever. Just for New Year. To show him off, how well fed he is, well

51

educated. So it's not a great time to have my head stuck behind a refrigerator, see?'

Amanda may have been horrified by all this, or maybe she just pretended to be. I couldn't tell. But Sam certainly wasn't. Actually, I remember being struck by this sense of calm surrounding Sam. No, she wasn't horrified, but she wasn't anesthetized, either. She was, strangely, at peace. Aware, accepting, but somehow moving beyond. Amanda noticed it, too, because she looked directly at Sam and asked her specifically, 'But how can you bear it?' A child's question, I thought, but I stopped myself from saying it.

'You bear what is,' Sam answered, quietly sipping her water. That would have been a perfect end of the conversation but Amanda needed more. You could almost see the synapses firing wildly behind her eyes, but the look on her face was one of a hurt little girl.

'I don't know. Maybe it's Buddhism,' she finally said. 'Yeah, maybe it's Buddhism that teaches you to be so accepting. God knows, nothing in my culture teaches you to let go of anger that way.'

'God knows?' I asked. 'I stopped asking God for anything a long time ago. Look around you. Do you see him anywhere?'

'No, maybe not,' Amanda agreed. But that broke Sam's silence.

'Or maybe yes. We have different ideas on the subject, Mother and I. Mother looks and sees trouble, and so she works hard to make things better. I look and see miracles. Mother brought those miracles. But maybe God brought Mother. You live. You wait. What must come, will come.' Amanda and I were now silent. Even I had never heard Samnang speak that way. She stood up and poured water into a large jug to bring to the others. We just watched her. I don't know what Amanda was thinking, but I know I was thinking that perhaps my job with Sam really was done.

52

Perhaps she now had even more to teach me than I had to teach her. 'But of course,' she then suddenly said, 'Mother has seen more trouble than I have. My life has been easier.'

Amanda moved into her flat soon after. Maybe she caught the cleaning bug. Maybe she realized she'd better be in and settled before *Chaul Chnam* came around. But for four days the following week she was away from the Home and busy with her own life. Of course, it was fine for her to take the time off. It just seemed slightly strange to me, I recall, that she didn't ask. She just told us. 'Oh, I won't be here next Tuesday through Friday. I'm moving.' I don't know if it was the way she announced it, with that sense of entitlement and authority, or if I found myself actually missing having her around. But I know I felt put out by it, irritable even, and the fact that I didn't understand why I was feeling that way only made it worse. So, on the spur of the moment, I decided, rightly or wrongly, to head on over there one afternoon and see what she was up to. I left Sam and Srey in charge.

'I could go to Amanda's with you,' Srey offered.

'Yes you could, but I think we could use you more here.'

'But I want to see Amanda's new apartment.'

'I bet you do. But the children need you. And Sam will need you. I'll only be gone a few hours anyway.'

'Oh, alright.' Srey could have been any petulant sixteen-year-old in any country in the world just then and actually, it thrilled me to see it. She has more spark than any Khmer kid I've ever seen. Certainly than any Khmer girl.

'You know. I especially need you to help with the homework. You're so smart. And I always think it's good for the younger ones to see how hard you work. They do look up to you, you know.' That brought a glimmer of a smile to her face. And to mine. It was good to know I could still outsmart a teenager – sometimes.

I spent the twenty-minute *tuk tuk* ride in a state of extreme suspicious agitation, not sure what I thought I was going to find. I had believed that the extent of her belongings was the contents of that backpack she was hauling around the first time I saw her. And the apartment was furnished. What could she possibly have been doing for four days? When I look back on it now I can see that something wasn't quite right with me. Something inside had become unstuck, as if an array of strange feelings were jostling around, knocking up against my ribs, stirring up my insides. I had become both more and less comfortable with Amanda, all at the same time. I liked her company. I appreciated the work she did for us. But when she was out of my sight I felt nervous, protective. I just couldn't shake this feeling of apprehension.

By the time I reached her house my heart was pounding. I pushed on the door. It swayed open so I ran up the stairs – imagine me running – and knocked. There was noise coming from inside. Peoples' voices. So I knocked again. Then, there she was.

'Deborah! How nice of you to come. I didn't expect you. Come in. Let me turn off the radio.' She looked genuinely happy to see me. I looked around. Everything was in order, very much like I had first seen the place. But there were some new things, too. A rug. A few throw pillows on the couch. Curtains. Now that I was there, I didn't know what to do with myself.

'I thought you might need some help. Just thought I'd come and check. We want to give you a housewarming gift, too, but we didn't know what you already had.' Of course I was lying, making it up as I went along. It could have been true, though, would have been true if I'd given any rational thought to anything before I had impulsively hopped into that *tuk tuk*.

'This is so sweet of you. Come in. Sit down. Tea?'

'Yes. Thanks. You have a teapot?'

'I have a teapot, two cups, four glasses, and knives, spoons and forks for six. Not bad, eh? I bought it all in the market yesterday. And I bought food. The basics. Tea, coffee, some spices, milk. It's been fun figuring out what I can get, what I can't. What I need. What I don't.'

She was chatting away happily as she puttered around her little kitchen. She seemed settled. She was definitely nesting, big time, and it made me wonder just how long it had been since she'd had a real home of her own.

'It all looks wonderful, Amanda. Really. It must feel good to have a place of your own at last after hostels and hotels.'

'It sure does,' she said, offering me tea.

'How long has it been?' I probed.

'A long time.' Period. End of discussion. She soon stood up and looked out the window. 'I can't believe this view. Last night, I brought that little table over here to the window, made myself some dinner, and sat watching all the people as I ate. It's so busy. There's so much to look at.'

'It is a great location. Maybe the best in the city. You were lucky to find it, and to be able to afford it.'

'Well, I deserve a little luck for a change.'

'Do you?' I asked, with my eyebrows probably a bit too raised.

'Sure,' she answered quickly, and walked away from the window. 'We all do.'

I couldn't disagree with that although it didn't provide the insight into her past that I had been hoping for. Nothing in the apartment did. The more I looked around, the less I could find of anything really personal. There were no photographs of family. Not even of her dead husband. There were a few books on the one bookshelf, but nothing that gave a hint of where she had been or what she had been doing before finding me that cold day in February.

55

Amanda was making a new life for herself. But so what? Why was I so desperate to know about her past? In Cambodia, weren't we all doing the same thing? Weren't we all turning our collective backs on the horrors of the past and looking only at the two inches in front of us?

I tried very hard to convince myself of all this as I sat on her new couch sipping her newly bought tea. I started to chat. 'So, I must be your first guest, right?'

'Well, no. Actually, last night Mr and Mrs Chea and their youngest son came to visit.'

'That was nice of them. What are they like?'

'Very friendly. They brought me a bottle of palm wine. Wow, was that strong!'

'They live on that out in the country. There are men who make their living wandering around village to village, field to field, with bamboo cylinders of the stuff hanging off their shoulders. So you tried it?'

'I had to. It was a gift, you know? But I just had a sip and then started to cough. They all had a good laugh at that. But then something strange happened. The little boy was laughing and he was so cute I went over and gave him a soft pat on the head.'

'Oh, no.'

'Yes. I obviously did something wrong because he ran to his mother and gave me such a look. I felt terrible. I still do.'

'Well, it's one of those cultural things, you know. Like not showing the bottom of your feet. You don't rub a child on the head.'

'But I've done that to some of the kids at the Home without trouble.'

'That's different. My kids have been around enough strangers and volunteers to know it's okay and I tell them that pretty regularly. But you have to be careful. You're not home.'

I left soon after. Amanda assured me she would be at work the next day and I was certain she would be. Her apartment was nice and clean and comfortable, but I had been right. It wasn't home. Far from it.

Once Amanda came back I promised myself to leave her past alone. She was happy. Sam was happy, as were all the kids. Shit – even I was happy. I told myself it would be my pre-New Year's resolution. If she wanted to tell me something, she would. Otherwise, let it be. And besides, I was beginning to realize that with my growing awareness of the arrival of New Year came an unspoken awareness of the expected arrival of Kyle. He had been gone a long time this time. We hadn't heard anything from or about him in ages. But, just as everyone else in this country migrates home for the holiday, Kyle always comes back to us. We hadn't spent the holiday without him in years. Although he never said as much, I guess we were the closest thing he had to a home anywhere. And, although I would never tell him, the Home wouldn't be a home at New Year without him.

So, I was suppressing my suspicion of Amanda. But, if I wasn't going to be suspicious of Amanda, I suppose I needed something else to suspect. Over the next few weeks I found myself getting more and more stirred up about the Tribunal. I had been following the news about that court debacle for a while, but now I was getting really incensed. When it first became clear that the world was finally going to recognize all that Pol Pot and his accomplices had done, that they would finally - finally - be brought to trial, we all couldn't believe it. First we were euphoric, as if war had been declared over at last. Then we were frustrated when we realized how long the whole thing would take and how much of the usual petty corruption was worming its way into the proceedings. Eventually it became just another thing we noticed but tried to ignore, like the weather, like the poverty. But now, suddenly, it all seemed to matter to me again. Now, every new bit of hypocrisy made me stamp my feet and pace around the room. The angrier I got, the more I scoured the newspapers for any sort of slightly objective reporting. And the more newspapers I read, the angrier I got.

I remember when the news broke about the Cambodian Bar Association's new fees for foreign lawyers. It was one of those excruciatingly hot days and Sam had taken the kids for an extra-long session at the nearby swimming pool. Amanda volunteered to stay behind to help me put the youngest ones down for their naps. We had recently been given several new fans by an NGO that had decided to consolidate its offices – in other words, give up and move to a more hospitable Bangkok. Phnom Penh's loss was our gain, though, and we were able to position these fans so they swiveled just above each pair of beds, each child getting his or her own fifteen-second blast of cool air. Together, Amanda and I dried off their sweaty little heads, placed light cotton throws over their diapered bottoms and bare legs, and watched them settle in. When all six were asleep, we sat ourselves in the shade of the banyan tree in a patch of our garden just under the nursery window. We listened to the soft hum of the fans in the room above and sat as still as we could, trying to generate as little sweat as possible. Unfortunately, I decided to use the quiet time to smoke a cigarette – okay, some days I have two – and read the paper. I think Amanda was reading a book or just staring into space. Everything was rather beautiful and peaceful until I hit upon the headline *Bar Fees: The Latest Obstacle*.

'Goddamn it,' I said too loudly.

'What?'

'Jesus Christ,' I muttered, trying to keep my voice down. 'Listen to this:

The Cambodian Bar Association has imposed fees in excess of $4,000 on foreign lawyers, effectively limiting their ability to appear at the Court.

The bastards. Now the Tribunal's stalled, again.' I was disgusted but couldn't stop myself from continuing:

...accused may now argue they have not been allowed access to counsel of their choice...

'Jesus Christ,' I muttered again.

'Yeah. So?' Amanda asked.

'So the government is perverting the whole process, that's all... finding a way to keep those monsters out of prison, making a mockery of the whole thing.'

'But you're not surprised, are you? Didn't you tell me that a lot of the same people from the Khmer Rouge are still in power?'

'Yes, of course they are. And they're all corrupt, and they say one thing and do another. All these elections, the Tribunal, it's just a hoax.' I was on my feet now.

It had been a long time since I railed at the injustices of the world, but I knew in my heart that my whole life had been built on the quivering foundation of one huge rant. Coming to Cambodia, leaving the US, running out of Ohio, boarding the bus off-campus with my nursing diploma still hot in my hand – all of that may have felt like another lifetime, but it was all still living inside me. Let's face it. We're never really free of our pasts. A country. An old lady. A young woman. None of us.

But my reaction was making Amanda nervous. 'Take it easy, Deborah,' she tried to calm me down. 'You're going to give yourself a heart attack. It's too hot. Sit down. God, it's not like you to react like this. Take it easy.'

I stopped and looked around me. Not only had I stood up, but I had paced myself back and forth so that I was now standing behind Amanda all the way on the other side of the garden. I was nearly shaking, certainly sweating like crazy, and my hand was turning white from holding the newspaper as if it was a sword clenched for battle. Jesus, I thought. What's come over me? Some inappropriate, misplaced rage had been unleashed and it really scared me. I tried to laugh it off.

'Yes, of course, you're right. I'm sorry. I know it's silly. The heat must be getting to me in my old age. Good thing I didn't wake the kids, eh?' Slowly I walked back to my perch under the tree and Amanda and I went back to our quiet sweating in the shade. I let go of my vise grip on the paper and gently turned the pages, looking at the ads but not daring to read any of the articles. Amanda brought me a glass of water. 'If only it was a beer,' I tried to joke.

By the time the kids came back from their swim I had calmed down. I had to. All the noise woke up the babies, and then there were diapers to change, sleepy eyes to kiss, and feats of aquatic glory to hear about. In an instant we were all back to living our moments of now, one after another the minutes of the day picking us up like a tidal wave and moving us to whatever might happen next. Keep your eyes in front of you and take one step at a time was the way I had learned to live my life, and I willed myself to remember it. From then on I tried to keep my rages to myself. Unwittingly, I had let Amanda witness a glimpse of me as the young, idealistic, romantic Deborah, and I wished I hadn't.

One Saturday night soon after Amanda moved into her apartment, Sam asked if she could go out with her to see the new flat and eat (or rather drink) at the journalists' bar across the street. The two of them ambushed me at my most vulnerable. The house was quiet. Everyone was well. Nita was cleaning up after dinner. Sam and Amanda found me in my office reading emails. I looked up to see them standing over me, smiling.

'Yes?' I asked, knowing something was up.

'Mother, Amanda has invited me to go see her new home and, perhaps, go to the journalists' restaurant after for a short time. May I?'

It may not sound unusual but this, indeed, was. Sam never – never – went out with friends. She had friends. Often as she was growing up girls would come over to the house to play, do homework, even help out. But as her friends grew up and started to do what other teenagers did, she saw them less and less. There was a time when I would encourage her to go out with them, but she never would. She would always say, 'After a long day, I am happy to be home with you and the children. Do not worry.' So I didn't. I was so pleased to have her company I didn't think much about it at all, but then the younger Srey became a teenager and I learned what *chomping at the bit* really meant – Srey who right now, I noticed, was peering around the corner of the office and listening to the conversation.

'Go out?' I said. 'Tonight?' I know I sounded startled. 'I suppose so. Okay. What time will you be home?'

'She'll be back by midnight, for sure,' Amanda said, rushing in. But Sam interrupted. 'Probably around eleven. Before you are asleep.'

'Can I go too, Mother?' This was Srey, of course, eager, adorable, clueless. I could see Amanda's eyes say, 'Sure, it's fine,' and Sam's saying, 'Absolutely not.' I, of course, sided with Sam.

'No, not this time, Srey. Let your sister have her time first.' Then came the look from Srey. 'Remember, you're still underage,' I added, as if our country was so very law-abiding. 'Your time will come.'

I walked Sam and Amanda to the door as if nothing special was happening, but I could feel the heat of panic

61

rise up in my chest. I was frightened, but not because I didn't trust Sam, not even because I didn't trust her to be out with Amanda. It was the rest of the world out there that scared me, that I didn't dare allow myself to trust. I ran back to the office calling behind me, 'Wait, girls. Wait just a minute.' When I came back I thrust some of my emergency stash of riels and American dollars into Sam's hand.

'Here. Money for a *tuk tuk* and anything else, just in case. Take the *tuk tuk* outside the house and have him wait for you, no matter how long. Okay?'

'Yes, of course, Mother. I know.'

Then I pulled Amanda aside. I probably held her arm too tightly as I spoke. 'Now listen,' I said. 'The fact that the bar is a Western one doesn't make it any safer, not for a Khmer girl like Sam. Do you understand?'

'Don't worry. I'll watch over her.'

'Amanda, I'm not being a hysterical parent,' I said, although of course I was. 'Sam isn't used to drinking and the Western sex trade is no joke.'

'Okay. Okay. I hear you.'

That was all I could do, so I waved and pretended to smile as they rode off, shouting after them, 'Have fun you two.'

I didn't spend the evening pacing back and forth waiting for her. I didn't call the bar to make sure they were all right. I was very well behaved, considering. I recall Srey and I watched a video of old *Gilligan's Island* shows. *Gilligan's Island* was one of her favorites. 'I know it is silly, Mother,' she said, 'but I think Ginger is so beautiful.' Jeez.

At about 10:45, as I was getting ready for bed, I heard Sam's footsteps in the hallway. She was home. I met her at the door of my room.

'Hi, Sweetheart. Come give me a kiss.' That was an old trick I remembered my mother doing to see if she smelled alcohol on our breath. Sam's breath smelled sweet. If she had had anything to drink, I could already tell it wasn't much. 'Did you have a good time?'

'Yes, I did. A very good time.'

'Did you like Amanda's apartment?'

'Oh, Mother, it is beautiful. So much room, just for her. I think she is happy there.'

'Why wouldn't she be? And what a view, right? And did you enjoy spending time with her? Did you have much to talk about?' I was fishing again.

'Oh yes. I am very comfortable with her. And then we went to the restaurant. It is lovely there.'

'Yes, I know.'

'Yes, you have been there, haven't you?'

'Ah, I suppose, once or twice.'

'I had one glass of wine and two Coca Lites. Amanda had a beer. I don't really like beer, though. And we shared some fried bananas. They were delicious.'

I almost laughed. What a sweet conversation to have with your eighteen-year-old daughter who's just come back from one of the hottest bars in a very hot city. My relief was bordering on giddiness. 'I'm glad you had such a good time,' I said, trying to be serious. 'It was nice of Amanda to invite you.'

'Oh, and Mother, before I forget. Guess who we saw? Kyle.'

'Kyle? You saw Kyle? Our Kyle?'

'Yes. Kyle Mackenzie. He is back.'

'He is? Since when?'

'Just a few days ago. He said he would come see us soon. I thanked him for the scarves and hats. He is so funny.'

'Yes, he certainly is. And how does he look? Is he okay?'

'Yes, he looks good. I think he is back for New Year's. Oh, and I introduced him to Amanda, too.'

'Amanda, of course. She's never met Kyle. Did she like him?'

63

'Yes. She thought he was very nice. Just like Indiana Jones, she said.' Sam was laughing. She thought that was funny. I thought it was pretty apt. 'Well, goodnight, Mother. In the morning, I promise.'

'In the morning, I promise.'

So Kyle was finally back. Kyle Mackenzie, our own Australian minesweeper. Funny, charming, good looking, straight-shooting, capable and irrepressible. His government should pay him for being such a perfect specimen of Australian manhood. He's so often out of town, usually somewhere dangerous, exploding landmines in farmers' fields or whatever. But when he does come home, watch out. Something funny always happens. He always brings little gifts for the kids and usually, bless him, chocolates for me. He knows my weakness – at least the one for chocolate. The ridiculous one I have for Kyle himself I keep hidden. But I guess we all love him in our own way, and I know we all rest a little easier knowing he's back. Phnom Penh feels much safer when he's around. And I was especially glad to hear he was at the bar when Sam was there. I knew he would watch out for her. Nobody messes with Kyle Mackenzie. Everyone in Phnom Penh knows him. And now he's met Amanda, too.

APRIL

New Year is Cambodia's joyous harvest festival. Every home has attractive decorations and all shrines have many offerings of food. For three days Khmer families celebrate together and play traditional games. It is a happy time.
A Touristic Handbook, p. 23

Everyone is talking about global warming, even in our little corner of the world. It's the new superstition. Each mega-hurricane in America brings knowing glances and solemn nodding heads. News of European floodings brings whispers of divine retribution. The street vendors selling floral wreathes outside the *wats* are making a killing. 'Please Buddha,' you can almost hear the fervent prayers coming from inside the temples, 'do not let the weather destroy us. We are good enough at destroying ourselves.'

February had been bizarrely cold. April is always blisteringly hot, but this year brought temperatures that used to be known only in tales of the mythic past. The record was something like 41 degrees Centigrade, that's nearly 106 degrees Fahrenheit, and even we natives found that hard to bear.

Coping with the heat and humidity is just something you learn to do when you find yourself living your life in these latitudes. In some ways how a person handles it is how we separate the so-called men from the boys, or actually, the Khmer from the *barang*. I remember when I stopped feeling like a foreigner. It was during the hot season, a couple of years after moving to Phnom Penh. Up until then, I wilted every time the thermometer reached above thirty, and I was no newcomer to the tropics. I may have been raised in Ohio, but I trained in the Philippines, and it gets pretty hot down there too. It took years not to be amazed by the fact that there were times when I could sit in the shade of a tree at night, long after the sun had set, not move even one muscle, and still sweat as if I had just run a marathon. Merely existing was enough exercise to make every piece of clothing completely drenched. That's what happens to foreigners, and you have to look out for them. They need to drink their liters of water. They need their cold showers three times a day. And, of course, they need to stay inside in the middle of the afternoon. The Khmers swing in their hammocks in the shade beneath their raised houses. The *barangs* hope to hell the air conditioning is working in their hotels.

Eventually, the more you live through it, the less it affects you. It's silly but I wear it as a sort of badge of honor that I can continue with my daily life despite the heat, even when it hits mythic proportions. I don't even think about it anymore. I just naturally slow down. It did surprise me, though, that Amanda slowed down as well. She, who was usually so full of energy, instinctively came to a resigned, uncomplaining crawl like the rest of us. I had fully expected that between Sam and I, someone would have to continually remind her to drink her water and cover her head. But we didn't, and that could only mean one thing. This weather was not new to her. Her body had already learned to adapt to extremes of heat and humidity, and that doesn't happen by backpacking around Thailand for a few months.

One day, when the temperature was nearing the record, Sam and Amanda were in the library with some of the kids. I was walking past on my way to do something or other when I overheard a bit of their conversation. Sam had obviously asked how Amanda was handling the heat and her answer was, 'I'm okay. I'm used to it.' Used to it? How could she be used to it? Where had she been? I lingered by the door. Yes, I was eavesdropping. No, I didn't feel guilty about it. All us mothers do it. I know my sister spent years volunteering to do the soccer carpool, just so she could eavesdrop on the kids in the back seat. How else would she know anything about their lives, she told me. Sometimes the kids forget you're there and all sorts of things tumble out. You just have to 'lie in wait'. Well, that's what I was doing. I was lying in wait and what I heard was worth waiting for.

'I lived for a while in the Philippines and East Timor before that. So I got used to it. The hot season's pretty bad there, too.'

East Timor, that crazy place? And the Philippines? What the hell was she doing there? That wasn't an answer to who Amanda was. That just brought up a zillion more questions. But just then it was still too damn hot to bother asking.

Because of those record temperatures, the New Year Water Festival was a special treat. The ritual of throwing water on people passing in the street spilled over into more days than was strictly necessary. I was as much to blame as any. Although this religious ceremony was really meant to ward off evil spirits, it turned into a sort of Khmer version of suburban American kids running through sprinklers. Every day for a week I set the kids up in the front courtyard with buckets of water mixed with talcum powder. The kids filled plastic cups full of the concoction and hurled it at passers-by. But that Kiri and his five-year-old sidekick, Sothy, got their hands on water pistols and were shooting everyone in sight, making those terrible machine gun noises boys insist on making. I hate that stuff, though, and I don't let my kids play with guns. It may be normal and harmless in other places in the world, but guns are no laughing matter here. 'Give me those things,' I snapped shoving plastic cups in their hands instead. 'No guns!'

67

'Sorry, Mother,' Sothy said.

Kiri stormed off in a pout, only to come back when I pretended I wasn't looking. He bombarded me, but I let him do it. A holiday standoff, I called it. We were both having too much fun.

When this gentle ritual of sprinkling family members turned into a national water fight, I don't know. But our Khmer Home for Blessed Children was squarely on the front line. 'Getting' me was what the kids loved the most, I think, and I actually loved it, too, but especially that year, in that heat, with my gnawing suspicion that evil spirits were hovering just over our shoulders. Actually, we did have a lot to be thankful for. None of our kids had died in the past year. This was more remarkable than it sounds. And except for the rheumatic fever Nary had had from birth, they were all healthy. So, although I always make sure we observe the holiday and that the kids participate in the ceremonies, I think I was doing it with a bit more fervor this year. Certainly I was grateful we had all lived through the year without any personal traumas or political upheavals. But, to be honest, I think I was giving in to my own superstitions as well. I was also praying to anyone who would listen that the nagging unease I felt about what the next year might bring would turn out to be nothing more than an old woman's paranoia.

Usually, the first day of the holiday is the calmest. It starts with the monks ringing bells in all the *wat*s around the city marking the arrival of the *new angel*. We light candles and we pray. It's lovely, really. A sense of communal celebration takes over and there's a quiet anticipation of all the excitement yet to come. But this year's first morning wasn't quite so quiet. Within an hour the kids had gone from adorable laughing to riotous whooping and hollering. Before I could rush out to see what all the commotion was, Sam had run inside absolutely dripping with white water and completely out of breath.

'Mother, come see.' She could barely speak for her laughter. I headed for the door, but then came Amanda, who was also a mess.

'Deborah, don't. You'll be sorry.'

Of course I went to see, and what I saw when I opened the door was Rambo. Kyle Mackenzie stood there with a bandana on his head, supersoakers strapped to each arm, another one across his back, and he was engaged in full-on water combat with all my kids who were, in turn, giving as good as they got. And here, so soon after I had so righteously proclaimed 'no guns.' But the battle was furious and, I had to admit, hysterically funny. There was only one thing I could do. I quickly closed the door behind me and rushed to the kitchen. When Sam and Amanda saw what I was up to they cried out, 'No, don't. You'll be hurt.' But it was too late. I didn't need a gun to do my worst. Oh no. Against the protests of poor Nita who was trying so desperately to prepare our lunch, I had taken the huge metal soup tureen, filled it full of water, and sloshed my way back outside and into the middle of the fray. Everyone stopped. It grew quiet.

'So, it's come to this, has it?' asked our Rambo.

'There's no escape. Give up now, or else.' It was his choice. He grabbed the rifle off his back and started to spray furiously. I walked straight over to him, my kids' cries of support ringing in my ears, and dumped the entire pot right over his head. It was glorious. The water ran off him and onto the pavement like the Mekong itself.

'I surrender,' he cried. 'Come here, old girl,' and he clapped his soaking arms around me, making me just as waterlogged as he was. It was a typical Kyle Mackenzie entrance – and just in time for lunch.

For years now, Kyle had been appearing and disappearing through our door. Despite my normal reservations about this sort of haphazard volunteerism, with Kyle it was different. It's strange but although the kids always loved to see him, they all instinctively knew not to expect him. They were happy when he was there – especially Srey who seemed to use him to practice all her newly found teenage coquettish charms. And I was happy, too, taking whatever time he could give us, and me, gratefully. But we didn't look for him when he was gone. Kyle had a way of showing he cared without making any promises and that, strange as it sounds, worked for us all.

'So - surprised to see me?' he asked, after we had all cleaned up and had our lunch of chicken and rice.

'No, not at all. Not really,' I said. 'I'm never surprised to see you. I'm just glad that when you do show up you still have all your limbs.'

'My limbs? Don't worry about that. I'm the best there is with these landmines. No way I'd blow myself up.'

'Not unless it's on purpose,' I wanted to say, but didn't. For all his friskiness, Kyle did have a dark side. I glimpsed a corner of it once soon after we met. I was just being curious about his work – why anyone would choose to do what he does, run the risks he runs in some Godforsaken place he has nothing to do with. But the more I probed, the more I could see a blackness come over his brow. It was a literal blackness as if he was suddenly standing in the shade. His usual adorable face turned vengeful, and it frightened me so much that I never asked him those questions again. After all, we're all playing hide and seek here in Phnom Penh, aren't we? All us *barangs*? In any case, I didn't allude to Kyle's suspected death wish, but instead I said, 'Well, if you *had* lost a limb or two, you wouldn't have made such a mess out there in front of the house. I assume you'll help clean it up?'

'Yes, Mother,' he said, laughing, knowing how much I hated it when he called me that. 'But I see you've got some new help around here.' He nodded towards Amanda who had appeared across the room and was busily feeding a toddler who had really already finished his meal.

'Yes. That's Amanda. Sam told me you all met at the restaurant the other night.'

'That's right. Imagine my surprise to see our Sam there, looking quite the young woman, sipping her wine at the bar.' Now my brow blackened. 'Don't worry, Deborah,' Kyle whispered. 'She was fine. It was Amanda I was more surprised to see.'

'What? Do you know her?'

'No, I never met her before in my life. I'm sure. But there's something…I don't know…familiar. Who is she, anyway?' We then exchanged one of those conversations held solely between two sets of eyes. In an instant, he saw my nervousness, I saw his interest, and we both concluded to let it alone, for now. He then let his voice get louder. 'Anyway, she was great with Sam. No worries. And next time I'll make sure to chaperone them for the whole evening.'

'Next time?' I asked.

'Of course,' he teased, following me into the kitchen. 'The horse is out of the stable now,' he said, or some such annoying quip.

The next day we were all up and ready early. All the kids were bathed, every last one of them. Their hair was combed, their clothes ironed. Amanda had slept over the night before to make sure she was here early to help, and even Kyle had agreed to join us by ten o'clock. It was to be a day full of ritual, and it started with one of my favorites. Everyone, beginning with Samnang, lined up in front of me as I sat on a stool in the back courtyard like something out of *The King and I*. Bowls of cool water with clean cloths were set on the ground beside me and, one by one, each of my children took turns washing my feet. Now there's a ceremony worth preserving. Everyone was quiet and respectful and, like every year, I was overwhelmed, not by the responsibility of being the only reliable parent for so many – no, it wasn't that – but rather, for being so loved.

When it was time for us to go to the *wat*, we lined up all the kids in pairs. We placed the youngest up front with me leading the way, the rest stretching back along the pavement. Sam and Amanda hovered in and out of the middle while Kyle walked behind the rest, Srey slinking her way beside him.

There were two *wat*s within walking distance of our house, but for New Year I always led us to the further, larger, more beautiful one. It was like walking into a carnival. Street musicians lined the painted walls surrounding the temple. The sound of drums and pipes drowned out the usual din of honking *motos*. Vendors sold nuts and candies wrapped in red and blue cellophane; puppeteers darted in and out of our line, dancing with the kids, drawing them into the celebration. The world was suddenly alive with colors: oranges, whites, gold and saffron robes on the monks, flags like sunbursts whipping against a blue sky. Once inside the walls, one of our favorite monks, one who always manages to come by just when some new child has joined the Home, led a small group of us to pray before the statue of Buddha, now adorned in its New Year robes of orange and yellow. Another group went to help build the ceremonial mountain of sand, each new grain destined to bring more health and happiness. By the time I set off to deliver our gift of food to the monks you could barely see them sitting there behind the bowls of rice, dried fruit, sticky sweets, pastries and cakes. No matter how little the Cambodians have themselves, there was always food set aside for the monks whose lives literally depend on the charity of the impoverished. As I placed my basket of coconuts and morning glories down with the rest, a boy's voice called out in English, 'Cool. Thanks. *Sursdey Chhnum Theiy!*'

'And Happy New Year to you, too,' I answered, peeking around to see the face behind the voice. He couldn't have been more than twelve or thirteen. He sat cross-legged, his bare feet poking out from his robes. The telltale cords of an iPod dangled around his shaved head. A teenager first. And, only then, a monk.

We spent the whole day at the *wat*, playing games, listening to music, praying whenever we could fit it in. After a few hours, the heat was starting to get to me. I found a piece of wall to perch on amidst the crowd. The stone was cool. A palm tree and the checked *krama* wrapped around my head sheltered me from the sun. I watched my kids rushing around the grounds as if they were at a fun fair. And I suppose, in some ways, they were. A Khmer fun fair – no artificial rides, just their spirits lifted though music, devotion and the knowledge that they were together, safe and loved.

Off to the side, I noticed Kyle's iconic Australian military hat sticking out of the crowd. It was unmistakable. He wore it everywhere, its wide brim clipped up to one side. If I turned a bit, I could see him standing behind a group of kids getting their faces painted. Srey was there too, of course, tugging on his sleeve, looking like she was talking a mile a minute. He seemed to be looking around and shielding his eyes as if trying to find someone in the crowd. He waved and soon I saw Amanda's head come into view. His entire body turned in her direction and they began to talk. Poor Srey. Her own body language was clear, even from a distance. She got quiet and then I saw her kneel down to be with the younger kids, their faces now

73

painted like lions. I didn't know where Sam was. But from my perch I watched Amanda and Kyle walk away from the crowd towards the cover of one of the smaller shrines.

'Mother, there you are.' I heard Sam's voice behind me. I turned to see her standing there, a sleeping Arun in her arms, Chak by her side. When Chak saw me he climbed onto the wall and slid into my lap.

'We have some sleepy boys, don't we?' I asked.

'Yes. And there are several more I left sitting with the old monks by the gate.'

'Okay. Help me get them home, and then you can come back if you want. I'm tired, too. But here – give me Arun. Go tell Amanda and Kyle what we're doing and I'll meet you by the street. I think I saw them go over there.' By the time I reached the gate with my two small boys attached to me, Sam was there, too, with the rest of the kids who were ready to go home. Srey was with her. 'Mother, may I go home now?'

'Of course. Have you had enough?'

'Yes. I've had enough.'

It wasn't until I was home and the younger ones were sound asleep, exhausted from the excitement of the celebrations, that I realized what I had done. I had left nearly a couple of dozen kids streets away, under the care of a distracted community of monks, some neighbours, and two volunteer workers I knew next to nothing about. Stranger than that, I felt more at ease about it than I believed I should have. But there had been a lot of sun, a lot of noise, and I was feeling tired and, to be honest, a little old. As I nodded off, I noticed my hands already asleep in my lap. My fingers were splayed as if I had just let something slip away.

Many things grind to a halt during the New Year holiday, and one of those is inevitably the mail. Just when school is back in session and you think life is back to normal, you find yourself plowing through a backlog of envelopes unceremoniously dropped at your door. It took me the entire morning, two cigarettes and two cups of coffee to get through it all. Some was junk, but not as much as you would think. How I've gotten onto the mailing lists of Australian travel agencies and Chinese jewellery companies I'll never know. But besides those few, there were letters from supporters, inquiries about volunteering, New Year's cards from old friends, political party solicitations, a few bills, several important donations (God bless them), and even an Easter card from my sister. That one surprised me. I had completely forgotten about Easter. As the years rolled by, my old Christian traditions seemed more and more out of place here. It is true that when I was negotiating with the nuns to take over the Home, they wanted to make sure I had come from a Christian background. They needed to feel that Jesus would still shine his grace on our 'Blessed Children.' I don't remember making any promises, but I don't think I disabused them of the idea, either.

I was certainly a Protestant like everyone else I knew, back in the heartland of America. Growing up, I did my share of Sunday school lessons and nativity plays. But it was never a big deal. My parents weren't great believers. We went to church because everyone else went to church, celebrated Christmas and Easter because all of America seemed to. I don't think I met a Jew until I was at college, and if I did I hadn't noticed much. And a Buddhist? Forget it. I may have grown up in the Sixties. I may have seen pictures of the Beatles in India sitting at the feet of the Maharishi. But all of that had nothing to do with me. As the eldest of four, the daughter of a father who owned a hardware store and a mother who was a nurse, I was too busy doing what I was asked and what I was supposed to do to think about anything else. I was a good girl. Maybe that's why when the tornado that was America back in 1970 finally did suck me into its eye and spit me out again with such ferocity and violence, I landed on the other side of the planet feeling nothing but anger and humiliation.

Easter now seemed beside the point, but it was still good to hear from Pat. 'PS,' she wrote on the left side of the card, 'Expect to hear from Admissions by mid-April. I wish it was just up to me. But think about visiting in any case. If Sam doesn't make it this year, we can try again next. Either way, the trip would be a nice graduation present for Samnang.' A graduation present? It took me a minute to realize what she meant. Sam was now eighteen. My sister was assuming that she was graduating from high school just like all eighteen-year-olds. I guess it never occurred to her that Sam's school might be different, might not have caps and gowns and pomp and circumstance on the football field. Pat just assumed that Sam was doing what all eighteen-year-olds she had ever known did. And what was that? Go to school, then graduate…then … then … Of course I had thought about Sam's future. I used to think about it a lot. Back when she was little, we had long discussions about what she wanted to be when she grew up. First, she wanted to be a nurse like me. Then a hairdresser. Then a movie star. For a while, it all seemed harmless. Let the girl dream. But as she got older, her sights narrowed. The more she understood what it meant to grow up where she did, how she did, the less she talked about her goals and aspirations. But I was wrong not to push. I had gotten selfish. I was seeing that now. My daughter had grown into an extraordinary person and it was my job to help her realize that and find her way out into the larger world. Why had I stopped dreaming for her? What was the point of devoting my life to saving these children if I didn't know what I was saving them for? Sam found me very quiet and distracted when she came to kiss me goodnight. She saw the Easter card and read it.

'Graduation? From what?' she asked.

'No, not from what. To what,' was my answer.

It didn't take long for the New Year to start showing its true colors. The holiday celebration might have been bathed in saffron and blue, but within a few weeks the color of this new year turned into an intense, opaque, troubling red – a red that got even more complex the more you peered into it: richer, fuller, seductive, but still disturbing.

It started with a pounding on the front door one Monday morning as the kids were lining up for school. Nita had just arrived to help with the breakfast dishes. She had barely closed the door behind her when the pounding began. I heard a shriek and then the hurried shuffling of bare feet.

'Miss Deborah. Oh no. Miss Deborah. Come!'

The kids were already massing around the door, and not knowing what I was about to find I had to push them firmly away. 'All of you, to the kitchen. Now. Sam? Take them.' It could have been anything. A deformed, disfigured beggar, not that that common sight would have troubled anyone. Or it could have been the police with their AK57s. Or an abused teenager, red with blood. The first thing I saw as I peered through the still opened door was a shot of red, but it wasn't the red of blood. It was the red of a cotton blanket within a reed basket, and squirming within the blanket was a baby. 'Goddamnit,' I breathed out loud. 'Don't tell me.' I bent down to look at it. Gently, I opened up the blanket, not so much to see the baby but instead to see if a note had been left as well. There was no note. That wasn't surprising, but still it would have been nice. It would have been nice to get a name, an age, or even a word of

77

thanks or sorry. But I've known mothers in this situation before and they are almost always so tormented by what they are doing that taking that extra time to write a few words is more than any of them can bear. I did understand that. But still.

'Oh Mother, a baby. Can we keep her? Is it a girl?' Srey was standing over me. I hadn't even noticed all the kids crowding around again, their curiosity having gotten the better of them.

'I don't know,' I said, lifting the basketful of baby. 'I haven't even looked yet. But it's time for school. Come on everyone. Line up. Who's walking with you? Sam? Amanda? Is Amanda here?'

'I'll go, Mother,' said Sam. 'It is my turn, and I have some classes this morning, too. Remember?'

'Yes, right. Okay, then. Let's go. It's getting late.' The kids lined up still staring at me but absolutely quiet. I remember that quiet very distinctly. No one knew what to say so no one said anything. Even the baby was completely still, lying in that basket which I had unceremoniously slung over my arm like some old load of laundry.

I didn't rush. I watched my kids march down the street to school like I usually did and only then did I slowly close the door behind me. 'Nita, take care of the kitchen, please. I'll take this to the sick room.'

What we called 'the sick room' was the old infirmary left over from when the nuns ran the place. It's a room with locked cupboards for medicines, a long, raised bed and two good, strong hanging lights. This is where I bring the kids when they're hurt or sick or whenever I don't quite know what I might find when I take a close look. I threw a sheet on the bed, placed the basket on the sheet, and slowly pulled apart the folds of the blanket. At first glance, the baby looked to be about six weeks old, but it's hard to tell when they're so malnourished. It was awake, though still

78

quiet, but when I slowly waved my hand in front of its face the eyes blinked and followed my movement. Okay. It wasn't blind. I continued the inventory. Breathing was slightly shallow though regular. The skin had color and elasticity, and although the ribs were protruding it seemed not to be actually starving. Two arms, ten fingers, and a reasonable gripping reaction. Two legs, ten toes, and sluggish, though existent, reflexes. And, not surprisingly, no penis. It's still easier to give away a girl than a boy. If anything, this one was lucky not to have been left on some rubbish heap to die alone.

Now that she was unswaddled she must have gotten cold because she started to kick her skinny little legs and cry. As she kicked, her makeshift diaper fell away. It was dry – too dry actually – but it was stained and old. I started to reach for a new, clean cloth diaper and noticed Amanda standing ghost-like in the doorway.

'Jesus, Amanda. You scared the shit out of me. Sweetheart, give me a hand, will you? Pass me that diaper? Amanda? Hey! You there?'

'Oh, sorry. I was …' she started to stammer and then slowly approached, handing me the diaper while never taking her eyes off the baby. She was moving in slow motion. It was weird, but now the baby was crying in earnest and I was too busy paying attention to the types of sounds she was making and her startled reaction to my touch to pay much attention to Amanda. I began to move more quickly, clicking into baby nurse mode. Bathe, dry, powder, diaper, dress, cuddle – but all that time Amanda just stood and watched. I could have used her help.

'Hey. What's up?' I finally said, once the baby had settled into the crook of my elbow and started sucking my knuckle (strong sucking instinct – another good sign).

'Huh?' she answered with a far-away voice. 'Oh, nothing. So, is it a boy or girl?'

'A girl.'

'What's her name?'

'No name. No nothing. No information at all.'

'Is she alright? I mean, will she be?'

'Hard to tell, but she's not in too bad shape, considering she's just been abandoned on our doorstep. She's lucky…aren't you, little one? Are you lucky?' I was now losing myself into baby talk as this tiny, helpless thing pulled me in and in and in with her huge eyes and soft gurgly sounds. 'Let's give you some water and see how that goes, okay? Some water first? And then maybe some formula?' I remembered I had a stack of mail I had needed to go through that morning and I thought about asking Amanda to take over with the baby for a bit, but one look at Amanda made it clear that this was one baby she was not ready to hold. I didn't think much of it at the time. Not everyone is comfortable with really little babies and the more I thought about it the clearer it became to me that this one couldn't have been more than two months at the most. That's much younger than any of the other babies in the house, far younger than I ever allow myself to take in. I learned that lesson early. For me, eight months was the absolute youngest – twelve months, even better. I just have too many kids with too many potential problems to take on the fragility of a newborn. And although this little one was superficially healthy, she was clearly going to have her own fair share of troubles. How could she not?

By lunchtime, I was pretty tired. Life was hectic enough without having a frightened, potentially sick and worrisome newborn on my hands. And Amanda acting like a deer in the headlights didn't help. Thank goodness for Nita. 'No Nonsense Nita' is what I call her and she really earned her nickname that day. After her initial outburst in the doorway, she became a housekeeping machine, cleaning the kitchen, dressing the little ones, making beds, sweeping floors. No chatter, no questions, no playing with the kids, no excuses. Nita saw a job and she did it. She had been like that for years. I could never be sure which days she would show up but when she did she worked like a fiend. She was one of the few people I had allowed myself to rely on. And thank goodness for that, because on that day Amanda was almost useless. She would do things I asked her to do – things she had been doing on her own initiative for months now – but after every chore she would come back to wherever the baby was and just stand there, staring. Finally, I lost patience.

'Listen, Amanda. Snap out of it, will you? It's just a baby, okay? You don't have to take care of her, but while she's with us I'll need you more than ever. If you're here, you're here. Got it?'

'Right. Sorry. I don't know what's come over me. She's just so...so...'

'...helpless?'

'...beautiful. What will we call her?' For the first time, Amanda started to approach. She even reached out to touch the baby's cheek who then grabbed onto Amanda's finger. I have never seen a more complex set of emotions surge across one person's face in my life. I didn't know what Amanda was feeling but evidently she was feeling quite a lot, and my instinct told me I had to put an end to it – quick.

'What will we call her?' I repeated the question. 'Baby. We'll call her The Baby. We're not the ones to name her. When I find a home for her, they'll name her. And hopefully, that won't be long.'

'What do you mean? You're going to send her away? You can't do that. She just got here. Who's going to take her? Where will she go?' Amanda was suddenly talking uncontrollably, rattling off arguments, near threats. And amidst all the 'you-can't-do-thises' and 'you-can't-do-that's' she grabbed the baby from me, stepped away and cradled her against her chest.

Time froze. All the background color of the world faded out to grey and I felt paralyzed. Amanda with The Baby in her arms looked like she could run, but I felt like I couldn't move. Whatever that complex set of emotions had been that I had seen on Amanda's face, they were now twisting around inside me. I stared at the pathetic image in front of me and I know I was, for one torturous moment, transported into a past of my own. There was Amanda with a newborn in her arms, but somehow they morphed into the memory of me, a young Kent State nursing student, kneeling beside another body and holding it in my arms, a larger body, a college kid, but a body nonetheless. Danger, anger, an old familiar panic threatened to swallow me up.

'Oh, Jesus,' I cried to myself. 'Stop it. Now. Don't do this. Not now.' I kept hearing those words in my head as I took enough deep breaths to bring me back to the present. Once there, I began to approach Amanda and The Baby, those two interlocked, lost beings. I reached towards them as if I was reaching towards a wild animal.

'Okay, Amanda. Take it easy. Give her to me. Come on now.' I was aware that I was talking to her the way you talk to a crazy person, choosing each word with precision and modulating my tone so everything sounded calm. Eventually, Amanda handed the baby over. 'There you go,' I reassured her. 'That a girl.' I noticed Nita and quickly handed her the baby while never taking my eyes off Amanda. Nita didn't speak very much English, but I could tell she understood everything that was happening. Taking the baby, she quickly moved away, leaving me cradling Amanda to my side.

But what was happening? Amanda wasn't crying. She wasn't hysterical, although I had feared that she had been heading in that direction. Instead, she was now standing

82

there, childless, trying to regulate her breathing, obviously trying to get back to normal. I guided her towards my office. I wanted to pull her towards me, to comfort her as we walked, but she was stiff, like a plank of wood leaning against a wall.

'Honey, are you okay? Do you want to talk about this?' I eventually asked.

'No. I'm fine. Sorry. I don't know what happened over there.' She pretended to laugh. 'But I'm fine. Really.'

'Okay. If you say so. But you do understand why we can't keep her, right? That she's just too little, too young?' Amanda was silent. 'Think of it this way...She's not really ours to keep. We're just holding onto her until we find her real home.'

'Okay. I suppose so.' She was reluctant, though she tried to appease me nonetheless. 'But it's just that she's so... It's heartbreaking.'

'I know. And we will do for her what we can. But we must find a proper home for her. She may be sick, but hopefully she's healthy enough and young enough for me to place her. To find her a real home with parents who can do much more for her than we ever could.' We reached the door of my office but Amanda didn't follow me in. Instead she just stood there staring at me. I hoped that she was taking in all that I had said, but I couldn't be sure. Her face had that same empty, stony look I had seen months before in my office when I had confronted her about her past. I put my hands on her shoulders and locked my eyes into hers. 'Amanda, you mustn't let yourself get attached.'

'Yes, I know.'

'Do you? Do you really?'

'Yes. I do,' she answered. Then she took a deep breath and moved away. 'But now, I think I better go help with lunch. I can hear the kids in the dining room already.'

And with that she walked away as if nothing had happened. She pretended to be back to her regular self, but as she walked I could see the effort it took her to get there. Each movement was calculated. Her shoulders moved up and around. She loosened her neck and straightened her back. She stopped, took a breath and smoothed back her hair. 'Okay, so who's hungry?' she chirped at the kids as she reached the table. It was a masterful, frightening performance and my own heart broke a little watching it.

Later that evening I had a quiet word with Sam. 'Keep an eye on Amanda and The Baby, okay?' I said as discretely as I could. But Sam didn't understand. 'I mean, she seemed a bit upset at first when The Baby came. Don't let her get too attached.'

'Too attached? Like she might want to keep The Baby?'

'Yes. Like that.' The idea seemed to be unfathomable to Sam. The idea of keeping the baby – and especially of Amanda keeping the baby – was so clearly irrational that Sam could barely believe such a problem could arise. 'Just watch. Don't let Amanda spend too much time taking care of her. And let me know if you have any ideas of where to place her. It's getting a bit easier to do Western adoptions again, but it's not as easy as it used to be.'

'Okay, Mother. But what about the doctor? Will you take The Baby to Dr Reith?' Sam asked. 'He is always such a help to us. I am sure he will know what to do.'

'Yes, I've already called him. I'll take The Baby there first thing tomorrow morning. He'll check her out and do some blood tests. But she doesn't look too bad to me. A little thin and frightened, poor kid, but not obviously sick. Whoever the mother is tried her best.'

'But of course, she could have HIV.'

'Yes, she certainly could.'

'It is a shame,' Sam said but not just as some common expression of sympathy. Rather, as a serious statement of fact. And of course, she was right. Shame is, indeed, what it was.

Over the next few days, we all incorporated The Baby's needs into our daily routine. Between Sam, Srey and I, and with the occasional supervised help of Amanda, The Baby got fed, dressed and cuddled with the rest of the kids pitching in however they could. The only problem, of course, was that The Baby was sleeping in my room. She was too young and frail to be down the hall with the others and she still needed her midnight feeds. With me was the only place she could be. I honestly didn't think it would be a problem. At sixty years old, I didn't need nearly as much sleep as I used to. Boy, was I wrong. By the end of that first week I was exhausted. And, when I get exhausted, I get cranky, and a cranky Deborah makes for a tense household. With each sleepless night I became more desperate to find a home for the kid. But with each sleepless night I became less and less able to take on the difficult task of finding one.

Amanda thought she had the answer. One morning when she caught me nearly falling asleep over my cigarette she shook her head and said, 'Deborah, forgive me for saying this but you're too old to be staying up all night with an infant.'

'Gee, you think so?' I snapped.

'Yes, I do. So why don't you let me help? I'll take her some of the time. Give you a break.'

'You? No way. She can't go off to your apartment. She can't leave the house overnight.'

'I know that. I mean I can stay over here. I'll do the night-time feedings.'

It was tempting. Very tempting. But, although Amanda seemed to have returned to normal after her initial freak-out, I just wasn't sure. I don't always listen to my instincts and, to be honest, they're not always right. I tend to be too cautious. Sometimes I can be, well, a little too cynical. But this time I was going to listen. 'Thanks, but I can't let you do that,' I tried to explain. 'Whoever left her here left her to be with me. She's my responsibility. You can help best by continuing to work with Sam as you do, making sure everyone else is getting what they need. As long as all the rest of the kids stay healthy and no other crises arise, we should be okay for the time being. I just wish I could have some help finding her a home. But you can't help with that. I need somebody who knows the system, has some connections. Somebody besides me.'

And then it struck me. It was obvious, really, and a testimony to just how exhausted I was that I hadn't thought of it before. Kyle. Kyle was the one who could help. Although Kyle was ostensibly employed by an Australian agency as a minesweeper, he had become much more than that. In Phnom Penh he had become known as a *fixer*. Those of us who lived our lives doing our work around the fringes of the establishment know that Kyle Mackenzie gets things done. How, we don't dare ask. Nor do we care. But he could be hard to find. I hadn't seen him since New Year's, but I had a sneaking suspicion that Amanda had. I was about to ask her if she knew where he was, but she had already marched off in a bit of a snit, I realized, not having her offer of help accepted. Too bad. I couldn't worry about her hurt feelings just then. I was now on a mission, reinvigorated by the prospect of assistance. I went in search of Sam and found her in the library, giving The Baby her bottle and helping Nary read a book for school. I picked Nary up, still so light and fragile from all her heart problems, and gave her a kiss on the forehead. 'No fever today, I see. I think you can go back to school tomorrow, Sweetie.'

'Yes, Mom,' she said. 'I am better. So I can help with The Baby now.'

'Yes, after you finish your reading homework,' Sam corrected. 'Homework first. Right, Mother?'

'Right,' I laughed. 'But Sam, a quick question. Do you know how I can reach Kyle? He hasn't been here since The Baby came. I need to talk to him.'

'Ask Amanda. He went away for a few days, I think. But she sees him sometimes.'

'Oh, does she? Okay. Thanks.' Just as I suspected.

I now went in search of Amanda, but my step slowed. No, I wasn't surprised to hear that Amanda was seeing Kyle sometimes. I could tell right away that he was intrigued by her, by the mystery of her. But still, the idea of it irked me.

Eventually, I found her in the garden playing with the toddlers. She had all four of them in a circle and had them rolling the ball back and forth to each other, calling out names of animals. It looked like a good game.

'Sorry to interrupt, guys. But Amanda, can I ask you something?'

'Of course,' she said, continuing to catch and roll the ball as it came back to her.

'Do you know how to reach Kyle Mackenzie? I want to ask him something.'

'Kyle? Well...'

'Sam said she thought you've seen him since New Year's and I need to talk to him.'

'Well, I have run into him once or twice, but...'

She was being evasive but I wasn't going to give up. 'It's important. Is he in town?'

'I'm not sure. I think so. Anyway, he said he would come by soon. I told him about The Baby.'

'Oh, really? Do you think he could come by today?'

'Today? I don't know.'

'Well, do you have his number handy? I seem to have lost it,' I lied. I had never had his cellphone number. I had never presumed to ask him for it.

'Yes, I have it. I'll go call him for you.' I would have preferred to call him myself but I didn't have the strength to argue. I didn't have the strength to do much but stand there staring at the circle of three-year-olds staring up at me with imploring eyes.

'Mama. Ball,' said little Khim, reaching up his hand to help me sit down on the ground to play. It would take more than one tiny hand to get me down on that ground, and as I lowered myself, making all sorts of grunts and moans on the way, the kids started to laugh.

'Mama's tired,' I said.

'Mama big,' said Khim.

'Gee. Thanks a lot, kiddo. Yes, I know. Big and tired.' But, to be honest, once I was down I couldn't think of a place I'd rather be.

Ten or fifteen minutes later I heard steps coming towards the garden, and then the smallest one jumped up out of the circle. Amanda was back, but so was Kyle and Khim bounded up into his arms.

'Here he is,' said Amanda. 'When I called he was already on his way.'

'I sure was,' Kyle said. 'I thought it was about time I checked in with you guys. I hear you've got a new addition around here.' Still holding onto Khim, he reached down and helped haul me up to my feet. He gave a noticeable smirk.

'Don't say a word, you. Not one word,' I threatened, teasing him. 'I'm an earth-mother type. I'm big-boned.'

'So you say.' And with one mighty tug I was up on my feet. Before I knew what I was doing I had thrown my arms around him as if I was another one of the kids. 'Hey, old girl. You alright?' He sounded concerned, and I couldn't laugh it off.

'Sorry, but Jesus I'm glad to see you.'

'Yeah. Figured you might be,' Kyle said, seeming to know everything even before I had told him. 'Come on. Take me to see this new kid.'

'Go see baby, go see baby,' the children were now all calling out, as they tugged and pulled Kyle into the house. Barely ten seconds with Kyle and the kids were already jumping and laughing and making a riot. It wasn't long before Srey also appeared, The Baby asleep in her arms.

'Oh, hello Kyle. And how are you?' she said in a terribly grown up voice. She was definitely more distant than usual with him, standing there looking all maternal and off-bounds. Maybe she was punishing him for not giving her the attention she had hoped for over the New Year festivities. I found her act pretty funny, and none of it was lost on Kyle.

'Good day, Srey,' he said, taking off his hat and giving a little bow. 'And who is this you're holding?'

'This, Kyle, is The Baby. Do not wake her, please. I just got her to sleep, poor thing. You see, I am helping with her very much now. It is quite a tiring job.'

What an act. But I didn't want to spoil it for her, so I stifled my laughter and said, 'Yes, Srey. I don't know what I would have done without you lately. Perhaps you could go put The Baby in her crib while I have a chat with Kyle?'

'Of course, Mother. I was just thinking that myself,' and she calmly walked away, giving a little smile to Kyle as she left. Honestly….

'And Amanda,' I continued, 'could you get these guys ready for their naps? We'll be in my office.' If Amanda was annoyed or disappointed at being excluded from this particular tête-à-tête, she didn't let on. Instead she corralled the kids and marched them down the hall.

I led Kyle to the office and offered him a chair. He seemed to fill up the room. 'So, Kyle,' I started. 'You steal in and out like a thief in the night. Where've you been since New Year?'

'I had a job out on the Vietnamese border. Just a quick there and back. Luckily, turned out to be nothing, just a couple of dud landmines. Scary for the villagers though. Didn't Amanda tell you?'

'Not that I remember, but it's been pretty crazy around here, as you can imagine.' So Amanda did know where he was, I was thinking. How much are they seeing each other, I began to wonder and blurted out: 'So, you two seeing a lot of each other these days, if I may ask?'

Kyle laughed and slung his arm over the back of his chair. 'You'd ask anyway, whether I let you or not. But I've got nothing to hide. We talked some over New Year's. And we've met for a drink a few times after. I admit I'm intrigued.'

'Intrigued is it? Not merely curious? Well, I suppose you're right. She's a puzzle, that one. I can't say I know much about her.'

'Me neither, though there's still something familiar, something I can't quite put my finger on. She's let a few things slip out, like that she was married briefly.'

'Yeah, that much I knew.'

'She sure can hold her drink, though.'

'What's that supposed to mean? Now Kyle, don't you mess with her.'

'Take it easy, love. What do you take me for? I just meant that even after a drink or two – two not eight – she's still pretty closed-mouthed about things. I mean, I know she was married and her husband died while they were in the Peace Corps. But that's about it.'

'Peace Corps? Well that's already more than I know.'

'I've got to say, Deborah, I'm a little surprised you've let her stay on like this. I mean, she's obviously got some sort of past. You've let your guard down on this one.'

'I know. Believe me, I know. But I guess we don't always do what makes sense now, do we? Look at you, just to take one small example.' Kyle gave no response to that. Just a half smile and a nod of his head.

'But anyway, is this why you called me here? To find out whether I've been bonking the new girl?'

'Jesus, Kyle. For God's sake. No, that's not it. But I will say, be careful. I don't think she's 100% stable, especially now with The Baby here. God knows what she's been through. Either of them, actually. I can't stand to think about it. But that's why I need you. Help me find a placing for this kid, will you? I'm just so tired from all these endless nights of feedings and diaper changes that I can't bring myself to make the calls, do the research. You know – like finding out who's doing adoptions now, who isn't; which functionaries will turn a blind eye, which won't. The regular political shit.' Kyle was smiling, almost laughing. 'Yes, you know more what to do than I do,' I acknowledged. 'Luckily I haven't had to deal with much of this stuff lately. But could you do whatever it is you do and help me out here?'

'Sure. Of course I will. I'll see what I can dig up, nose around a bit. There must be some movie star out there looking for a quick family. But you have to tell me what you know about the kid. Health-wise, I mean.'

'Again, I don't know much. Dr Reith did some blood work a few days ago but we haven't gotten the results yet. When we do, I'll let you know.'

'Yeah, well, it might not make much sense to make any serious enquiries until we do know. I mean, if she's really sick, forget it. I don't know what you'll do then.'

'God, don't say that. I gotta get her out of here. I tell you, Kyle, it's not that I'm too old. It's not that. It's just that – shit. I don't know if I can take on a sick infant. I mean a really sick one. It wouldn't be fair to the other kids. It wouldn't be fair to Sam.'

'Sam? Why Sam?'

'Maybe you haven't noticed, especially with Srey mooning around after you, but Sam's eighteen now. She already thinks I can't run this place without her. And with a sick baby to raise, she'd be right.' I didn't want to talk anymore about that, about Sam or about me, so I stood up. Kyle had already promised to help find a home for The Baby. That was enough for now. But as I went to open the door and head back to the kids, one more thing did occur to me. 'Oh, and Kyle,' I whispered, 'actually, there is something else. If you do happen to find out anything about Amanda….I mean, anything you think I need to know…anything pertinent to us here…'

'Leave it with me,' he said, giving me his old seductive wink. 'Leave it all with me.'

In the midst of all this work and worry, April ended with some good news for a change, not only for us specifically at the Home, but for all of us here in Cambodia. Against all odds, the Khmer Rouge Tribunal had made some progress. I had all but given up on it, thinking it was just another lie, some new cruel joke. But then the Cambodian Bar Association gave in to foreign pressure and cut all those exorbitant fees they had been levying on foreign lawyers. It was in all the papers and everyone thought it was a big deal. One evening, after dinner, Sam found me reading about it while I tried to rock The Baby to sleep – one hand held the paper, one foot rocked the cradle.

'Everything quiet here, Mother?' Sam asked. I put down the paper and gave her my attention.

'Quiet enough. How's everyone else? Is Thom helping the boys with their dancing? He promised, otherwise there'll be hell to pay with Madame.'

'Yes,' she laughed. 'They are practising. I think some are afraid of Madame.'

'Yes, it's funny, isn't it? Madame is one of the gentlest people I know, but man, she can look scary...And Amanda, where's she?'

'She's getting the little ones ready for bed. Do not worry. You have ten or fifteen minutes before they start looking for you.' Sam then took over the rocking while I went back to my reading.

'Good. I just want to finish this article.' I read for a few more minutes and then put the paper in my lap and sat there smiling. 'Sam, did you see the paper today?' I asked, knowing she hadn't. 'Listen to this. Some good news about The Tribunal.'

'Good news? Really?'

'Yes. Remember those foreign lawyers' fees – nearly five thousand dollars a year they were asking, just to work here? Well, after the stink everyone made about it, they backed down. They actually backed down. Now it's only five hundred dollars once instead of five thousand dollars each year.' Sam nodded her head as she listened to my latest civics lesson. 'Do you understand how important that is?'

'I think so. They are caring about what other people in the world think. Yes?'

'Yes.'

'And now, maybe, they will be more objective?'

'Yes, I hope so. And more honest.'

'More honest, yes. And more just.' Now Sam was smiling, too. She was beginning to get it.

'That's right. Can you imagine? Justice? Here in Cambodia?'

'Justice,' Sam said again, as if learning a new word.

'Yes,' I asserted, finding myself feeling much more optimistic than usual. 'If enough people want there to be. People like you.'

'People like me, Mother? What can I do?'

'Maybe not much right now. But in the future, sure.' Then something popped out of my mouth that I hadn't even realized was sitting there. 'You could become a lawyer, for instance.'

'A lawyer?'

'Why not?'

Sam stopped rocking The Baby and stood up. Her smile was gone. 'Mother, it is not like you to tease me in this way.'

'Sweetheart, don't be upset. What do you mean? I'm not teasing.'

'Well then you are being silly. I cannot become a lawyer.'

'And why not?' Sam said nothing but just looked at me as if I had suggested she might fly to the moon for a holiday. 'Listen to me, Samnang. You can do anything. Anything…' I was about to give her an impromptu you-can-be-anything-you-want-to-be-when-you-grow-up lecture when a loud squirting noise came from The Baby's bottom, followed by a high-pitched cry. I went to pick her up. 'Jesus, will you look at this! She has diarrhea again. What a mess.' Sam was already on her feet and coming to the rescue.

'Here is a new diaper. I will get some warm water,' she offered. 'Do you think we need to change her formula again? Are you fine for a moment without me?'

'Yes, I'm fine. Go get the water. Yuck…Oh, and tell Amanda to stay with the kids for a few more minutes until I can get there to tuck them in. Jesus Christ,' I muttered to myself. 'This is not good, poor thing.' Sam was already heading towards the kitchen when I looked up again and called after her. 'But listen, Sam. I want to talk about this

94

some more. Later.' She stopped and looked at me. 'Tonight. Before bed, okay?'

'Yes. If you wish, Mother.' Sam rolled her eyes at me in a way that was much more like something Srey would do than any look she herself had ever given me before. 'But first, Mother, The Baby…'

We didn't get to have the rest of our talk that night. It took a long time to get The Baby cleaned up, and then there were the other kids to settle down, tuck in, give their goodnight kisses to. By the time the house was quiet for the night, I was too exhausted to talk about anything. When Sam came into my room to say goodnight, I was already in bed, half asleep. 'I'm sorry, but I'm so tired. We'll talk some more tomorrow,' I told her.

'Okay, Mother.'

'But think about what I said. Okay?'

'Okay. I promise.' She bent down to kiss my forehead and tuck me in, as if I was just another one of her charges. 'In the morning, Mother.'

'I promise,' I said. I had no idea what she was thinking. But she was smiling again as she left the room. I could only hope that the beginning of our talk had exposed at least the tiny corner of a thought.

Then the theoretical became real. It was nearly the end of the month and the letter I had been trying not to care about finally arrived. The large airmail envelope with *Kent State Admissions Office* stamped on the corner stuck out amidst the pile of the day's bills and circulars like a diamond in a mud puddle. It seemed to shimmer with expectations as I held it in my hand, turning it over, feeling its weight. But it wasn't mine to open and Sam had taken the kids to the park. I knew I had to wait until she got home. It was a long thirty minutes. First, I left the envelope on my desk as if it was just any other letter. I went to the kitchen to check on dinner preparations. Nita was busy and shooed me away. I went back to my desk, picked up the envelope and held it to the light. Of course I couldn't see anything and the damned thing almost made my palms itch with frustration. So I marched myself off to Sam's room and placed it firmly on her bed.

'There,' I said out loud to no-one.

'There what?' I heard behind me. Amanda stood in the doorway. On her hip she held The Baby. A pile of clean laundry was in her arms. I moved aside so she could see the envelope propped up on Sam's pillow. 'Oh my,' she laughed. 'Here we go. You can't open it, you know.'

'I know. And it's torture.'

'You can't open it, but that doesn't mean you can't figure out what's in it. May I?' Amanda put down the laundry and picked up the package. 'Oh yes. This is good news. Definitely good news.'

'How can you tell?'

'Look how thick it is. There are at least five or six sheets of paper in here, and something hard, like cardboard.'

'So you think she got in?'

'What else? Feel it.' She began to laugh. 'If they didn't want her, they wouldn't have written page after page of rejections. How many ways can you say no?'

'Oh God. Jesus. I can't believe it.'

'Can't believe what? What are you two up to?' Busted. Sam was suddenly in the room staring at us and the envelope that we were holding between us.

'Sam, I didn't hear you come in,' I stammered. 'But look. This came in the mail for you. We didn't open it.' Sam took the envelope out of our hands and stared at it. I remember the room felt as if the sun had just gone behind a dark cloud.

'Oh. Here it is then. Thank you.' And she placed it back on her bed.

'Aren't you going to open it?' I asked.

'Yes. Later. I have to help Nary with her reading first.'

Amanda and I looked at each other in disbelief. Even The Baby whimpered. Amanda began to speak as if carefully setting each word one by one in its perfect place. 'I can get Nary started while you read the letter. From the size of it I can tell they have a lot of information they want to give you. Come on, Deborah. Let's give Sam some privacy.'

'Really, Amanda. It is fine. This can wait,' Sam argued. I remained silent, but Amanda persisted.

'No, Sam. I think it's better if it doesn't wait. Go ahead. We'll be in the library,' and she firmly ushered me out of the room. 'Come on,' she whispered to me. 'Let her have her moment.'

I guess I hadn't realized just how nervous and conflicted about it I was. Of course, I wanted Sam to get in. I couldn't bear the thought of anyone rejecting her for anything. But I also knew that getting in wasn't the same as going. I felt Amanda's hand on my back and I think I leaned into it because her touch went from a stationary pressure to a pat to a rub.

'It'll be okay,' she told me, half laughing. 'Don't worry. Whatever happens, we'll sort it out together, old friend.' Old friend. That sounded so good to me just then. I don't really have many old friends, but an old friend was exactly what I needed as I walked down that long hallway towards the other kids.

Amanda stayed by my side until Sam reappeared. The twenty minutes felt like a lifetime, but then Sam was standing there in the library, staring at us. She was quiet, as usual, and there was no special look of any kind on her face.

'I am sorry it took me so long. There was much to read.'

'And....?' Amanda and I both asked.

'They have accepted me, and they have been very generous. It would cost us almost nothing, if I go. I have some time before I must give them my answer,' she said and then sat down next to Nary to look at her homework.

I felt robbed. There was no excitement, no jumping up and down. Where was our celebration? 'Oh, Sweetheart, congratulations! I'm so very happy for you!' I threw my arms around her but I couldn't help but notice that she didn't hug me back.

'Thank you, Mother. But really. It is not so very important. We will see.'

Again, I found myself looking to Amanda for help. I didn't know what to do. I admit I had tried to imagine what it would be like when the letter came. I thought I had played out all the possibilities in my head. But this one I hadn't imagined. This real life scenario was instead just like any late afternoon on any normal day with nothing special happening. Nothing special. Nothing, except then there was Amanda handing over The Baby – something she never did once she got her hands on her – and saying, 'Deborah, can you check her diaper? She might need a change. I'll stay here to help Sam with the kids' homework.'

Before I realized it, I was holding The Baby and standing outside the library door. I listened for a moment but heard nothing except one kid reciting :

6 times 2 is 12, 6 times 3 is 18, 6 times 4 is 24…
and another kid reading:

…there was so much crying and screaming and pulling and pushing that the mother finally said, 'Enough!'

I went to change The Baby, but she didn't need changing. I was the one whose stomach was churning. I puttered around the house as long as I could before I headed back towards the library. Before I went in, I heard Amanda's voice: 'You know, it almost doesn't matter whether you go or not. The important thing is that now you can see what's possible for you. And remember, all of this is possible because of who you are and what you have already accomplished. That's worth celebrating, don't you think? That's worth being proud of.' And, although I didn't hear Sam's response, I did see her nod and momentarily lean her head against Amanda's shoulder, just like an old friend.

MAY

Kep and the beaches of the South...once the playground of the rich and famous, now rediscovered for its beautiful beaches and delicious crab. Visit close-lying Rabbit Island or experience the deep green jungles of the National Park. A holiday in Kep has something for everyone. Come to this paradise and you will truly fall in love with Cambodia and its people.
A Touristic Handbook, p. 14

The Baby's blood tests were inconclusive. When Dr Reith rang to say the HIV test was negative, Amanda happened to be in the office with me and overheard the conversation. Her hands involuntarily flew up to her mouth as if she needed to physically keep her joy caged in.

'Negative? She doesn't have HIV? Is that what he said?' she was asking even before I had hung up the phone.

'Negative...for now, Amanda.'

'For now? What does that mean? It's either negative or positive, right?'

'Wrong. It's not that simple. Even if a baby's mother is positive, the mother's antibodies can stay in the baby's bloodstream for up to eighteen months. But that doesn't mean the baby isn't HIV positive. It just means we can't see it yet.'

'Then what's the point of taking the test?'

'Well, she could already have been out and out positive, I guess.'

'So, it is good news.'

'No. It's nothing news. It's still wait-and-see news. And in the meantime, she's still got diarrhea and she's still very weak.'

Actually, I was getting more and more worried about The Baby all the time. The diarrhea was never-ending. It

100

seemed as if she couldn't keep anything in. I had tried all the home remedies I knew. I had switched the formulas over and over, but nothing was working, and no one can live on sips of boiled water alone. I had certainly dealt with sick children before and had watched enough of them slip into the relief of death. But this was getting to be too much. She was just so helpless and I was so tired. There had already been too many difficult nights when she would cry from hunger and I wouldn't know if I should try feeding her or not. Something was wrong. Here, I had assumed that the mother (whoever she was) had left her with me thinking that anything I could do for her must be better than what she could do herself. But now I wasn't so sure. Maybe the mother had just given up. Maybe she was just too tired and at her wits' end – just like I was getting to be. In reality, it didn't matter whether this tiny person had HIV or not. It was looking more and more like she wasn't going to make it anyway. But Amanda refused to believe it.

'Look Deborah,' she said once again. 'Let me help. There must be something we can do, but you're just too exhausted. You're going to get sick yourself if you don't watch out.'

So I gave in. Just this once, I told myself.

'Okay. Tonight. You stay with her tonight. Set yourselves up in the library if you want.'

'Oh, thank you. Thank you.' She was so happy, so excited, it made me immediately regret what I had agreed to.

'Okay. But just one night.'

'Yes, of course. But you get some sleep.'

'And take lots of boiled water and diapers with you.'

'Yes, of course.'

'And don't try to give her too much. Barely an ounce. She seems to be worse at night.'

101

'Okay. I'll give her little tiny sips, but often. She'll be fine. We'll be fine. You'll see.'

'Yes, well, in the meantime, we still have the rest of the day to get through. And something's going on with Chak. He's getting quiet again. With all the tumult, I haven't been able to spend as much time with him as he needs. I better go check on him now.'

'Okay. And I'll go see to Sam and The Baby. Sam probably needs a break herself.'

And so it started. Desperate times call for desperate measures, they say. Against my better judgment, I let Amanda get more involved with The Baby, and once she started there was no stopping. Their first night together went well enough. I got some sleep. Amanda reported that The Baby only made one mess at two in the morning, but was able to keep in nearly three ounces over the rest of the night. And Amanda looked fine…actually, better than fine. It was becoming clear to me that she wasn't only happy to be taking care of The Baby, she needed to be taking care of The Baby. After nearly three weeks that felt like three months, I couldn't say no.

By the end of a week of shared night duties, Amanda was still fine. I was less cranky and The Baby was – well, she just was. No better, no worse. Sometimes she could take her feedings, sometimes not. She wasn't losing more weight, but she wasn't gaining any either. Sometimes she was responsive – I think I even heard her giggle once, although it might have been gas – but usually she just lay there looking around, sometimes yawning, sometimes kicking her tiny feet. We each took turns holding her as much as we could, as much as we dared given her unpredictable gastric explosions. The rest of the children just accepted her as they accept everything, as one more piece of their present reality.

But it was now deeply into May, and each day was getting more humid. The rainy season was bearing down on us.

'Mother, Mrs Lang at the school asked if we wanted to borrow her car again this year,' Sam reported one day. 'She said we could, but I did not know what to tell her.'

'Oh, Sam, our holiday. I completely forgot.' I felt awful. 'But how can we go with all this? I can't leave The Baby.' I was in despair. Every May we went away for a bit. Sometimes it was just a long weekend, sometimes as much as a week. Sometimes I took the older kids; sometimes it was just Sam and I. But every year at this time, before the monsoons came, we got out of Phnom Penh. One way or another, we made our escape into the countryside and it was always a lifesaver. If I ever needed a holiday, I needed it now. But how could I possibly go? 'I'm so sorry, Sam. I don't know what to do, how we can manage it. I hate to disappoint you.'

'Do not worry about me, Mother. I am happy to stay at home. It is you I worry about. It is you who needs the holiday.'

Sam wasn't the only one who was wondering about our annual holiday. Srey had gone with us the previous May and she now started to ask about it, too. But her question was not what I had expected:

'Mother, I was thinking. What if Amanda and I stay at home with Sam and we all take care of the others together while you go away?'

'What, me go away? By myself?'

'Or you can go with someone else, but you do need to get away. You work so hard.'

'Oh, Srey. I don't know. I really don't know if I can. How can I leave The Baby?'

'We can take care of her. All of us together. Really.'

103

'Let me think about it. But thank you.' I gave her a kiss and realized how tall she had gotten. I couldn't kiss the top of her head anymore, and she was looking at me eye to eye.

'I know it is hard to go now,' she said. 'But you must. You so need it.'

Clearly, everyone was worried about me. I wasn't looking that bad, I didn't think. Okay, so I'm an exhausted, overweight sixty-year-old woman, but it would take more than one poopy baby to lay me low. But let's face it. I was desperate to go away, too, just for a few days. However, I wanted to go with Sam, especially since I still hadn't gotten her to talk about her college acceptance. If she didn't make a decision soon the choice would be taken out of her hands. Maybe that's what Sam had been planning all along, but it wouldn't do for me. No, a few days away would give us time to talk. We had to talk. We needed to go and now that the idea was in my head, it was all I could think about.

Once again, Kyle came to the rescue. He had gotten into the habit of coming by most afternoons. He would take a bunch of kids to the swimming pool or the park and, I noticed, basically be wherever Amanda happened to be. I remember once carrying The Baby on my hip as I passed him in the hallway and making the mistake of asking him to hold onto her for a minute.

'What, are you joking? Get that thing away from me,' he said, and he wasn't laughing. But that's when he had this great idea. 'You know, why don't you take the kid back to Dr Reith? Check her in for a few days. Face it, something's not right. And if you don't get it sorted now, you'll never get her adopted. Nobody wants a poop machine.'

And that's what I did. I took The Baby back to Dr Reith. To be honest, this follow-up visit was really overdue. Dr Reith's clinic is always so overloaded I had wanted to try to get the kid better myself. But although The Baby did have

104

some good days, those were sporadic and unpredictable. She still wasn't stable. And, I guess, neither was I.

Dr Khim Reith is a hero, pure and simple. A Khmer himself of indeterminate age, he has that wonderful round face and those deep soft eyes that hide a lifetime of concern and frustration. I don't know his whole story. It never seemed right to ask even though we've known each other for years. But I do know he's young enough to have grown up after the War and to have managed, probably by sheer brilliance and determination, to get a decent education. Somehow he attracted the attention of a well-meaning French family and they paid for him to go to medical school in Paris. It's not all that unusual a story, to be honest. These incredible acts of generosity are played out in all sorts of unsuspected places and ways around this country. You usually don't hear about them, but they're there, inching everyone forward, keeping dreams simmering under the surface of despair. There have been the occasional quiet evenings when I've been visiting some sick kid or other at the clinic when he's sat with me and had a medicinal glass of brandy. After a sip or two he often gets nostalgic about his life back in France. How could he not? His stories are wonderful, mostly about food. Sometimes he talks about midnight walks along the Seine, standing on a darkened bridge watching the lights play with the ripples on the river. Then his eyes sparkle, the weariness starts to leave his face and you can catch a glimpse of the brave, idealistic young man he used to be. Then, as soon as his training was over, he came back here, to Phnom Penh, under the aegis of the French Red Cross. He helped set up the clinic, worked for a while as the junior doctor under a series of consultants who came and then left again as soon as they could. But Dr Reith always stayed. Even after the funding stopped. Now he runs the clinic on his own, with the help of a few local nurses, some so-called trainees from wherever he can find them, and whatever money he can extract from wealthy, guilt-ridden Westerners. I say he's a hero, but who knows? Maybe he's just another quixotic madman in disguise.

I called to let him know The Baby and I were coming, but even so we had quite a long wait before he was able to see us.

'Oh, Miss Deborah. I am so sorry you had to wait.' He always calls me 'Miss Deborah'. I once urged him to drop the 'Miss' but he refused. 'I call you that out of respect. My respect for you is great. Please do not ask me to stop.' Not much I could say to that. So, despite our friendship, I am still 'Miss Deborah', and he will always be 'Dr Reith'.

He led us into a small examining room, one of three cinderblock cubicles with a narrow table and strong overhead lamps. Gently, he took The Baby from my grasp. She was so small I could hardly tell the difference. 'And how is she?' he asked.

'Fine. Not fine. I don't know. No change.'

The Baby let herself be examined and then, helpfully, she gave a little poop for him to test. Not too big. Not too disgusting. Throughout, he was very thorough and although he chatted with me as he worked, he never smiled.

Loosely swaddling The Baby and still holding her in his arms he finally spoke. 'Miss Deborah, I have two concerns. The first is the child. She is very young, maybe three months at most now. And, as I explained, we cannot know about AIDS for certain yet. But it does not matter. She is not thriving. For some reason her stomach still cannot digest properly. There is some more I might be able to do for her, but if she does not respond soon…'

'That's what I was afraid of, Doctor. I just don't know what else there is to do for her.'

'I know you are doing the best you can.'

'I am, but…' Neither of us needed me to finish that sentence. Instead, we both stared at the child, letting her quiet smallness finish it for us. 'But you said you have a second concern?'

'Yes. My second concern is you.'

'Me? Oh, I'm alright.'

'So you always say, but I am not so sure.' Then he proceeded to examine my eyes, my throat, my glands, all with one hand while still holding The Baby in the other. I complained, of course, with every touch. Although a trained nurse, I always hate being around doctors. I don't hate working with doctors; I just hate being a patient. I hate being prodded and examined, being made to feel like I'm not all I should be.

'Please, enough,' I said. 'I'm fine. Really. I'm just tired.'

'Yes, I can see you are tired. And Kyle…'

'Kyle? What's he said?'

'Not very much. He was here the other day making some inquiries and mentioned the strain you were under. That is all.'

'Goddamnit.'

'Now, Miss Deborah, don't say that. Kyle is your friend. Let him worry about you. It is good for him to worry about someone. I believe he needs it as much as you do. Now, here is my suggestion.'

Then he mapped out a plan of action which nearly reduced me to tears. I was to take The Baby home for two nights – no longer – during which time I would prepare for my holiday somewhere 'by the cool of the sea' as he called it. Then I would bring The Baby back to him for more tests and observation. I must go for no less than five days, and I must not argue about it. 'Then we will see,' he said.

I went home and called a meeting of 'the group': Sam, Amanda, and Kyle, whose phone number I now had firmly etched in my brain. But I also included Srey and Thom, the two kids next in line. I outlined Dr Reith's plan and asked them what they thought. Not surprisingly, all of them thought it was a wonderful idea and each of them offered to stay home.

'What? You're sending me off on some ten-hour hot and dusty cross-country drive all by myself? Are you guys trying to kill me?' I turned full-faced towards Kyle and sneered. 'And I thought you were so worried about me.' Of course, he just laughed.

Amanda spoke first. 'Deborah, of course you shouldn't go alone,' she said. 'And of course I am the likely one to stay. After all you've done for me, taking me on, giving me work, it's the least I can do to repay you.'

'Repay me? You have already more than done that. But yes, I guess you're right. I guess I would need you to stay. But what about you, Kyle? Could you spare the time to stay with the kids, too? This stupid holiday is all your fault, after all.'

'Okay, okay. So I butted in a bit. Not unheard of around these parts. And anyway, I can see you're protesting too much. You know you want to do this. You've probably already got the whole thing sussed out in your head.'

I had to laugh. Of course he was right, and of course everybody knew it.

Then Sam spoke. 'Mother, I will go with you. I know there is no other way, if the rest will forgive me.'

'And I will stay to help Amanda,' Srey added. 'Kyle will be a big help, but we need another woman here, too,' at which point The Baby let her own agreement be known by producing a new explosion. We all laughed and groaned and scurried around to get her cleaned up. Thom stood off to the side wanting to help but not quite knowing what to do. I went up to him and put my hand on his shoulder. He looked so old, so strong, I remember getting all choked up as I tried to speak. Clearly, Dr Reith was right. I was an emotional wreck. The exhaustion from taking care of this baby was getting the better of me. 'Thom, you are the oldest son. Kyle is here to help, but you must be the responsible one. The girls will show you what to do, but I rely on you to keep everyone safe.'

'Yes, Mother. You can rely on me.' Even now I can see the smile that came over his face and, to this day, the thought of it slays me.

Two days later, as promised, Sam and I delivered The Baby to the waiting hands of Dr Reith and then set off in our borrowed car with its intermittent air conditioning towards Kep and the southernmost coast of the country. Our Khmer Home for Blessed Children was left in the care of a most unlikely quartet: a 16-year-old girl with delusions of grandeur, a shy powerhouse of a 17-year-old boy, and a wild Australian with shady connections and a death wish. But the biggest question mark of all was still, of course, Amanda.

It didn't really take ten hours to get to Kep. Now that we were nearly two-thirds of the way through this first decade of a new century, a road had been created to parallel the Mekong and connect the capital with the southernmost portion of the country. Notice I said 'created' and not 'paved.' Although tarmac was occasionally in evidence, just enough to make us feel as if the land beneath our borrowed wheels was under our control, more often than not the road turned again to dirt, slowing our progress as if to remind us that this, indeed, Cambodia we were crossing and nowhere else on earth. But given that it was May and the entire country was aching for rain, all that dirt had turned to dust. We kept the car windows closed for as long as we could, but eventually we had to open them. There is only so much that the air conditioner in a twelve-

109

year-old Toyota can do. We hardly cared, though. Sam and I were happy to inch along, in and out of tiny nameless village after tiny nameless village, smelling the sweet scent of ripe mangoes and bananas baking in the afternoon sun.

It had been a while since we had ventured into this part of the country. Whenever we were able to get away I tried to take us somewhere new. For all its faults, I do love Cambodia and I want my kids to love it, too, but not for its new luxury hotels and gilded palaces; not for its sharp-eyed entrepreneurs and go-getting hustlers; not even for the tradition of its monks or the beauty of its art. I want them to love their country as it is in its heart, where the need to recreate life with each new season is accepted and respected, where generations hold each other's hands and turn towards tomorrow, where hope refuses to die and laughter is used like fertilizer to keep their spirits growing. Some years we ventured north towards Siem Reap and the ancient temples of Angkor. Two years ago I took a group of boys to Tonle Sap Lake where pigs live in water and alligators are raised like sheep. But Dr Reith had said to head for 'the coolness of the sea', so we headed towards Kep and the Gulf of Thailand. Sam hadn't been there since she was little and her excitement was growing with each kilometer. How much had changed, I wondered?

Not much. One benefit of going slowly is that you can take your time to see what is outside your window and beyond the dust clouds. The countryside is so harsh and so beautiful. Fields of rice paddies stretch for miles studded with the bony frames of oxen, white against dirt brown. Distant hills are clouded with haze like oases, mirages in a sun-parched expanse. Your eyes water as you stare and you can almost remember that in just one month or two all of this will be flooded by the rising waters of the monsoon season. Trees will then look like bushes; those distant mountains like outcrops. This scenery has lasted forever, will last forever, ebbing and flowing with time and the seasons, green turning to brown and back to green again, earth becoming water becoming earth, reminding us that of all the constants in this world, the most reliable constant is change.

The roads are never empty. Far from it. Roads here are not just ways of getting from one place to another. They are places in themselves. People live beside them. Animals walk in them. On their edges makeshift shops sell everything from lotus flowers to transmission fluid. There are no curbs, no sharp delineations between spaces to move and spaces to stop. Everything is everywhere. Motos pull up beside oxcarts beside bicycles-built-for-five beside open-backed trucks carrying thirty workers to the fields beside air-conditioned buses filled with American tourists beside Mercedes with government license plates and rolled-up windows beside horses pulling trailers full of construction equipment beside barefoot children walking walking walking. Like the earth that transforms to water, here the past merges with the future leaving you with nothing else to do but work if you can in the mornings, rest as you must in the hottest part of the afternoon, and sleep as best you are able at night.

Kep itself is a fairytale. Once a resort, a Riviera of sorts for wealthy Frenchmen and American film stars, it is now scarred with the remains of the Khmer Rouge's reign of destruction. As we drove along the beach road we saw long-deserted villas looming like vultures over hotel construction sites. It quickly became clear that, although we were too early for Kep's renaissance, we had certainly left its dark ages behind. I was beginning to wonder where this guesthouse of ours could possibly be among all this new construction. A friend from the school had recommended it, and with such short notice I barely had time to make the phone call to reserve our room. The owner assured me, though, that we would have air-conditioning, a private bath and a view of the Gulf of Thailand. But who knows? We drove almost to the end of the road before Sam was finally able to say, 'Look, Mother. Up there. Can that be it?'

'Even if it isn't, it's going to be.' I pulled the car into one of four spaces at the foot of a series of steps leading to a two-story pink building nestled against a hill amid acres of trees and flowers. No sooner had our car door slammed shut than two young Khmer men came scurrying down the steps. They took one look at Sam and smiled. Then they saw me and bowed respectfully, reaching for our luggage.

'You are new guests from Phnom Penh? Yes? Please follow.'

'Look, Mother. A swimming-pool!' Sam said.

'And look at that view,' I answered. We were standing just across the road and slightly above one of the most beautiful stretches of sea, inlets, coves and clouds that I had ever, ever seen. I was feeling better already.

If we just spent four days sitting by the pool and sleeping in the air conditioning I would have been content. But after only one day of doing nothing Sam came up with an idea for an 'adventure' (just what I needed).

'Mother, we are very near the boat to Koh Tonsay. Do you remember? Let's go, please!'

Koh Tonsay, otherwise known as Rabbit Island, is a small island of pure magic just a few kilometers offshore: white sandy beaches, fresh crab and phosphorescent coral. We had been there once before when Sam was about seven years old, and I too remembered it as one of our most glorious adventures. As I recalled, there was nothing there but a few huts and a zillion palm trees, but I also seemed to remember a thirty-minute death-defying ride in a leaky motorboat driven by an eight-year-old local boy. The hotel proprietor assured us that the island was still there and that it was one of the most beautiful spots in the world with the best swimming anywhere. Progress had reached its shores, though. About ten families lived there full-time now and acted as fishermen, cooks and hosts for the handful of huts they now provided for tourists. 'They even have mosquito nets,' she told us, 'and all for only five US dollars.'

'Really? You can stay overnight now?' Sam was nearly jumping up and down with excitement. 'Oh, Mother. Just think!'

Just think, indeed. Sam wanted us to leave the air-conditioned comfort of our newly renovated bedroom with its two queen-sized beds and clean white sheets, for a night in a hut in the middle of a bay. Not exactly my idea of fun, but how could I say no?

And so, the next day after lunch, we put a few necessaries into a string sack and set off for Rabbit Island: an afternoon of heaven, I was sure, followed by a long, buggy, snake-ridden night of hell. It was a short walk down the strand to the dock, if you could call it that. Actually, the dock was a shelter with a thatched roof – sort of a Khmer version of a bus stop – and next to it was a wooden sign painted green and nailed to two tree limbs staked into the ground. It announced, in both hand-written Khmer and English white paint: 'Have Boat for Visit Island.' A very old, very fat Cambodian woman approached us, her hand already outstretched.

'You go to island? Three dollah. Wait here for boat. Boy come soon.'

I looked out across the sea to the island. Sam could tell I was nervous. 'Oh, Mother. Don't be silly. We will be fine. I am sure the boat is safe.'

'Yes, yes. Of course. But just in case…' I walked a few feet away from the mooring to a little shrine which had been set up, nestled into the trunk of an ageless tree. On a tall, patinaed copper base stood the most beautiful tiny gold model of a temple and, in it, a tiny weather-beaten

113

Buddha. I wasn't sure if this was a good sign or a bad one, but just in case I proceeded to have my own little silent moment there with bowed head and closed eyes. You see, raised in the landlocked expanse of the Midwest, I've never really felt happy in a boat.

'Madame. Come now.' I turned to see what looked like a six-year-old boy waving to me. (Could it have been, after all these years, the same boy, now even younger, lost in time ferrying passengers to their doom like some Cambodian Charon?)

'Okay. Okay. Where's the boat?' I asked, but then I saw Sam wading out into the water, following our captain to what could only be called a rowboat. Yes, it was brightly painted green and red. Yes, it had a flag on one end and something that looked like a rudder attached to the back. But a rowboat it was nonetheless, and there Sam went, the most precious person in the world to me, happily climbing aboard, helped by a four-foot-tall Cambodian boy who was now looking my way. The things you do for love.

I nearly toppled the whole thing over as I hoisted my bulk into the boat. Hearing the laughter of Sam and island-boy didn't help. Even before I could settle myself down on the bench and start to complain, a lawnmower motor jerry-rigged to the back revved up and we smoothly, gently, slowly glided away.

'You see, Mother. Not so bad,' Sam said, patting my hand which had already turned white from clenching onto the side for dear life.

'Not bad. Good,' the boy agreed, as he steered us across the Gulf so effortlessly, so happily that by the time we were slowing down and 'setting anchor' I was completely convinced that this ageless, timeless small being was indeed the master of all he surveyed.

I climbed out and onto the white sands of the empty beach which was shaded by a grove of palm trees.

Everything was silent but for the easy lapping of the sea against the land. Looking around, I started to laugh. Srey would have loved this, I thought. Her own real-life Gilligan's Island. Already Rabbit Island was working its magic, because I had quietly promised myself to bring her back here one day.

'See you tomorrow,' the boy called to us as he jumped back into the boat and sped away as if he was now riding a Harley. Before I could say 'Now what?' a man came up to us, bowed and directed us to a small group of huts about a hundred yards down the beach. A woman was setting banana leaves over an open fire, while another was cracking open coconuts. Nearby, a man was heaving a net-full of the day's catch onto the beach. Scattered around were makeshift picnic tables, benches, hammocks and a large square wooden platform covered with hand-dyed cloth. Our guide motioned towards everything we could see and said, 'All for you. Enjoy.' We spent the rest of the day rocking ourselves to sleep in hammocks, collecting shells and broken bits of coral, swimming – or rather, floating – in the cool sea water. I hadn't felt so at peace for a very, very long time. And Sam looked like the girl she really was, the weight of her responsibilities, real or imagined, left behind with each footprint in the sand.

As dusk approached, we were shown our hut – simple, but dry and clean, with two solid army beds, yes, complete with mosquito netting, and behind it a cleared path to the facilities – rudimentary to be sure, but at least there was a roof, four walls and a door (which was more than I had originally expected). By that time I couldn't care. I was so content to be where I was, with my daughter, comfortable and relaxed and then...extremely well fed. While we had been lazying through the day, the Rabbit Islanders had been preparing a feast – fresh crab steamed in banana leaves, chunks of coconut and fried bananas, sticky rice topped with steamed fish, coconut juice and, for me, a bit of palm wine. As we ate, we watched the sky preparing itself for sunset, streaks of cloudy pink arising out of the blue, yellows becoming orange and then bright, deep, bottomless red.

Plum wine and beautiful skies loosen tongues, and before I knew what I was saying, I was in the midst of the conversation that had so abruptly ended a few days earlier with the sound of exploding poop. Almost as if talking to myself, I picked up exactly where I had left off. 'I hope you don't misunderstand what I meant before, Sam, that time when we were talking. I hope you know I would never tease you, and certainly not about something like your future.'

'Yes, I know. I was wondering when you would remind me of that talk, Mother,' Sam joked. 'But, since you want to be serious now I must ask – how could I become such a thing as a lawyer even if I wanted to? I am not smart like that.'

'Sam, it's me, your mother, you're talking to. Come on! You know how smart you are.'

'Okay, yes. I know I am smart. But I do not mean smart. I mean educated. I have only gone to Khmer school. It is not enough. You know that is true.'

Of course I did, and maybe that was why I had dreaded this conversation. Guilt. Maybe I should have sent her to the International School. I could have found a way if I had tried hard enough. But she never pushed for it, and there were the rest of the kids to think about. Even if I could send Sam, I could never afford to send them all. 'I know,' I admitted. 'I have always felt bad about that.'

'No, Mother. Do not. It never would have made sense. And I have been happy at school.'

'And you have done well, well enough to show everybody how much more you can do if given the chance.'

116

We then sat in silence for a few moments, listening to the waves, watching the sun disappear behind the horizon.

'This is so beautiful, Mother. Thank you for bringing me here. I told you you would like it. I do know what is good for you sometimes.'

'I admit it, you do. Sometimes. But not always.' Sam looked at me with a questioning hesitation that seemed almost like a warning. I started to pick my words carefully. 'Sam, our lives – yours and mine – will always run together, next to each other, parallel. But the line your life takes does not have to be the same as mine. You do not have to be a nurse because I am. You do not have to run the Home because I do.' And this was, I now realized, the other reason I had feared this conversation. Sam needed to know that she could leave me, that she must leave me in order to find her own way. But I also needed to convince her that I would be fine when she did, even if I didn't quite believe it myself. 'Sweetheart, what about university? Wouldn't you like to go?'

'Oh, Mother, it is too hard to decide…'

'But you have to tell them.'

'I know.'

'What is stopping you then?'

She started to laugh. 'Stopping me? Do you really not know?'

'I want to hear you say it. I don't want to guess.'

'Alright. I will say it. You, and forty children, and everyone who needs me.' Of course I knew this was the reason, but I was silly to think hearing her say it out loud would make it any better. If anything, it made it worse. I took a minute before I responded.

'Okay. But what about what you need?'

'Everyone else needs me more.'

'No, Sam. That's not true. That can't be true. Listen, sweetheart. You must believe me. I'll be fine. We'll all be

117

fine. I'll get help.' Now it was Sam's turn to wait before she spoke.

'You will get help?'

'Yes.'

'Who? Amanda?'

'Maybe. Probably not.'

'Why not?'

'I'm not sure.'

'But then…?'

Like bullets – boom boom boom – each question pierced another target. I could see Sam's brain clicking into action, reloading with each new thought, aiming for the next issue. She pulled the trigger again. 'Perhaps, if Amanda stayed.'

'I don't know about that. I doubt it would be Amanda. But I'll find somebody.'

'Who?'

'I don't know. That's not your concern.'

'But it is. Mother, it is my main concern. You ask, would I like to go to America? Would I like to go to university, become a lawyer, have a better life, help my family, my country? Become someone special? Yes. Of course I would. Especially now with the Tribunal, so many things seem possible. But, Mother, I will not leave you on your own. It is as simple as that.'

My heart was breaking. I thanked all the gods that I could think of that the sky had darkened enough so that Sam wouldn't see the tears in my eyes. I took a few moments to collect myself and then said, 'If I find some help, will you think about it?'

'Yes. I will think about it. But not tonight. No more now, please. And not you, either. Let us just sit and listen and enjoy where we are. Yes?'

The sun had completely set and we were sitting in moonlight. It sparkled on the sea like tears dropping from my own heart.

I didn't sleep very well that night. Sam, in her youth, was able to turn off her brain and lull herself to sleep with the sounds of waves and distant cicadas. I had no trouble falling asleep, but I didn't sleep soundly. For me, it was a night full of nightmares. I've been plagued by these crazy misfirings of my brain my whole life long, on and off. Sometimes I knew why the night terrors came and stayed, and sometimes I didn't. It had been years since I'd had a bad one, though, but to be honest, it was silly of me not to have realized one would come along now. I may not have admitted it to my waking self, but my sleeping self was now all too ready and willing to explain to me why I had really been so worried about my conversation with Sam. No, it wasn't guilt over her schooling. It wasn't even my continuing worry about Amanda. It was something much deeper, much older, something I had left behind thirty years earlier, never talked about, never acknowledged. It was fear. No, it was more than fear. It was utter, extreme terror.

The recent news out of America didn't help. I saw the item in the paper and, of course, it was all over the television. It was the sort of thing I always tried to ignore with each more frequent, more deadly occurrence. But these events, and especially the most recent one, don't just fade away. They lodge themselves in the back of my brain and wait to jump out and arrest my heart when I least expect it.

On April 16, just a few weeks earlier – I remember the date exactly – a twenty-three-year-old student walked into a Virginia Tech classroom building and killed thirty-two students. The news report said that his subsequent suicide made this shooting the most deadly in US history. And so it continues. Children go to American colleges to learn. Then, for no reason other than random insanity and the 'right to bear arms', some of them die, are murdered with guns as they sit at their desks, cross grassy quads, lean chatting with friends against library pillars. That night on the paradise of Rabbit Island, as I slept beneath palm trees just beyond the easy waves, my dreams were filled with images of bleeding, dying schoolchildren. First, I saw them cowering under desks as I imagined they must have in Virginia, in California, in Pennsylvania and Iowa. But that wasn't what woke me up covered with sweat, my head full of my screaming choking voice. What woke me up was another image, a thirty-year-old image of my own college campus, my own fellow students bleeding on the ground, a row of rifles still shooting, triggers pulled but not by random madmen. The triggers of my nightmare, both waking and sleeping, were pulled by policemen, American policemen, storming the campus of Kent State, killing my friends. And me? I was a young nursing student, first cowering behind a statue of a man on a horse, then holding the hand of a student as we rushed him to the hospital. Helpless. All I was was helpless. That boy died later that day, and I knew that something inside me had died, as well.

Luckily, Sam didn't wake up to see me in my fright. Somehow I must have kept my screaming to myself, just as I had kept my story to myself for all those years. No, I hadn't been the girl in that famous photograph crying over the body of her dying friend. But I had been there nonetheless, standing just behind, not understanding how this could be happening, but understanding all too well what it meant. We were not safe. There were murderers everywhere. Innocents, everywhere. Although I knew I must, how could I think that I could send my beloved daughter back there now and still be 'fine'?

I think Sam mistook my quiet of the next morning for peacefulness. We woke as the birds and the sun had barely begun their day. I moved from the army bed in the hut to a hammock under a tree and watched Sam take a morning swim. My head was still full of the terrifying visions of my sleepless night. Even after I stopped seeing them behind closed eyelids, I still felt their effect in my heart and my limbs. But mothers have to hide these things from their children. So I smiled as I watched Sam dry herself in the sun, and I chatted with the women as they brought us our breakfast. Sam herself was quiet, but hers was due to a genuine contentment, not to mention a mouth full of papaya, rice and fried bananas. Mid-morning, one of the women came up to me on my hammock and pointed out into the Gulf.

'Madame, look there. Your boy comes.'

And there he was, first a dot on the horizon and then larger than life, rocketing towards the beach, our hot-rodding, six-year-old captain. 'Sam!' I called out. 'I think it might be time to go.'

'Oh, Mother. How sad to leave this place,' she sighed. She was right. It was sad. How easy it would have been to turn my back on the worries and responsibilities of the real world and live my remaining days on Rabbit Island, cracking coconuts, mending the occasional torn hammock. Plenty of people had already accused me of turning my back on reality when I picked up and headed off to Asia in the first place. 'If you must save the world, start here at home where we need you,' my mother begged with tears in her eyes when I told her I was leaving. She never understood why I did what I did with my life. But how could she? I could barely explain it to myself.

This time, as I clambered into the motorized rowboat I wasn't afraid. The boy knew enough to drive slowly and the sea was very calm. Sam sat facing forward and watched the shores of Kep draw closer and closer. I faced backwards, trying to convince myself that I was leaving my fears behind.

'Look, Mother. There she is,' Sam soon said, pointing to a rocky jetty stretching like a note of caution into the sea. Atop the jetty sat 'The Woman of Kep', an enormous statue of a seated woman facing out towards the Gulf and the hostile countries beyond. She had one leg folded beneath the other, one hand demurely resting in her lap, wavy hair cut short, and an enigmatic smile. She was completely naked except for a red cloth inexpertly draped across her chest, concealing only one of her breasts. As a piece of artwork, she was hideous, her stony flesh glaringly white against the blue of the sky and the green of the trees. But the ridiculousness of her form didn't seem to bother her as she sat there year after year, not exactly welcoming her guests, but at least acknowledging their arrival on her shores. The locals clothed her every year to satisfy their delicate sensibilities. That's why so many people call her 'Modesty'. But to me, she looked more like 'Acceptance' with her reluctant smile devoid of emotion, supported by a base of huge, rounded hips and buttocks. The old girl had seen a lot, you could tell. But she's still there, accepting whatever the natural and human forces may throw at her, unyielding in her perseverance.

I spent the rest of that day asleep in our air-conditioned hotel room. Hours of dreamless sleep was just what I needed. Sam eventually roused me around dinnertime.

'They have roasted a pig for dinner. We can eat by the pool. Are you alright?'

'A pig roast? By the pool? Yes, I think that's just what I need.'

The closer we got to Phnom Penh the faster I drove. No more lazy glances out the window at the peasantry and the countryside. Each kilometer was drawing me back into the world I had not left behind, but which was still there, waiting for me with all its complications and mysteries. I had called home twice while we were away. Both times Kyle answered the phone. Neither time was Amanda available, although Kyle assured me that everyone was well and everything was under control. Srey came to the phone each time, too, and confirmed his report.

'Yes, Mother, we are well. You do not have to worry. The girls all help and the boys are behaving,' she promised me. 'But we miss you so. When will you be home?' she asked, and that was even more reassuring.

We pulled up in front of the house just after dinner. Everything was quiet and clearly in order. I stood inside the doorway and listened for a minute before I called out, 'Hello? Anybody miss me?' Soon they were all crowded around me, hugging my knees, asking to be picked up. It was funny how much I had missed them, even after only a few days. 'Look at you,' I laughed. 'Have you all grown while I've been away?' Thom came up, quietly kissed my cheek and took my luggage. Then Srey ran over, talking a mile a minute and asking a million questions. I barely took in any of it, but her energy filled me up. And behind them all stood Kyle and Amanda, smiling, obviously a bit tired, but clearly at ease. And in Amanda's arms was The Baby. I gave both of them a hug and dug out of my bag the thank you gifts Sam and I had bought: a necklace of shells for Kyle ('All the island men wear these,' Sam assured him). And for Amanda, a silk sari. I took The Baby out of her arms so Amanda could try it on. She looked beautiful, not only in the sari, but in general, I remember thinking. She looked beautiful within herself, well rested, at peace, happy.

'And how's The Baby doing?' I asked. 'I thought she would still be at the clinic.'

'I just collected her a little while ago,' Amanda said. 'Thought I'd save you the trip. She's doing fine.'

'Fine?' I asked, a bit incredulous.

'Well, certainly no worse,' said Kyle. 'You can call Doc when you're ready. He's got some ideas, I think.'

I knew he would have some ideas, but I decided to wait until the morning to find out. I wanted to take her for the night and see for myself. First, though, I wanted to sit with my kids and tell them stories about our adventures. I wanted to hear them laugh as they imagined me climbing into the boat. And I wanted them each to look me in the eye, not only so I could see that each of them really was okay, but so that each of them could see me: could see that I had gone away, but that I had really and truly come back home.

My first night back went surprisingly smoothly. I was all geared up for a sleepless night, changing diapers and sterilizing water. But nothing happened. I put The Baby down to sleep and as I watched her, waiting for the first explosion, I fell asleep myself. When I woke to her whimpering and rustling around, it was nearly six hours later. She had slept through the night. 'How the hell did he get her to do that?' I wondered, and that was the first thing I asked Dr Reith when I called him right after breakfast.

'Doc, she slept through the night,' I said in amazement as soon as he picked up the phone.

'Yes. She has done that twice before. I think the trick is not to feed her too soon before bedtime. She may be hungry during the night, but it is the diarrhea that wakes her, not the hunger. But tell me, your trip was good?'

'Yes, it was wonderful. Just what the doctor ordered, literally.'

'Excellent. And now?'

'Now? You mean The Baby?'

'Yes. We must talk about her. Can you come in later today? I have some time free at four o'clock.'

I spent the rest of the day cautiously watching everything to do with the child, recording diaper changes, ounces drank, as if she was some sort of science experiment. I noted how often she slept, the times she played, *if* she played. But I especially watched Amanda. She came early and went about her work with her old enthusiasm, only now she did everything with The Baby cradled against her chest in a homemade cotton sling. I had never seen that sling before. She told me one of the nurses at the clinic had given it to her. 'The Baby loves it,' she said. 'We both do.'

When the time came to go see Dr Reith, it was actually hard to pry them apart. Amanda was reluctant to let The Baby go, although she tried to hide it. 'Oh, does she need to go to the clinic with you? Really? Are you sure?' The Baby wasn't so happy either when I lifted her out of the warmth and took her into my own arms. If I didn't know better, I would have thought I had heard The Baby give a prolonged 'Noooo' as she was detached from Amanda's chest.

The Baby felt feather-light as I carried her the few minute walk to the doctor's. She clearly hadn't gained any weight in my absence, or could it have been that I had forgotten how incredibly tiny she was? By the time I was sitting in Dr Reith's office, she was soundly asleep in my arms. There was no need to mince words, so I asked straight out, 'How bad is it?'

Dr Reith took a deep breath, clasped his hands behind his back and slowly nodded his head, not as if he had an answer, but as if he was still pondering the question.

'Is it bad? Yes,' he said. 'How bad? I do not know. I do not think we can know. She is very ill, very small, not very responsive. I cannot be sure how old she is, but I do

125

believe she was born prematurely. Her digestion is very much underdeveloped. Her reflexes are sluggish.'

'But maybe, in time…'

'If we were in a big modern hospital in the West, with round-the-clock care and excellent neo-natal facilities, then maybe, yes…in time. But we are not. And so…' He hesitated to continue. But he didn't need to continue. I knew what he was trying not to say. In my heart, I had known it all along. 'The real question then is: What do we do with her, for her, until…?'

I looked down at this tiny being in my arms, so helpless but yet so real. I knew the doctor was right, but as I looked into her peaceful face I couldn't help but still feel that smallest glimmer of hope. I had seen many horrible things happen in Cambodia. But I had also witnessed miracles. Who was I, who were any of us to say that this baby's life couldn't still be another one?

'Deborah, I see in your face how you feel. Of course you feel this way. We must not give up hope. This child's mother did not give up hope, and that is why the baby sleeps in your arms today. But we must ask, who will be the… I am picking my words carefully now… the custodian? Who will oversee whatever fate awaits her? Forgive me, but I do not believe it can be you.'

Anger, surprising anger, was what I first felt at those words. Did I want this job? No. Did I think it was best to bring a sick, perhaps dying, child into my home like this? Of course not. But this was my job, nonetheless. The mother had left her with me. No one else. 'But Doc, what the hell can I do? She's here. I have more ability to oversee her fate than anyone else I know of around this city. What the hell else can I do?' I waited a moment before continuing, as did he. But then, under my breath, I muttered, 'And certainly, adoption is now impossible.' I made it sound like a statement, but we both knew it was

126

still a question. But unfortunately, it was the one question he could easily answer.

'Yes, I am afraid adoption is now out of the question. No one would take this child on as their own. Except...' and then it was his turn to mutter under his breath.

'Except?'

'Except? No, this is not a real answer, either. But I must tell you that Amanda was here every day while you were gone, helping us with her, sitting with her. She is quite attached, I fear.'

Sometimes it's horrible being right. I knew this would happen. I knew that if I left for a few days Amanda would find a way to take this baby into her heart and it would become stuck there, wedged into that dark place that she'd been hiding from us all these months. And Amanda would feel as if some light had grown in that place, the light which I already saw pouring out of her eyes the minute I walked back into our Home. That light might be able to nourish Amanda but, goddamn it, it could not nourish the infant, not enough to keep the child's fate from enveloping them both. And when that inevitably happened, The Baby would be gone, and Amanda's dark place would devour her. Then what would I be left with? Two losses to explain to my kids. I could see it all unfolding as if it was some horrible movie. 'I'm sorry, Doctor. But we can't let this happen. This is what I was afraid of all along and it just can't be. I have to protect my kids.'

'Yes, I understand.'

'I have forty other kids who must come first.'

'Yes, I know.'

'They must be my priority. It may sound cruel but...' I was beginning to rant and, even worse, beginning to feel my eyes fill with tears.

'Miss Deborah, please. I agree with you. Do not feel bad. You are right. But unfortunately, there is no choice for now. The Baby must stay with you until we find a place for her that is better. And if she stays with you, she will inevitably be staying with Amanda. Whether we like it or not, that bond now exists between them. We cannot pretend that it doesn't. But I do have a few ideas. It will not be easy, but let me make some calls.'

'And Amanda?'

'Her fate is her own. You cannot protect her. You already have too many children in your care and she is not a child.'

It was a long, slow walk home. Dr Reith was right and I knew it. I can't change people's fates, no matter how much I may want to. But I refused to believe that there was nothing I could do. I could not just stand by, bowing my head in helpless acceptance. I am not, after all, a Khmer and never will be. I held The Baby close so she could feel the deep, steady rhythm of my breath. With each slow footstep I urged her to breathe along with me, to take in that life force the monks always talk about. And then, for the first time in many, many years, I realized I was praying. With every step I said a silent prayer to whichever deity was willing to listen. Please, for all these fragile fates around me, let me be the custodian. That is what I prayed for. Let the ferryman be me. And let me at least provide shelter and warmth and as smooth a ride as these choppy waters will allow.

The end of May seemed to bring a new shuffling of position throughout the Home. I had noticed over the years that this happens every now and then. Some seemingly inconsequential thing will happen and then suddenly, it's all change. Like ducks in a row, one moves up and another one takes its place. After my holiday, I started to notice that Kiri, my not-so-little eight-year-old gladiator, had started hanging around with Thom. He followed his older brother around like a shadow, mimicking his gestures, his serious big boy stance. I couldn't have been happier – Kiri, the would-be thug, coming under the influence of Thom, my gentle muscleman. It did make me concerned about Sothy, though. Who would he play with now? Would he become jealous? But soon I saw that, just like in some carnival game, the vacant position was immediately filled by a new little head popping up to complete the line. Chak, of all people, our newest family member (not counting The Baby), had become Sothy's new playmate. Chak, who had never even been willing to leave my side let alone leave the house, was now confident enough to chase Sothy down the road on the way to school, allowing himself to be teased and bossed around like any good, adoring little brother should.

There were two other changes as well. The first shoved itself in my face on a sweltering Saturday afternoon. I had made special arrangements to have my kids get some extra time at the local school's pool. Kyle was around – he was often around now, much to the kids' delight and my own hesitant appreciation – and was willing to act as chaperone. Sam was busy doing something or other, and so I wanted Amanda to go as well. I was inundated with paperwork and there had to be another adult in the group. But Amanda balked: 'It's so hot. It might not be such a good idea for The Baby to be outside in this heat.'

'Maybe not. Leave her with me.'

'But I thought you were going to do the bills? You can't take care of her now. I should stay back with The Baby.'

It *was* hot and I was getting annoyed. Amanda works for me and she should do what I tell her to do, was what I was thinking. But what I didn't realize was that Srey was standing nearby and had overheard the conversation.

'Mother, why don't...' she started and I almost interrupted her, assuming she would offer to 'help' Kyle with the kids instead and let Amanda stay home with The Baby. In that nanosecond between words I was already gathering up my arguments, namely that in my book a sixteen-year-old is not an adult, and anyway, it's my Home and everyone will do what I say, Goddamn it. But before I could start, I heard Srey continue, '…why don't I stay back with The Baby? I can watch her for a couple of hours. I know what to do. And that way Amanda can take the children.'

Srey offering to stay behind? Not to go swimming on such a hot day? Not to go parading around in her bikini in front of Kyle? I could barely believe my ears and had to use all my self-control not to leap up and throw my arms around her in gratitude.

'You know, Srey, that would be such a help. Thank you so much for offering.'

'But don't you want to go swimming?' Amanda asked.

'I can go later,' Srey said. 'I don't need a chaperone like the other children do. Right, Mother?'

'Yes, right. Maybe you and Sam can go later. Maybe this evening.'

Then I watched Srey calmly, yet purposefully, take The Baby from Amanda's reluctant arms.

'I guess I'll go get my bathing suit then,' Amanda seemed to sigh instead of speak.

'That would be great,' I said. 'The kids are waiting.'

As I sat there trying to take in the significance of this amazing change in Srey's behavior, I noticed Kyle in the next room. He watched Amanda walk down the hall and then he followed her. They spoke too softly for me to hear, but they were still close enough for me to see Kyle reach down, place a tentative finger under Amanda's chin, and a small kiss on her cheek. That was another change.

By the time the hot season draws to a close, the air feels pregnant. That's the only word for it. There is so much humidity, so much moisture in the air that you almost feel like you're breathing under water. And like any pregnancy, by the time you get to the end of it, all you want is for the waters to break. Forget about the streets that you know will be flooded. Who cares about the mud that will overwhelm the fields. Just bring on the rain and the blessed relief that comes with the end of unrelenting weight and unreleased pressure. Those last days of May almost suffocated us with its heat. We knew the rainy season would bring its own set of troubles, but we longed for it nonetheless. And then, like they always do, the rains came.

JUNE

The monsoon rains arrive in brief afternoon showers. With them also come the cooling monsoon winds which are very pleasant. When the sun comes back out of the rain, the world smells and looks newly born. A glorious time!
A Touristic Handbook, p. 28

What a mess. The streets were flooding. The sewers were backing up. Wet, gloppy soot seeped in though every window, under every door. This happens every year, I know. But, as with childbirth, you forget the pain and the mess until you're in the midst of it all again. Then you remember, or so I'm told.

Keeping up with the weather was now a big part of our daily schedule. Of course, everyday life continues during the monsoon season. Kids go to school. Shops open up. Monks pray and beggars beg. But now it all must be timed to the rhythm of the rainstorms which actually has a funny effect on time itself. You can't just decide to go buy mango juice, for example. If you're heading for the shop and the heavens open, you have to duck under cover and wait. If you walk along your normal route and find a road temporarily washed out, you have to backtrack and find a new one. So everything takes longer. You can't really set your own schedule and life seems to move along in spurts. But for us at the Home in 2007, this was a pretty good way to live. Too much had already happened that year, for my money. The monsoon seemed to force us to lessen our expectations and be grateful for whatever little we could accomplish, whenever we could accomplish it. And this new rhythm suited me. It was as if the universe was giving me permission to relinquish control. Relinquish – now there's a word I never thought I'd learn to love quite so much.

In a funny way, the more vehement the weather, the more comfortable life became. I could tell Sam noticed all this, too. She noticed how life was taking on an easier, *whatever* sort of a feel. The change in her was subtle at first; the kind of thing only a mother would see. Her step was a little less urgent. Instead of rushing to be the one to do some chore she would first stop to see if anyone else was taking on the job. And somebody else almost always did. I once even found her in the boys' bedroom doing nothing. I was walking past on my way to somewhere or other and I saw her sitting on a bed next to The Baby, absent-mindedly playing with her feet while Amanda folded laundry. Sam didn't take over the job or even offer to help. She just sat there, sometimes staring into space, sometimes chatting. I didn't want to make too much of it, but I did notice it and I guess I stored it away in the back of my mind someplace for later reflection.

I watched it happen again and again. Sam wasn't shirking her responsibilities. No, not at all. She still always did everything that she needed to do. But that was exactly the change. She did what *she* needed to do, not what everyone else needed to do as well. Sam was loosening her grip on the minutiae of the everyday functioning of the Home and she was letting the rest of us get on with it. And that left her with time: time which I discovered she was using to dream.

'Amanda - tell me - what is it like to live in America?' I overheard her ask. And then on another day, 'Amanda, were you nervous when you went to university? Did you miss your family terribly?' I sometimes stopped to hear Amanda's answers. Amanda's answers about her past, even her more distant past, were still of some interest to me. I discovered she had gone to Yale which was where she had

133

met her husband, Tim. That was news. But honestly, those little tidbits of irrelevant information were now less intriguing than Sam's questions about her own future. Most interesting of all, though, was the fact that Sam was now finally beginning to ask those questions.

One morning, Sam walked into my office with a stack of mail. It had been days since the postman had been able to make a delivery, and we were suddenly flooded with circulars, catalogues, bills and inquiries. She stood by my desk and watched me flip through envelope after envelope. I looked up to see her standing there, peering over my shoulder.

'Yes, my dear? Can I help you in some small way? Expecting something?'

'Oh no. I was just wondering.'

'Wondering?'

'Yes, wondering if you have heard from Aunt Pat lately.'

'No, but I do owe her a letter, as do you, now that you mention it. Why?'

'I don't know. I was just...wondering.'

Now, Sam doesn't just 'wonder' for no reason. Maybe that's not such a good thing, but it's true. I realized then that the wheels of change which I had reluctantly set in motion were finally starting to pick up speed. Whether I wanted to or not, I now had to help them move on even faster. I started to push. 'Yes, I think I will write to Aunt Pat. And when I do,' I asked as nonchalantly as possible, 'would you like me to tell her about that conversation we had on Rabbit Island?'

'About college? About really going?'

'Yes. About college. About really going.'

'I don't know, Mother. It is such a hard decision. I just do not know how to make it.'

'Well, you know it's possible to tell them yes, but then go at a later time. Now or next year. That's possible, too, you know.'

'Yes, I know. Maybe that is what I was wondering. It does not help me make the decision, but it does give me time, I suppose.'

'Sometimes just a little more time is all we need…' I suggested.

'Alright then,' she said. Her voice was caught somewhere between excitement and fear. 'Alright. Tell her I will accept. I will send back the card telling the university. But please, do not make a big thing about this, Mother. Okay? Do not tell my brothers and sisters. This is not a decision. Just a little move towards a decision.'

She then left the room and I asked her to close the door behind her. I sat for a minute with the stack of letters in my hand and willed my brain to stop racing. 'Just a little move towards a decision,' Sam had said. But I knew that entire movements of history began with such 'little moves.' That very first step can create cataclysmic change. I opened the bottom drawer of my desk and rustled around in the back. I pulled out a secret bag of imported Hershey's Chocolate Kisses. There were twenty-seven left. Sitting all alone, I disrobed them from their foil coverings, gently laying them down in perfect order across the desktop. Staring into space in silence, I ate each one.

I sent an email to Pat right away, before I lost my nerve. Who knew if the mail service was really working? Who knew how long it would take a letter to fly from Phnom Penh to Ohio? At least email was fast, and it was already June. If Sam really did decide to go to school in September, I had to get her over there and settled by August. August – just two months away. When I started to think about it, it seemed impossible, despite what I had told her. There were flights, clothes, living arrangements to consider. Money.

135

Where the hell would I get the money? And even if Pat and I could pull this all together in just two months, there still was Sam's big reservation. Who would help me with the Home? Sure, I could find assorted hands to wash the dishes and feed the toddlers and take the kids to the park and cook the rice and do the laundry and and and. But who else, besides me, would be the responsible one, the one not only to do the chores, but to think about them before they even needed doing? Who else, besides me, would care? My heart sank. This was what Sam had been worrying about all along. And although she couldn't be right to worry – she just couldn't be – I was afraid she was right. Truthfully, I didn't know if that made me happy or sad, but I sent the email off to my sister anyway. Short and to the point:

Hi,

She still hasn't decided for sure, but is telling them 'yes'. Dare we start preparations, just in case?

Xoxo,

D

It took me twenty minutes to compose those few words, then another ten to stare at the screen while I mustered up the courage to press 'Send'. When I heard the little chime signal that it was on its way, I stood up and walked down the hall to the bathroom. I had to wash the stray tears off my face quickly before anyone could see them.

A few days later, The Baby had to go back to the clinic. She had a slight fever and a runny nose, nothing all that alarming under normal circumstances. But none of the circumstances around this baby were normal, and I couldn't take any chances. Amanda insisted on coming with us.

'It doesn't take two adults to walk one baby down the road. It does take at least two adults to watch the other forty kids left behind,' I argued.

'But most are at school, and Sam is around and Nita's here. They'll be fine.'

'That's not the point,' I started to say, but then The Baby began to cry and I saw one of the three-year-olds wobbling towards the kitchen and I suddenly thought, this is it. I'm drawing the line. The rains could start any minute. It was hot. I was hot, and I was tired and fed up. Finally, I was ready to tell Amanda, 'Enough is enough. You'll damn well do what I tell you to do or you can pack your bags and leave.' I was getting angrier and angrier and I could feel myself getting ready to let it rip, but then I saw Sam watching us from the kitchen as the toddler fell into her arms, and I stopped myself. At that moment I realized that I now needed this stray cat, this Amanda, even more than she needed me. Despite my reservations, my supposed better judgment, I had chosen my love for Sam over everything else and, as I stormed out the door with Amanda chasing after me, I cursed myself and my bloody weakness.

Amanda saw I was angry and I think that scared her. She started to speak but I was in no mood for it. I couldn't even hear what she was saying to me. All I could hear was the honking of speeding *motos* and my own voice ranting in my head. It had all escalated so quickly. Everything was fine and calm and then suddenly I snapped, or so it would seem to Amanda. I knew if I said anything to her then it would be too much, too angry, too hurtful and I couldn't let that happen. If Sam was to be able to leave, I needed to keep Amanda on board, at least for a while longer, at least through the summer. But I hated it. How had I let it get to this point? Why hadn't I listened to myself, relied on my own judgment from the start? Who the hell was this question-mark-of-a-person I had let into my perfectly controlled world, anyway? When we reached the door of the clinic I realized Amanda was still talking, making apologies, trying to calm me down, and I was holding The Baby much too tightly. She had stopped crying and for a nanosecond I thought, 'My God! What have I done?' as if I had smothered the little thing with all my suppressed fury. But, no. She was fine. I took her out of the sling on my chest and held her over my shoulder. My hands were shaking. I took as deep a breath as I could.

'Before we go in here, Amanda, I just have to say one thing.' I stopped us both right there on the pavement in front of the clinic, under a very dark and threatening sky. 'Now listen to me. Months ago you arrived on my doorstep and asked if you could work for me. If you could help. Well, you're not helping. Do you understand? This is not your baby and your need to be with her all the time is making my life harder, not easier. You're not helping at all.'

Inside the clinic the nurse apologized, saying Dr Reith wouldn't be able to see us for another thirty minutes or so. I didn't say anything else to Amanda. I just sat down on the folding chair to wait, placing The Baby on my lap. Amanda stroked her head and said, 'Alright then. I'll go back home,' and walked away.

I didn't get home for another hour or so. Dr Reith thought The Baby was probably fine, but decided to keep her overnight, just in case. *Just in case* there was something else going on with the child, or maybe *just in case* I was on the verge of losing my marbles completely. He didn't say so much out loud, but we know each other well enough to understand each other's looks. Needless to say, I was happy and grateful to leave the kid behind for the night. I started to walk back home but halfway there the rains came. I got soaked in an instant. There was nothing to be done so I just continued walking at the same slow pace, ignoring the people now rushing all around me, newspapers hopelessly covering their heads. I turned the corner and found myself calf-deep in monsoon waters and for some reason I stopped. I just stood there and laughed. The raindrops were so intense they felt like iron pellets bashing onto my shoulders. I didn't care. The waters were warm and insistent. They took control of me, plastering my cotton blouse against my back, straightening out the curls in my hair. My shoulders released under the weight and I felt caught in its power. Caught, not trapped. Held. Stopped. And it felt good. Minutes or hours later I heard a young man's voice insinuating itself into the pounding noise of the rain.

'Mother. Mother. Come here.' It was Thom, hurrying home from a quick trip to the hardware store. He grabbed my hand and pulled me towards him. 'Mother, what are you doing?' he cried as he all but carried me the last few yards back to the house. 'You will get sick and we will have to take care of you,' he scolded. I have to say, just then the idea of everyone else taking care of me sounded pretty damn good.

I did get sick, of course. Nothing terrible. But I suppose the combination of The Baby's germs and the soaking and everything else landed me with a murderous cold. Luckily, I didn't have a fever so I didn't have to stay in bed. But with all the sneezing and hacking and nose blowing, I wasn't much good to anybody. When the time came to bring The Baby back home, I just sent Amanda off to do it. I didn't have the strength for anything else.

On the thirteenth of June Sam had an adventure, and it was all because a few mornings before then the house had been so unexpectedly quiet that I had allowed myself a second cigarette and second cup of coffee. While I indulged myself, I read the newspaper through to page eight. An incredible headline caught my eye. It was resting hidden below the fold:

ECCC to Swear in Investigators

I have saved that article ever since. It described the opening of a door, a very heavy, seemingly impenetrable door. On its own sitting there towards the bottom of the page, stuck between ads for a hairdresser and a new noodle bar, the article looked like nothing much at all. But if you read it carefully, and that morning I did, you could see that the article said much more than it seemed to say.

I couldn't believe it and I rushed off to find Sam. She had just arrived back from her computer class and was settling down in the library to help Nary with her reading.

'Sam, look at this! Look at this!' I was excited. I thrust the paper into her face. 'Do you understand what this means? They tried to hide it in the middle of the paper, but I saw it. I saw it. Do you understand?'

Sam started to laugh. 'Look Nary. Look how excited Mother is. What is she talking about?'

'Can I read it?' Nary asked as she intercepted the paper on its way from my hands to Sam's. Slowly she began to read. 'After near—ly a year of nego—nego-' Then Sam realized this was not a joke and read it out loud for us, with me mouthing the words behind her:

After nearly a year of negotiations, the judges of the Extraordinary Chambers in the Courts of Cambodia (ECCC) approved the internal rules which will govern the proceedings of the Tribunal established to investigate crimes potentially committed during the reign of the Khmer Rouge between April 1974 and June 1979. The Pre-Trial Chamber will hold its first session on June 13. ECCC investigators will be sworn in. These sessions will be open to the public at no cost.

'The Tribunal? It is starting?' she asked. 'Really?'

'Really. It's happening.'

'But what about all the problems? The arguments?'

'Resolved, I guess. Hard to believe, but true.' I watched Sam sit there and take it all in. First, she placed the article in her lap and just stared off into space with a sort of quizzical, mystified kind of look. She turned towards Nary, who was now nestled next to her staring at her own book, following each word with a tiny finger. Sam gave Nary a kiss on the top of her head.

'This, Mother, is very important, I think. This, I think, is the beginning of change, isn't it?' Each word was chosen carefully, and, as she spoke, I could see an entire lifetime of thoughts clicking into place. I couldn't possibly know what those thoughts were, but their existence was plain to see in the arching of her eyebrows, the slow movement of the corners of her lips. I realized then that as important as this Tribunal was becoming to me, it was even more important to Sam. Sam is the Khmer one, after all. Not me. And anyway, my life is set. I have made my choices. Yet a change like this in Cambodia can mean a world of changes for Sam and for all her generation.

'Sam, you should go,' I blurted out. 'Yes, you should. This is history being made and it's just a bus ride away. It says here the sessions are being held in the Dangkor District Courthouse. That's just a short ride down National Road 4. Yes. Go.'

'Can I? Really?'

'Why not? It says it's open to the public.'

So two days later, Samnang left the house early and headed to the bus stop. She took with her a bag with a container of fried bananas and sticky rice for lunch, a change-purse full of more money than she would need, and a small notebook. At breakfast, she tried to convince me to go with her. I was tempted. I would have loved to have been there to see the swearing in of those judges, to see the starting off of what could be the end of a generation of injustice. Nevertheless, I knew it was better for me not to go. Better for Sam. Perhaps I was reading too much into this, but I believed that this journey, which seemed like just a few miles down the highway, was actually the first step on Sam's own much longer road.

141

The day passed very slowly for me. I admit I was a little nervous about letting her go off on her own. In this country anything can happen, any seemingly innocent event can turn into trouble without notice. Every time I looked at the clock I gave myself a little talking to: about trust, about faith, about letting go – three things I was especially bad at. There was more than enough happening at the Home, of course, to keep me diverted. I remember Nita wasn't around that day so it was left to me, Amanda, Srey and Thom to get on with all of it. I realized that ever since my trip to Kep in May I was beginning to rely on Srey and Thom more and more. They seemed to slip seamlessly into their new roles of eldest children, and Thom especially thrived on it. He had always been so quiet, so self-contained, but now he was blossoming in this new sense of responsibility. Suddenly I could hear his voice from rooms away, giving instructions to the smaller kids, calmly intervening in arguments. He started to stay longer after meals, not only to help clean up, but also to listen in on our conversations. Sometimes he even participated. I can now see how important it was to me, to all of us, that Thom began to grow up just when he did.

There was also the added distraction of The Baby's new medicine. When Amanda brought her home from the clinic she had also brought with her a new regimen of antibiotics. Dr Reith told me he had been waiting for this new supply from Hong Kong. God knows how he got the stuff. It couldn't have been completely legal, but I wasn't going to question it. Dr Reith had begun to think that perhaps there was some parasite in The Baby's gut, something we all live with but which she was just too weak to fight off. He had hesitated to put her on antibiotics before. She was so tiny and these medicines were so strong – who knew what harmful side effects they might have? But as The Baby made less and less progress over more and more time, he knew something had to be done. But she hated that stuff, I tell you. It took Amanda and I and all our strength to give it to her – one of us to hold her and one to squeeze the dropper into her mouth. More often than not she threw it back up, but we had to keep trying to get some of it into her, regardless of the waste, despite the cost. It wasn't easy and it lent that much more tumult to the whole post-dinner pre-bedtime process. It was especially annoying that evening because what I wanted to be doing was standing vigil for Sam's return, not wrestling with an infant and mopping up its mess. Having Kiri standing their laughing, eight-year-old Kiri with his posse of five and six-year-olds egging him on, just infuriated me all the more. Kiri's blossoming devotion to Thom had quieted him down a bit. But Thom can't always be hovering around him and Kiri can't always contain himself. I don't know what it is about that kid, but he does have a knack for being there at the wrong time, always making fun of the wrong thing.

'Kiri, enough!' I yelled. 'You, all of you, go to the library, now! Thom, get them out of here.' That was enough to scare the younger kids, but Kiri gave me a look that said, 'You'll have to do more than that to quiet me, lady.' I do love that kid's spirit. I really do. But just then I could have killed him.

It was nearly seven o'clock when Sam finally came home. The house was now quiet. Amanda had gotten The Baby to sleep and was heading home herself. 'Are you sure it's okay for me to leave?' she asked. 'I can stay 'til Sam gets home.' But then Sam burst through the door. 'Burst' is definitely the right word because she was still full of energy, full of a momentum which had carried her all the way home from Dangkor.

'Finally, you're here,' I called as I ran up to give her a hug.

'Oh, Mother, it was amazing.'

143

'I was getting worried that…'

'You should not have worried, Mother,' Sam interrupted, but I interrupted right back.

'I wasn't worried. I just couldn't wait to hear all about it.'

'Me too, Sam,' Amanda said. 'But tell me about it tomorrow. If it's okay, I better get going. I told Kyle I'd meet him for a drink. It's his birthday.'

'Kyle's birthday? I didn't know that,' I said. How could I have not known after all these years and yet Amanda did after just a few months? Come to think of it, I didn't even know how old he was. It just never seemed to matter. But it annoyed me that Amanda knew and I didn't.

Then Sam said, 'Yes, that's right. His birthday is today. Tell him Happy Birthday for me.' Now how did she know, I wondered? There was only one thing I could do – pretend.

'Yes, of course it is,' I said. 'It completely slipped my mind. Tell him to come by so we can celebrate.'

'Will do,' Amanda said and rushed out the door.

I sat Sam down at the table and placed a plate of food in front of her. 'Now eat and tell me all about it.'

'Mother, it was…a miracle,' she began. And then, between bites of chicken she described every detail, from her nervousness on the short bus trip out to the courthouse, to the rainstorm that caused her trip back to be three times as long. She told me about the grandeur of the building with its massive pillars and wide steps leading up to a heavy door inlaid with gold. She told me about how they took everything out of her bag and checked it all thoroughly before letting her go towards the chamber. She said the man doing the checking was a young soldier and he teased her about having to keep her sticky rice and bananas for himself. She said she was one of about twenty spectators who had come to watch, although there were lots of photographers, many of them Westerners.

'I sat in a large room with rows of chairs,' she said. 'There was a big glass window between us and the actual courtroom. A nice older man in a suit gave me his seat in the front row so I could see everything. And there were speakers hanging from the ceiling so we could hear every word being said.'

'So they're really taking this seriously? It wasn't just for show?' I asked.

'Oh Mother, no. This is very serious. Very real. You could see the separate round area where the accused will sit and give their testimonies. You could see the bench where the judges sit. And behind them are flags – one is the Cambodian flag, the other the flag of the United Nations. And everything was clean and quiet. The tables were all shiny, light-colored wood. The chairs were all leather, and there were microphones in front of everyone who might speak. It was beautiful, really. And then, when it was time for the investigators to be sworn in, they each stood up with one hand raised and one hand on their heart and repeated the oath. And they did it in three languages: Khmer first, then English, then French so that everyone would understand. And we all did understand. We spectators sitting behind the glass all turned to each other and smiled. We nodded to each other as if we knew one another. One older woman even started to cry. And you know, they are saying that they will arrest them all. Even that horrible butcher, Duch, himself.'

I took hold of Sam's hand. It was warm and very present. She then squeezed my hand in return as if to try to explain something important that she hadn't yet found the words for. I understood anyway. I knew which words she meant. She was struggling to find the words hope, justice and humanity, but I decided to let her discover them for herself. I knew those words, although I still couldn't let myself believe in them. That was just fine, though, because

145

my daughter was beginning to believe in them enough for the both of us.

I was never a big fan of birthdays. They always seemed more trouble than they were worth. Growing up as the eldest of four with two parents working full time, it always landed on me to organize the party, make the cake, decorate the house. I know there are people who like doing that sort of thing. They're usually the same people who spend weeks sewing homemade Halloween costumes. My sister Pat's like that – homespun. But not me. A Betty Crocker cake from a box. A plastic Superman mask from Woolworth's. That would have been my style, if I'd had a choice.

But things are different here in Cambodia, especially when you have up to forty kids in your care. It's always somebody's birthday, and each extra year that each of these kids lives does feel like a reason to celebrate. So, even though Cambodians don't usually make a big deal about birthdays, I do. I've even gotten good at cakes. We have a big bag of birthday decorations and we can make the place look festive in less than five minutes. Bowls of morning glories and lotus leaves decorate the table. And there's a gold plastic crown that the birthday kid gets to wear at dinner. So deciding to make an impromptu, last minute birthday party for Kyle was no big deal. It was Srey's idea really. She had known it was his birthday, too. Everyone seemed to know but me.

The day after Sam's trip to the Tribunal, Srey asked if she could have a private chat. I knew she couldn't possibly have become interested in the trials herself, and so a party had to be what she had in mind. I sought her out before bedtime and found her rattling around in the kitchen.

'Srey, you were looking for me? Sorry it's so late. I've been so busy.'

'Do not worry, Mother. I am busy too.' She was down on her hands and knees, speaking to me with her head buried in one of the back cupboards. I could barely hear her. I stuck my head in, too.

'What are we looking for?'

'Here they are,' she said, hoisting herself and me up off the floor. 'Those cake decorations that the English family brought us. Remember? I thought I'd put them on Kyle's cake.'

'Kyle's cake? Are we having a party?'

'Yes. Please. That was what I wanted to ask you. It was his birthday yesterday and he has never been here for his birthday before. I thought we could make him a party. May we?'

'Do you think he would like a party?' I asked.

'Of course. Everyone likes to have a birthday party,' Srey explained. Was that true, I wondered? Did everyone really, secretly like to have their birthdays celebrated? I wasn't so sure. Some people don't like thinking about the years passing by. For some people each new page of the calendar turned is a reminder of what they still haven't accomplished. Or even worse – what they still haven't forgotten. It's trickier than it seems, this whole birthday business. But who was I to spoil Srey's innocence? Who was I to insist on dark realities, especially if a sunnier fantasy might achieve something more. And anyway, wasn't that the Khmer way? 'Yes, I'm sure you're right,' I said, deciding to agree. 'It will be a lovely way to thank him for all he has done for us.'

'Yes. And for all he will do!' she added, laughing.

The next afternoon was spent in preparation. The house was decorated. An extra-large cake was baked with an Australian flag and 'Happy Birthday Kyle' drawn in imported English 'hundreds and thousands.' But it wasn't just Kyle's adoring women who were hard at it. All the kids

147

were involved, making gifts, drawing cards, even preparing after-dinner entertainment. It was really quite touching. They loved him. I guess we all did. And this year he had been around so much more often. I would have liked to think it was for me. The two of us had witnessed a lot together over the five years we had known each other. And five years in Cambodia is an awfully long time. But I'm not that silly. I had to admit that his more frequent arrivals at our door probably had more to do with Amanda than anything else. I wasn't really surprised. I had asked him to find out about her after all, and how else would he do it if not by getting close? And anyway, let's face it – she was attractive, and young and easy to be around, despite her obvious troubles. Or maybe because of them. Whether she was happy about all his attention was hard to tell, though. Sometimes she would seem close and comfortable with him. They'd joke; she might give him a playful push against his arm. But at other times her face would go blank and she'd walk away, leaving him standing alone in some hallway. I couldn't avoid watching the two of them. How close they had really become, how much he had really learned about her, I still didn't know. What I did know, though, was that all of a sudden his work didn't take him out of Phnom Penh quite as often as it used to.

Kyle knocked on the door at precisely six o'clock. Considering he supposedly knew nothing about this party he was being remarkably prompt. A bunch of the kids ran to open the door and before he was even inside they were crying 'Surprise!' and jumping all over him. By the time he reached the dining room he had three kids in his arms, another on his back, and one hanging off each leg. He looked like a kid tree.

'Alright, alright,' I said, laughing, and tried to disengage him from his fans. 'Let the old man breathe. Remember, he's not so young anymore.' Once I had peeled the kids off, I put my own arms around him and gave him a hug. 'Happy birthday, kiddo. Glad you're here.' And clearly he was glad, too. He went through the room tickling, tousling, tugging, lifting, punching, hugging every last one of us. Nita nearly collapsed from the attention. And even 'The Poop Machine' held onto his finger and gurgled. Each person got their own private greeting, their own private moment. Sam was given a clasping of both hands and a brotherly embrace. He gave Srey a killer smile and a stroking of her cheek. For Amanda there was a whisper in her ear just before he stole a quick kiss on the lips, which produced a chorus of giggles and whistles but which Amanda, I couldn't help but notice, didn't seem to like. And I got a second hug, a knowing look into my eyes, and a mysterious smile. It was quite a display and like nothing I had ever thought possible from the macho Kyle Mackenzie. We gave Kyle a party, some cake and a few cards. But that night, Kyle gave each one of us a little bit of himself.

The birthday feast lasted hours. Some of the kids did a traditional Khmer dance performance that would have done Madame proud. It did me proud. And then Srey led some of the younger girls in their own rendition of that horrible song I've hated for years:

Kyle, Kyle, you're so fine. You're so fine you blow my mind.
Hey Kyle!

There was lots of strutting and pre- (and post-) pubescent wiggling. I could barely stand to watch my precious little Khmer flowers delight in the worst that Western culture has to offer. Kyle seemed to like it, though. In the midst of it all, Thom sidled up to Kyle and quickly passed a package to him under the table. I had to laugh. Thom was nervous he'd get into trouble. His gift was a large bottle of Angkor beer, a real no-no in our house. I decided not to ask how he got it. Kyle looked at me with such joy, such desperate longing.

149

'Go ahead,' I said. 'Of course you can have your beer.' And then, making eye contact to my charges of various ages sitting around the table, '*You're* old enough. But give me a swig, too.' The sight of their mother actually sharing a beer with the big man himself was almost more than the youngest kids could bear. The room filled with laughter, cheers and whistles. Then, amidst the noise, an unspecified small voice called out: 'How old are you?'

'How old do you think?' Kyle asked. Guesses were volleyed from all directions.

'Twenty-five, thirty-one, twenty-three, seventeen.'

'Seventeen?' he asked in mock astonishment.

'Seventeen is a big number,' five-year-old Chak quietly explained.

'Sixty?' I suggested. Kyle just scowled at me. 'Well, a girl can dream....' I teased.

'Okay, okay. I'll tell you. Two days ago, at 7:42 in the morning, I turned thirty-nine.' A hush came over the crowd. All the kids looked at each other in disbelief. 'What?' he asked. 'What's wrong with thirty-nine?'

'Oh, nothing, of course,' Srey eventually, timidly, spoke up. 'It is just that...well...some of the younger children might be surprised. Thirty-nine is, after all, nearly forty.'

I let out such a hoot and a holler I had to leave the room. I couldn't help myself. Tears streamed down my face. That Srey – gotta love her.

Not surprisingly, it took a while to settle the kids down and get them to bed after all the excitement. Kyle offered to help as the rest of us scurried around, but I insisted he sit and relax while he had the chance. Amanda and I still had to endure the evening medicine struggle with The Baby. She actually didn't put up too much of a fight that night. Maybe she was as partied out as the rest of us. Once I finished kissing and tucking everyone in, I headed back to the dining room half expecting to find Amanda or Srey in

150

some tête-à-tête with the birthday boy. But it was actually Sam who was deep in conversation with him. She was telling him all about her trip to the courthouse and asking all sorts of questions about the various NGOs in town and what the Australians were doing to help. There was no bravado or fooling around in Kyle's voice as he answered her questions. He was listening to her carefully and giving the most honest and considered responses he could. As I sat down at the opposite end of the table I heard him say:

'Sam, I really am so impressed by you. Look at how you're getting involved, how you're learning about what's happening around you.' Sam then surprised me, as she had been doing so often lately. She took Kyle into her confidence.

'Thank you,' she said. 'I do want to learn more. Actually, I was not going to say much about this yet, but you know, I have been accepted to university.'

'Really?' he asked, shooting me a quick glance down the table.

'Yes. In America. Kent State in Ohio, where Mother comes from. I can go this autumn, if I decide to. But that is so very soon. It is difficult to decide. What do you think?' Kyle now looked over at me for a longer time, long enough to see me smile, sigh and nod my head in a cautious 'yes.' When he didn't answer her immediately, Sam began to speak again and now Amanda was also pulling up a chair. 'I know it will be hard for me. It will be hard for me to leave. But it will be harder for everyone else, I fear. It is such a difficult question. I would like your advice, Kyle.'

She had really put him on the spot. At first I thought of suggesting that she have this conversation with him in private. But I saw the way she was looking at me and I saw how aware she was of Amanda now also sitting across the table from her, and I understood that Sam knew exactly what she was doing. It took a great deal of self-control for

151

me not to butt in, not to add my opinion or assurances, especially since Kyle was staring straight at me, clearly asking for permission to proceed. For once in my life, though, I kept my thoughts to myself and let my silence be his answer. 'My opinion?' he asked. 'Truthfully?'

'Yes,' Sam said. Amanda nodded as well.

Kyle stood up and drew a chair right next to Sam so that he was now facing her directly with his back towards the rest of us. He spoke to her in as purposeful a manner as I had ever heard him speak. There was no joking around, no teasing. 'Sam,' he said, 'you are probably the most intelligent, most mature young person I have even known. I think you should go. I think you should go this year. You owe it to yourself. Actually, you owe it to all of us. That is my opinion.' Sam's nod showed us that she had now, finally, accepted this truth. The look on Amanda's face was much more inscrutable. And I have no idea what they all thought of me sitting there, my hands clenched white atop the table, my head bowed.

The next morning, Kyle arrived at the house soon after Amanda and just as Sam was leading the kids off to school.

'Good morning everyone,' I said. 'Perfect timing. Amanda, can you take The Baby? I'm dying for a smoke.'

'Of course. How did she do last night?'

'Not too bad. One mess at about four, but it was still that dark, greenish...'

'Jesus, do we have to do this, first thing in the morning?' Kyle pleaded. 'Can somebody get this out of here,' he begged, pointing at The Baby who was now making some minor threatening noises from her bottom. 'I want to watch Deborah smoke cigarettes and drink coffee.'

'With pleasure,' Amanda said, threatening to pass The Baby in front of Kyle's face. 'Deborah, don't worry. I'll look after the toddlers too, finish off breakfast, get them playing. Hey guys, weren't we going to do some animal drawings today?' she called out to them.

'Grab a cup of coffee for yourself and I'll meet you in my office,' I said. Kyle soon found me there, staring into the back garden, blowing smoke rings through the opened window. 'So, did you like your party?' I asked.

'I did. Very much. Thank you,' he said, sitting down and putting his feet on my desk. I let them stay there. What the hell.

'You looked like you did. I'm glad. You were wonderful with the kids, you know. And with Sam. I thank you for that.'

'Well, that's part of what I wanted to talk to you about before I head off.'

'Head off? Where are you going?'

'Siem Reap. In an hour or so.'

'An hour or so? That's sudden,' I said, a little too startled I suppose. Kyle's answer was apologetic.

'Yeah, I know I should have said...'

'No, I'm sorry,' I answered. I couldn't get the words out quickly enough. 'Really. You must never think that I make any assumptions about what you do or where you go. Please.'

'I know, I know. Really, I do. It's okay. And I'll only be gone for a few days, anyway. But there's an awful lot going on here. Things are changing, my dear.'

'They certainly are,' I agreed with a tired nod of my head. 'But I guess they have to, like you said last night. I just have to figure out how.' That's when he told me about his plan. It seems there had been a conspiracy brewing, but it wasn't between Kyle and Amanda as I might have expected. It was between Kyle and Dr Reith.

'Listen. There's a hospital,' he started. 'In Siem Reap. It's run by this Swedish doctor who's a bit of a character, a bit of a proselytizing do-gooder, if you know what I mean. But he has a lot of funding and he's poured a heap of money into the place.'

'Yes, yes. I've heard about this guy. He's like a one-man show up there, a real savior type.'

'That's the one. Well, there's some work I need to do around the temples up there and I – I mean, Dr Reith and I – thought I could pay this guy a visit.'

'About The Baby?'

'About The Baby.'

'But I thought he only helped Siem Reapers. That's part of his thing.'

'It is. But Dr Reith gave him a call.'

'Oh…'

'And I think he's willing to do…something. It seems this guy and our own Dr Reith go way back.'

'Yes. I see.' So this was Dr Reith's last resort. And I knew exactly what it meant without being told. By sending The Baby off to Siem Reap it might look like we were sending her off to be cured. But really, whether this godlike doctor could help The Baby or not, there would be no returning back for her from this trip. I leaned forward so Kyle could hear me whisper. I don't think I could have spoken louder even if I had wanted to. 'But, Amanda?'

'She doesn't know about any of this. And I don't propose to tell her until I know for certain we can do it.'

'But how will she react?'

'Not well, I suspect. But look. We both know Sam needs to leave. That became crystal clear last night. But it's simply not going to happen as long as The Baby's here. I know it sounds simplistic, and maybe even cruel, but listen. You've got a good set-up going here. It works. But it's precarious. Take something like this baby, and then take away Sam, and she's right – the whole thing falls apart. I'm sorry to say it, Deborah, but it's true.' Of course it was true. I had known it all along. But it was horrible hearing it said out loud. 'Now come on,' he continued. 'Let's be honest. We both know The Baby won't last long no matter what. It looks to me like she's got less and less life in her every time I see her. Poor kid. But if Sam goes away, she goes in less than two months. That's really soon. Probably too soon. Do you know what I'm saying?' Unfortunately, I did know what he was saying. I knew exactly what he was saying, both about the likely end of The Baby's life, and about the fragile beginning of Samnang's future. But I also knew that the situation at our Home had become even more complicated than just this. There was still more going on here than just the needs of two Khmer children.

Without thinking, I blurted out, 'Kyle. What do you know about Amanda?'

'Amanda?'

'Yes. She's part of this mess as much as The Baby is. Before The Baby arrived, it was all going well, despite my hesitations. Amanda was starting to fit right in. The kids fell in love with her. Hell, even I did. She became my friend. But since The Baby's arrival, since her determined attachment to it, it's like the two of them are one unit. It's "Amanda-and-The-Baby" all the time. Them separate from us. And that just doesn't work.'

'I know. I've seen it.'

'Okay then. I had started to let go of my suspicions. I really had. But now I need to know and you promised to tell me if you discovered something.'

'I know what I promised, but there's nothing I can say about that right now.'

'What's that supposed to mean? Do you know something or not?'

'I know some things. I'm guessing others. She won't let me in, Deborah. And believe me, I've tried.'

'Well then, tell me what you do know.'

'No.'

155

'No? What do you mean "no"? You promised.'

'Yes, but I'm going to have to break that promise for now.'

'What? How can you say that? Jesus Christ, Kyle!' I was now standing up and glaring down on him. I could feel my arms shaking with fury and fear. 'You can't do this to us. You just can't!'

'Okay, calm down. I'll tell you this.' He looked out the door to make sure we were really alone, but that just made me even more panicky. 'Remember when I first saw her I told you there was something familiar, something I couldn't put my finger on? Well, I remembered. There was an article in one of the Agency's newsletters a while back. A year ago or more. It was about a kidnapping and a killing of some foreigners down in Mindanao, in the Philippines. They didn't say for sure but they suspected the victims were some American Peace Corps volunteers. They kept it as hush hush as possible, but there was this grainy photo and I'm sure it was Amanda.'

'Oh my God. Did you ask her?'

'Yeah, but she wouldn't talk. I bet I'm right, though.'

'That poor girl. That poor girl.' I sat back down in my chair and could feel my eyes welling up with tears as I stared out the window. I knew there was endless horror in this world, but to have it, again, right here under my own roof was nearly unbearable. 'And to think she's kept it in all this time. Never saying anything to anyone? Never confiding in anyone, not even you? But, Jesus, how long have you known?'

'I've suspected it for a while now.'

'A while now? Wait a minute.' And like that, all my sympathy turned to anger. 'You've known this for a while and didn't tell me? With everything that's been going on here, you didn't tell me that I might have some time bomb under my roof? Kyle, is she going to go nuts on me?' He

156

didn't answer. He just looked down at the floor. 'Kyle?' I found myself back on my feet and staring down over him like some cartoon shadow of death. But still he said nothing, until finally he looked up at me and quietly, almost inaudibly, mouthed the words:

'Trust me.'

Just as quietly I shook my head and whispered, 'Fuck you.' Then he stood up and gripped me by the arms.

'Deborah, trust me. You have to. Look around you. Admit it. Who the hell are you? I don't know. Who the hell am I? You haven't a clue. What the fuck are any of us doing here anyway? Any of us? But the point is, it doesn't matter. Haven't you learned that yet? We don't have the luxury of letting it matter. None of it, none of our pasts, none of the boatloads of shit any of us may have done or suffered. We are here now and we have to trust each other. That's all we have.'

It was a standoff. Part of me might have believed what he was saying, but there was still a big part of me that wasn't ready to give in to it. But I knew I couldn't argue. There were no arguments probably because there were no facts, no single truth. So I said nothing and let him hug me, and when he did I held onto him so tightly we both thought I'd never let go. Then, five minutes later, he was gone.

A few days after that confrontation, I was sitting in the kitchen making up the schedule for the next week. I was doing a rush job of it. I used to take my time over that job. Once, a while ago now, I could sit down, mentally peruse the list of who could do what, calmly muse about the progress we were all making in our lives. I'd give easier jobs to the kids who might have been struggling in one way or another. Sometimes I'd even allow myself a private moment of Machiavellian glee when I would decide to give some especially distasteful chore to a kid who had been particularly annoying that week. I had grown to allow the creation of that schedule to become my own small weekly moment to pat myself on the back for a job well done. Now there was just too much to do, too much on my mind to be able to take the time to think it all through. Not surprisingly, the kids were feeling the effect. My recent slapdash plugging in of whatever name into whatever slot meant that I was no longer taking the time to think about each individual child – I mean, really think about them – how they were feeling, who their friends were, what they were thinking, or *if* they were thinking. Not that it took that much time to do it. It just took space, mental space. And that's what I had none of.

So, I hadn't noticed what was happening with Netra. She was one of those kids who could easily fall through the cracks no matter where she was. Netra was sweet, quiet, dutiful, undemanding, accepting. A good little Khmer girl who was slowly, at age twelve, edging her way to becoming a good little Khmer woman. Easy-going, but heart-breaking, because if you really looked you'd see that her placid smile was just a mask concealing a hollowness where her sense of self should be.

I walked into the hallway to put the new schedule up on the bulletin board, and Srey hurried over to me.

'Hey, what's up?' I asked.

'Oh, Mother. Netra is in the bedroom crying,' she said with a mixture of concern and annoyance.

'Why? What happened? Is she hurt?' I was already rushing towards the other end of the house.

'No, she's not hurt. I do not know what it is. But Amanda and The Baby are with her. I thought I should tell you.'

'Yes. Good girl. But wait…' A little light bulb went off in my head. 'Did you and Netra have a fight about something?'

'No, Mother.'

'You know how she looks up to you. Did her feelings get hurt somehow?'

'Mother, I didn't do anything.'

'Okay, sweetheart. I'm not saying you did. But sometimes you can say something and not realize that it makes other people sad.' I stopped walking and stroked her hair. I didn't want to be accusing Srey of hurting her sister for no reason. But Netra had always looked up to her so, followed her around like a little lapdog and sometimes Srey could be, well…a teenage girl. Not the most sensitive of species.

'We were talking about taking care of The Baby, I think. And then she started to cry.'

'Okay. Don't worry. Look, can you go check on the boys in their room, see that they're not up to mischief?' I went to the girls' bedroom as quickly as I could. The voices I heard coming from the room sounded calm and controlled, so I decided to stand in the doorway for a minute and peek in. Amanda and The Baby were sitting on the bed next to Netra comforting her, smiling at her.

'It's hard being twelve, isn't it?' Amanda was saying. 'I remember it so well. You're not a little girl anymore, are you?'

Netra shook her head 'No'.

'But you're not a teenager, either. You don't know where you are.'

Netra nodded her head 'Yes'.

'You know, I think it's one of the hardest ages of all. So much harder than sixteen. Sixteen is easy,' Amanda laughed. 'You can do all this stuff. You think you're a big shot.'

Now Netra was nodding her head more vigorously.

'But there's something special about being twelve. Do you know what it is?'

I could see Netra look up at Amanda. A lifetime of questions and hopes were in those eyes. 'What is it?' she whispered.

'What's special about being twelve is that you don't have to choose. For a few special couple of years in your life, say from the end of eleven to the middle of thirteen, you can be both little and big. If one day you want to play with the little kids, you can because you're not really a big kid yet. But if sometimes you feel like being a big kid, you can do that too, until you don't want to anymore. It's nice not having to be a big kid all the time. Believe me.'

Perfect. For my money, Amanda had said the perfect thing. I knew I couldn't have done it better, and if anything that made me feel worse. Here I had been steeling myself against Amanda again, accusing her of separating herself and The Baby from the rest of us, and now here she was comforting another one of the kids, knowing what to say and taking the time to say it. There was nothing I could add to the resolution of today's little drama, so I walked back to the kitchen. When I saw Netra at dinner she was smiling again, sitting in between Amanda and Srey but laughing with young Nary across the table. She was fine and so I was pleased. But I was also annoyed with myself for having been so oblivious to Netra's struggles.

I didn't get to thank Amanda until long after dinner when we were cleaning up the kitchen for the night.

'You know Amanda, I overheard your talk with Netra this afternoon,' I said.

'Oh, did you? Yeah, she was in a state, I guess. But I can remember being twelve. It's such a hard time.'

'And you knew exactly what to say. Well done. And thank you, so much. I should have noticed she was struggling a bit.'

'Oh, I think it was just one of those things. A mountain instead of a molehill. But you can't be everywhere, doing everything.'

'Unfortunately.'

'It amazes me what you're able to do here. Really. I hope you know that.'

'Yes, well, thanks. But it seems like it's never enough.'

It was one of those lovely, content sorts of moments which we hadn't had much of lately. The kids were all occupied. The Baby was lying quietly, staring at her feet, in an old laundry basket we had jerry-rigged into a portacrib. Amanda and I were working seamlessly side by side, chatting.

'So, do you really think Sam will go to the States?' Amanda asked, slipping the question into the conversation as if she was asking whether we had enough eggs for breakfast.

'She can if she wants to. My sister's a whirlwind, getting it all arranged at the university. It's all there waiting for her. She just has to decide when.'

'And Kent State, eh? *The* Kent State?'

'Yep, *the* Kent State.' I tried to laugh it off.

'*Four dead in O-hi-o*...That song?'

'Yes, yes. That's the one.' I kept trying to laugh, but it wasn't so funny. 'But you know, that was over thirty years ago so...'

'Wow. Hard to imagine, really.'

'Yes, I know,' I said, although I was no longer sure what she was referring to. I tried to get the conversation back to Sam and her future, but I wasn't so sure I wanted to talk about that, either. 'It's hard to imagine Sam going away.'

161

'But it would be so good for her to go, don't you think?' Amanda asked.

'I hope so.'

'Oh, I'm sure of it.' That's where I wanted the conversation to end, but Amanda kept on talking as she climbed on to the stool to put away the double boiler. 'I know it will be scary for her. It is for everyone. But she's so capable. It will change her life.'

'Well, that's the idea.'

'At first I was afraid she wouldn't go because of all the work to do here. She had to be convinced to leave you.'

I stopped scrubbing the frying pan, my hands still in hot water. 'And did you convince her?'

'Me? No. I thought you did. I just told her I agreed with you, that it was the right thing to do.'

'Oh,' I said, looking back into the sudsy water and scouring more vigorously than was strictly necessary. 'Well, there's still a lot to be figured out.'

'Sure, but you know you can count on me.'

I should have left it at that. There was nothing more that really needed to be said just then. But there was something about Amanda's complacency that got to me. Maybe it was again that sense of entitlement that I had noticed months before when she first landed at my door, assuming she could just walk into our lives. Or maybe it was the memory, still so new, of that horrible conversation with Kyle just before he left for Siem Reap. Or maybe I just have a big mouth. I didn't mean to make a scene, but I should have known that when I muttered, 'Well, we'll have to see,' Amanda would jump on it.

'What do you mean?' she persisted. 'You know I'm not going anywhere.'

'Oh, Amanda, let's be honest,' I said, trying not to sound too irritated. 'I don't really know anything of the sort.' She was about to argue with me, but I stopped her. 'Look.

162

Okay, you've been here a few months and that's fine. I mean, more than fine. It's been great. Very helpful. But anything can happen. Anything, to you, to The Baby...' Of course, The Baby picked just that moment to start fussing. And I'm sure I gave some sort of look in its direction. A look of exasperation, maybe. Or even despair. But before I could dry my hands, The Baby was in Amanda's arms and Amanda was glaring at me.

'Deborah, I don't know what you're talking about. I'm fine. The Baby's fine. But you're always acting as if I'm going to run away any minute, no matter what I do. Well, I'm not going to disappear. Not unless you want me to. But if you want me to leave you should just say so. If not, then please, will you accept that I'm here and let me get on with it?' She didn't even try to hide her anger. 'Now, I believe it's my turn to be with The Baby tonight, so if it's alright with you...' and she walked off to her makeshift bedroom in the library.

'Oh, Jeez,' I said to myself. 'Goddamnit,' and I went back to putting away the dishes and puttering around aimlessly. The problem was that I knew Amanda was right. Nobody knows the future; we barely even know our pasts. But still I had a choice to make: accept her or not – one thing or the other. I wasn't a bloody twelve-year-old.

By June's end we were all firmly settled into the season. The late afternoon rains were predictable and they brought an evening of cooler, clearer skies. Our heads felt cooler and clearer, too. As we waited for Kyle's return from Siem Reap, each one of us seemed to adapt to our understanding that strong currents were driving our lives forward to some new state, some position that was just beyond our sight. Whatever new set of circumstances was to be our future, it was already there waiting for us. The rushing waters of each new flooding carried us closer and closer to it. The Baby's

163

own life, though, seemed but a whisper. She locked onto whoever was carrying her like an appendage, a bothersome growth that sometimes required tending, sometimes not. The child herself barely had any force within her at all, or at least that's how she seemed to me. She had no fight left, and to my eyes she looked like she had already given her tiny self over to the torrent of her own fate.

Kyle arrived back all boisterous and full on. It was 11:15 on a Thursday morning: the older kids were at school, the little ones were napping, Amanda was changing The Baby's diaper again, and I was finishing up some business in my office. I happened to meander down the hall half-reading the latest newsletter from *World Vision* when I heard his voice deflate from an overblown balloon ready to burst to a sad little hiss: 'I'm home everyone! Miss me? Hello? Anybody here? Hey guys, where are you?'

I nearly ran right into him, standing alone in the foyer. 'Kyle!' I cried. 'Where the hell did you come from?'

'Well that's a fine way to welcome back your conquering hero.'

I gave him a hug and took his rucksack. 'When did you get back?'

'Just now. Came straight here. Haven't even been home yet. Where is everybody?'

'Out doing things. Living their lives. We haven't just been staring out the window pining away all week.' Although maybe sometimes some of us were.

'No? And why not?' He put his arm around my shoulder and I gladly sank into it.

'Coffee?' I asked.

'Yeah.'

'Cigarette?'

'Sure.'

And we headed toward my office. 'Amanda here?' he asked.

'Yeah, somewhere with The Baby, of course. Do you want me to call her?'

'Nah, I called her this morning. I'll see her la...' He stopped himself. 'You know, I think I'll go say hi. I'll meet you in your office in five.'

I watched him stride off towards the library and I thought to myself suddenly, for the first time, that maybe Kyle was actually in love with Amanda. It took the wind right out of me and I stood there, deflated. Maybe this wasn't some minor flirtation or temporary diversion. Maybe this was the real thing. 'You old fool,' I murmured to myself as I inched my way back to the office, holding a lit cigarette and staring into space. 'You old fool.'

I suppose that's how he found me a few minutes later, lost in thought, lost in a tangle of distant feelings. I heard him clear his throat and I turned to see him staring at me from the doorway, nearly laughing. 'And where are you, may I ask?' he teased, taking his usual seat and hoisting his feet onto my desk.

'Oh, I'm here. And everywhere, I guess.' I forced myself to laugh, too. 'So tell me. What's the news?'

'The news, my dear, is good.'

'Is it really?'

'Yes. He'll take her.'

'What? He'll take The Baby? Just like that?'

'Well, not just like that. Give me some credit. I had to charm and wheedle and beg. But I did it.'

I put out my half-smoked cigarette and stared back out the window. I was stunned. I knew Dr Reith had spoken with this legendary Swede. I knew Kyle went in person to plead our case. But I had never allowed myself to dream it would work. I was speechless, momentarily. 'Holy Mother of God,' I finally said. 'I can't believe it. I'd given up hope long ago.'

'Well let that be a lesson to you. Kyle Mackenzie works in mysterious ways. But don't relax yet. The one caveat is that we bring her up straight away.'

'Meaning?'

'Like yesterday. Now. Certainly in less than a week.'

'Less than a week? But why the rush?'

'Because, as he said: "This is not a morgue. It's a hospital." He wants to have at least the chance to save her, and every day is crucial. I suppose he's right.'

When things happen around here, they really happen. No window-dressing. No prettying up. It makes it both harder and simpler at the same time. 'Right. Okay,' I said, letting it sink in. 'Now let me think. I suppose I can take her by myself.'

'No, no, no. I'll go, too.'

But before I could even thank him, we heard Amanda's voice asking, 'Go where?' She was standing in the door with The Baby asleep in the sling across her chest. How long had she been there? Kyle and I looked at each other. We must have looked like we had been caught smoking in the bathroom. When neither of us spoke, Amanda asked again, 'Go where?'

'To Siem Reap,' I answered, knowing that would never be enough of an explanation.

Amanda looked at Kyle. 'Kyle?' she asked. There was a drawn out, schoolmistress sort of cadence to her voice. He shot me a glance as if to say, 'Keep quiet and leave this to me.'

'Yeah, Siem Reap,' he confirmed, but now he was sounding excited. 'This is my big news. There's a fantastic private hospital up there and I got talking to the head honcho about some minesweeping he's interested in. And I mentioned Little Miss Poop over here and he said he might be able to help.'

166

'My God! Really?' Amanda cried, clinging The Baby even closer to her. 'That's so wonderful! I can't believe it!'

'Well, don't get too excited. He can't be sure if there's anything he can do. He has to examine her first and then he'll see.'

'Yes. Of course. Of course. But it's a chance. A real chance. And I'll go too, of course. We can leave tomorrow.'

'Now wait a minute, Amanda,' I said, trying to hide my rapidly building anxiety. 'Not so fast. Remember…'

'Yes, I know. The rest of the kids. But we won't be long. And Sam and Nita are here. Do you think Madame can come and stay?'

'Now wait a second, love.' Kyle was now standing next to her and drawing her close to him like a skittish child. 'You don't need to go.'

'Don't be silly. Of course I'll go.' She moved away from him and her hands automatically drew The Baby even closer up to her heart. 'I have to go. Of course I do.' Then trying to make light of it all, she added, 'And besides. I've never been to Siem Reap.' And, as if on cue, The Baby pooped in her sleep and Amanda rushed off to clean her, calling back to us, 'This is wonderful news. Wonderful.'

Kyle sat back down. An ocean of troubled silence lay between us. It took a long time for us to overcome it.

'There's no way…' I finally started to say.

'There's no way she'll stay home,' Kyle continued, beginning to argue. But we were in agreement.

'That's what I was going to say. There's no way we can make her stay home. And maybe this is better anyway.'

'Yeah. If –when – something happens, she'd just end up blaming us. She needs to see the truth for herself.'

'But Kyle, please. You'll have to promise to stay with us, then. I can't face this on my own.'

'Of course not. I'll be with you the whole time.'

'Please, say you won't leave us.'

167

'I give you my word.'

That night, we told the kids. I told them that Kyle, Amanda and I would be taking The Baby to a special hospital to see if she could be helped. I told them Sam would be in charge, along with Thom and Srey, and that Dr Reith would also check in with them if needed. I tried to sound happy and optimistic. I tried to sound as happy and optimistic as Amanda looked. But I'm not that much of an actress. The children were all quiet, solemn even. Somehow they knew not to probe too deeply into all this. I know they sensed that there was more to it than I was telling. Amanda looked too happy, and Kyle looked too serious. They were all silent until one of the kids asked the question that was on everybody's mind. It was Nary – her seven-year-old body may be fragile, but of all the younger kids, her mind is one of the sharpest.

'When will you all be coming home, then?'

At first I didn't know what to say. But I couldn't lie to her. I had never lied to any of my kids and I wouldn't start now.I chose my words carefully. 'In a couple of days,' I tried to reassure her. 'I promise, *I'll* be home in a couple of days.'

JULY

Siem Reap is a city full of history and change. Now a World Heritage Site, the magnificent temples of Angkor are not to be missed. Watch the sun rise over Angkor Wat and have the experience of a lifetime! Siem Reap and its temples are truly heaven on earth.
  A Touristic Handbook, p. 18

Leave it to Kyle to make an already fraught trip even more exciting. There we were, three Westerners and a Cambodian infant, boarding an unmarked private junk-of-a-plane Kyle had commandeered from some mate. I shouldn't complain. The flight was free and the only alternative, namely crawling along flooded roads for hours in some overheating jalopy, would have been the death of us all. But I do hate those little prop planes. I can never believe they won't just drop out of the sky. The pilot seemed nervous, too – Mike, another one of those Australians with a touch of insanity in his eyes.

'Come on in. Make yourself to home,' Mike said, encouraging us to scramble up the metal steps and into the steel pipe with wings. He gave me a quick look and then nodded in Amanda's direction. 'Lightest up front. Right next to me. Just don't push any buttons,' he said, laughing. Big joke.

'What about the kid, Mike?' Kyle asked. 'She okay up there, too?'

'Good call. Better put her in back.'

'Yes, I'll take her,' I said, reaching up across Kyle. 'Come on, Amanda. Give her to me.' Amanda hesitated and I had to push. 'She'll be safer.'

'Yes, she'll be fine. Just strap her in with you back there,' Mike agreed and, before I had even finished buckling the

169

strap, he was revving up the engines. 'No time to waste. Don't want to attract too much attention, eh?' Then I heard him say to Kyle, 'You know, this Tribunal is great but it's making my life harder, to be sure. There's a lot more questions, a lot more nosing around in my business.' As the engines began to roar I was just able to hear him joke, 'I may have to go legit, and where's the fun in that?'

I reached for a seat-arm to hold onto but there wasn't any. So I held onto The Baby, closed my eyes and tried to breathe as deeply and as slowly as I could. A phrase, like a mantra, kept echoing through my head: 'This is not how I will die. This is not how I will die.'

Credit where credit is due, though. Once we were up, the flight was remarkably smooth. The sky was absolutely blue and felt like it was ours alone. No clouds. No distant planes. Not even a wayward bird. Just us, suspended in time and space, hovering. I heard the others laughing in the front, but I couldn't focus on their words. Their voices mixed with the drone of the engine to create a reverberation in my ears, a meaningless thick white noise that seemed to surround The Baby and me in some cocoon, separate from the rest of the world, in tune with each other only. The flight couldn't have lasted more than an hour or so, but it seemed to last forever. I remember glancing back and forth between the sky and The Baby and thinking how strange it was that nothing was changing. The view out my dirty, tiny window was a constant sea of blue. The look on The Baby's face was that of an immutable, undifferentiated blankness. Mostly, she slept. The few times she opened her eyes she barely saw me. She wasn't really looking then, just seeing. When she closed her eyes again it was as if she was saying there was nothing worth looking at. It was barely worth the effort.

I was abruptly snatched out of my reverie by a sharp increase in sound and a worrisome banking to the left.

'Oh look,' I heard Amanda say. 'It's beautiful.'

The temples of Angkor jutted up into the sky below us. I had visited that sacred, tourist-ridden site many times before, but I had never seen the temples from above, and from that distance they took my breath away. Ziggurats of stone reached up towards heaven from reflecting pools of blue. Ant-like tourists clambered over steeply pitched steps. Ancient gnarled branches of brown and green ripped through crumbling marble. Thousands of years of lingering prayers sliced by the edge of our wings. We landed with a jolt. For the first time that day, The Baby began to cry. I gave a surreptitious check of her diaper but it was disturbingly clean. No poop, which was a good thing. But no pee either, which was decidedly bad. I held her over my shoulder and whispered, 'Ssh. There, there,' while we managed the few steps onto land.

'I can take her now, Deborah,' Amanda said. As I handed The Baby over, her eyes briefly locked onto mine. To the end of my days I will swear that The Baby then told me she knew her time had come and she was ready.

Kyle took charge of everything. He led us from the airport into a taxi seemingly in seconds. In barely a minute more we were standing in the hallway of the hospital waiting to see the doctor. Time was playing games with me, and until I was actually being introduced to the great man himself, I felt displaced and out-of-synch. It took the warmth of his hand and the firmness of his shake to snap me back from wherever I had gone.

'Welcome. You must be Deborah Youngman,' he said. Then, turning towards Amanda, he added, 'And this is the child? May I? Please?' He took The Baby and held her like a football in the crook of his arm. She was so tiny she barely reached to the palm of his opened hand. He gave her a little bounce to feel her weight. 'Quite small. And how old do you think she is?'

171

'We can't be sure, but we guess about four months by now. We've had her since April,' I explained.

'Since April and now it's July. Well, you've certainly had your hands full. I can see that. I'll give her a quick examination and then we'll talk. Nurse?'

Kyle and I watched the doctor and his nurse take The Baby into the examining room. Amanda followed behind them, but the nurse motioned no, and closed the door before Amanda could enter.

'Come on. He won't be long,' Kyle said and drew her away from the door. 'There are chairs right down the hall where we can wait.'

As I sat in the waiting area, I looked around in wonder. This was a hospital. A real hospital, with clean white walls and steady bright lighting, nurses in crisp uniforms and a hush throughout the corridors. I had never seen anything like it in Cambodia. I had never seen anything like it since my last visit to see my mother back in Cleveland Memorial. I started to speak to no one in particular. 'Can you believe this place? It's amazing. There's nothing like it in Phnom Penh, at least nothing that the Cambodians can use.'

'I know. He's rolling in it,' Kyle answered. 'He's funded by everyone and he never stops asking, from what I hear. Good on him, though. You know?'

Amanda was quiet, though she couldn't stop fidgeting. She could barely contain herself in her seat. I put my hand on her knee to try to calm her. 'Don't worry,' I said. 'I'm sure they won't be long.'

'I hate this place. I hate hospitals. I hate this place,' she whispered over and over.

'How about some fresh air?' Kyle asked her.

'No.'

'A cup of coffee?'

'No. I can't leave.' But to me it looked as if Amanda had already left. I don't know where she went to, but although

172

she was physically there beside us in her chair, she was actually somewhere else, somewhere very disturbing for her. Was it her Peace Corps days? Was she now lost again in the jungles of the Philippines? I couldn't know for sure, but I did know what it was like to have your past and your present merge together into some wakeful nightmare. I feared that that nightmare which Amanda had been trying to fend off all this time might now, sadly, be coming true. But I had been right about one thing. It wasn't that long a wait. Perhaps just fifteen minutes more and the nurse came to find us.

'Miss Youngman, will you come with me?' I got up to follow her. Amanda stood up too. 'No. Just Miss Youngman, thank you. The doctor was very clear.' Kyle stood up to hold Amanda back, putting his arm around her shoulders. As I followed the nurse down the hall I could hear Amanda complaining, 'No, Kyle, let me go. I need to go too.'

When I entered the room, The Baby was lying in a clear plastic bassinet with wheeled legs as tall as a tabletop. She had on a new disposable diaper and was wrapped in a fresh cotton blanket. The doctor was sitting behind the desk. He shook my hand and motioned for me to sit as well.

'Now, Miss Youngman, your friends - Mr Mackenzie, I believe it is, and of course Dr Reith - have told me all about this child and the good work you do up in the capital. Actually, I believe I have heard about you and your Home before this. I congratulate you on all you have done.'

'Thank you, Doctor. But I'm surprised you've heard of us.'

'Well, yes. Your reputation does precede you, as they say,' he chuckled. 'I hear you are a trained nurse and you are also a...let us say, a no-nonsense type of person. Am I right?'

'Yes, I suppose you could say that.'

'Then you must realize the truth of the situation here,' he said, motioning to The Baby. 'This child is not thriving. Will not thrive. She cannot digest food. There can be any number of reasons for this, but at this point in time it barely matters.'

'She's dying, isn't she?' There was no more denying it, no more fighting and fretting. And honestly, to say it out loud was a relief.

'Yes, I am afraid so. And I must tell you, I consider it to be a miracle you have kept her alive this long. When was the last time her nappy was wet?'

'Yesterday afternoon.'

'And has she been awake at all today?'

'Barely.'

'As I thought. She slept through the examination. She did not cry or move. She has barely any reflexes. Her breathing is shallow.'

My eyes filled with tears, but they weren't only for The Baby. Without realizing, I was also looking towards the door.

'Yes. The young woman. Perhaps a more difficult question. Would you like me to talk with her? You must realize, though, that I will tell her the truth. I will not make it any easier than it is.'

'But she will listen to you. She'll believe what you say. Otherwise, I don't know…'

'Very well. Nurse, will you ask them to come in?'

There are times when your brain shuts down. Your senses stop working or they work in weird ways. You can hear but you can't understand. You can see but nothing looks real. The next several minutes were like that for me. Even remembering it now, so much later, I can't be sure what actually happened or what I just imagined. I can tell you that Amanda came into the room, followed by Kyle. She stood with her back against the wall, staring at The

174

Baby. The doctor spoke. She said nothing, but she went up to the bassinet, took The Baby out and held her, swaying back and forth. I think the Nurse was afraid Amanda might try to steal the child and she barred the way out of the room. But Amanda didn't try to run. Instead, she slowly lowered herself to the floor and sat there, rocking, with The Baby in her arms. The horror and pain of that scene brought me back to myself. I knelt down beside her, and tried to reason with her. 'Come on, sweetheart. Let her go. Let her go.' But Amanda had drawn herself and The Baby so deeply within she couldn't be reached. I began to get really frightened and looked up to Kyle for help. Instead, the Doctor intervened. He took Amanda firmly by the shoulders, stood her up by sheer force of his will, and spoke to her distinctly, face to face.

'My dear. Please listen to me. Children die for many reasons,' he explained. 'They live only for one. Love. Without love no child can live. With it, they can hold on even when their bodies are gone. This little baby has lived because you have loved her. But she is tired and has very little life left inside. Be proud of what you have given her, but please, let her go.' He motioned to the nurse who took The Baby away from Amanda. Hardly five minutes passed and The Baby was dead.

Somehow, Kyle and I got Amanda to leave the hospital. The doctor had been so kind. Here, we had landed on his doorstep, just one more unasked-for problem, and he had shown us charity and understanding. He even offered to take care of 'the body'. God knows what else we would have done. We couldn't have brought The Baby back to Phnom Penh. 'We have facilities here,' he offered. 'Facilities which, unfortunately, we have to use all too often.' Even waiting and bringing back her ashes seemed too much. After all, we really weren't her family, were we?

175

'And when we get home, we can arrange some sort of service for her, if you want,' Kyle told Amanda. 'Something meaningful to us all.' But Amanda didn't respond. She didn't say anything at all. She just walked out of the room and down the hall.

I turned towards the Doctor. 'I don't know how to thank you,' I said.

'I have done nothing. If only I could have done more. But take care of that young girl. She is your big concern now.'

'Yes, I know. I know.'

'Here are a few tranquilizers, just in case. She may have a few bad nights and might need these – one per night only, please.'

I took the small envelope of pills, but in my heart I knew it would take much more than that to get Amanda through these nights.

The hotel Kyle brought us to was run by his old, Khmer friend, Finn. It was basic and clean, with ensuite bathrooms and air conditioners that produced a hum of continuous crescendos and decrescendos. Finn was waiting for us when we arrived. A quick conversation with Kyle and an even quicker look at Amanda and he was ushering us up to our rooms.

'Let me know if you need anything,' Finn said with a smile of sympathy and compassion. 'Have you eaten? No? I will bring you up a plate.'

'Thanks, mate,' Kyle said. 'Come to think of it, I'm pretty hungry.'

'Me too,' I said. 'Amanda – are you hungry?'

Silence.

I looked at Kyle. 'Maybe sleep is more important anyway,' I told Amanda. 'How about you get into bed?'

Silence again, but now, without undressing or washing her face or anything, she pulled down the covers and got

176

in, turning her back away from us. Kyle shut off the light, tucked her in and stroked the top of her head with a light, tentative touch. 'Get some sleep,' he whispered.

The hotel room had a terrace just beyond a set of sliding doors. It wasn't much, just a concrete floor surrounded by a wrought-iron rail flaked with peeling black paint. A small metal table with rusty legs hosted two plastic chairs. Off to one side stood a waterlogged potted palm. A striped awning tried to keep out the sun and I stood beneath it for a few minutes, waiting for Kyle. The air was fresh from the latest rain and a shallow puddle made its way towards the drain in the corner. I was beyond tired. I thought nothing. I felt nothing. All I could do was lean against the railing and stare into the distance at the shadows of the hotel being constructed across the way, as they faded into those of the ancient temples lying just beyond.

'Here. Sit down. Finn sent this up.' Kyle was suddenly with me on the terrace carrying a tray of food.

I let out a sigh. 'God, I'm tired.'

'It's been a long day.'

'And it's not over yet…Wow, this looks great.' Finn had sent up a plate of sliced fruit, some cold chicken, a bottle of mineral water and three beers.

'Yes,' Kyle agreed, opening up two of the bottles even before sitting down. 'Finn's a good friend. I've known him for years. Another one who's survived despite it all…he said to let her sleep as long as she can.'

I nodded my head but didn't stop to answer. Once I started eating I realized I wasn't just hungry, I was ravenous. It was now about five o'clock in the evening. We had missed lunch, but this hunger was about more than just one missed meal. The beer was cold and wet and smooth as it slid down my throat. I started to come back to life.

'What time do we meet Mike in the morning?' I asked.

'I told him I'd give him a call.'

177

'Okay, because I'd like to get home as early as possible.'

'Well, we'll have to see,' he said, nodding in Amanda's direction.

I stopped eating and looked off into the distance. All the life that had started to come back to me flooded away. Yes, The Baby was gone. Yes, it was sad. But I had a Home to run, living kids to raise, kids who needed me, who were helpless and innocent, who were waiting for me to return, relying on me to return. Kyle could see what I was thinking. 'We can't just leave her like this,' he pleaded. 'I'm afraid she's having a breakdown.'

And that's when I realized, to my surprise, that I wasn't just tired and sad and drained. There was a large part of me, a growing part of me, that was angry, too. And this anger wasn't only about needing to get home to my kids. I was also angry for myself. I don't have many friends: there never seemed to be enough time for them. But I had allowed myself to consider Amanda a friend. And, although I might have hated to admit it, I needed her. I needed Amanda's friendship. I wanted her friendship, so she had to be okay. She couldn't have a breakdown. She had to come through all this and come back to life, back to us, to me. But the thought that I might now lose her didn't make me reach out to her. No, it infuriated me all the more. If anything, I pulled away.

'I don't know if she's having a breakdown or not. But I do know one thing – I've had enough.'

Both of us were shocked: Kyle, that I could be so heartless; me, that I had actually said it out loud.

'Deborah, listen…' he began, but I wouldn't let him continue.

'No. You listen,' I said. 'I'm sorry. You can think of me what you want. Call me cruel and uncaring. Call me a dried-up heartless spinster. But I have a responsibility, and it's not to that young woman in there. I told her not to get

178

attached. I told her this would happen. But she wouldn't listen, and now she's lying there as if she's the only one in the world who's ever lost anything. You can stay here for weeks, nursing her, psychoanalyzing her to your heart's content. But I just can't anymore. To me, she can't come first.'

'But Deborah, it's not like that. You don't know…'

'That's right. I don't know. She hasn't told me anything about herself. All you've told me are rumors and suppositions. And yet, I'm supposed to blithely accept her hysteria, her secrecy? And yours? No, Kyle. I'm sorry. This has to end now.'

'Okay, Deborah. You want to know? Do you really want to know? I'll tell you.' It was Amanda. Perhaps Kyle had left the glass door open a bit too much. Perhaps my voice had become louder than I had meant it to be. But for whatever reason, Amanda had woken up and heard everything. And now she was standing there, a glowering Medusa with knotted hair and steely eyes. Kyle reached out to her but she brushed him away as she went back into the room and sat like a statue on the bed.

'Okay, Amanda,' I said, following her inside and sitting on a wooden chair just inches away. 'It's time. Tell me.'

And so I finally got to hear Amanda's story, the great mystery I'd been waiting to hear for months now. But as chilling as her story was, it was the way she told it that has lasted with me, haunted me, and taught me the depths of destruction one person's actions can wreak on another. Every word of hers was uttered with the same blank pitch. I don't think I ever saw her eyes blink the whole time she was speaking. There was no anger in her voice. No pain or feeling of any kind. Just the words, the facts, and they felt like they had been chosen to sting into my flesh like rusting bits of barbed wire. Amanda spoke as if she was already dead, or even worse, dead again.

179

'I married Tim right after college,' she began. 'We joined the Peace Corps to save the world. We spent almost two years in East Timor. Tim dug wells and worked with the farmers. He was good with his hands. I helped the children. Then they closed down the program there. Terrorists. We could have gone home. Tim wanted to go home. Back to graduate school. Back to Connecticut. But I didn't. Not yet. Maybe not ever. They gave us jobs in the Philippines, in the south. Tim loved fishing and there's good fishing there. So I was able to convince him to go. He agreed because he loved me and didn't want to lose me, he said.'

At this point Amanda paused. She didn't move; she just stopped speaking. Kyle gave her a glass of water which she took, drank two sips, and then gave it back to him. All that time I just stared at her, motionless, but my mind was running marathons, jumping hurdles between Cambodia and that island in the Philippines. I had lived on that island once, a long, long time ago. It was a dangerous, impoverished place back then, full of hopelessness and simmering violence. From what I had heard, not much had changed over the years. If Amanda had left her story right there with what she had already told us, I probably would have been able to piece together the rest of it for myself. But she continued.

'We got started but we weren't there long. I began to feel sick in the mornings. I didn't tell him. I didn't tell anybody. When he asked me about it, I lied. I told him not to worry. I told him I didn't know. But he knew and he was worried. It didn't matter, though, because soon enough the rebels came. "Commander Robot" himself with that sneer. Those eyes. He tore our shirts and tied us to poles with rusty nails. Those nails – like daggers in our backs. We escaped, somehow. He sent his men after us. "Yankee scum!" they screamed. I watched them shoot Tim while I hid in the bushes. Branches held me. Like tentacles. I didn't say anything. When they knew he was dead they forgot about me. I ran further into the jungle. All night. Eventually, someone found me. I was hurt. My back was sliced open like a mango. Thorns, barbed wire, rusty nails. You felt the scar. I know you did. And I was bleeding, like my whole uterus had burst and was emptying out. And it was. Right there I lost the baby. Just a fetus a few months old, but big enough for me to know what she was, that she was real and that now she was gone. I bled for a long time, forever.'

She stopped again, but this time she looked as if she had stopped completely. She got back into the bed and sat there with her arms folded and a ferocious look that seemed to say, 'So there! Are you happy now?'

There was a pause. I don't know for how long. I remember Kyle standing in the corner and being surprised by the look of horror on his face. I guess I was surprised by that look because I didn't feel horror. Not at all. I didn't feel shocked or even like crying. Instead, I paced around the room, thinking. I took my time. I think I even went out to the balcony for a bit. Yes, I did, because I remember the sun was setting and I could see it turning the sky pink and orange behind the distant ruins of the temples. I remember thinking, 'Another day is over. One more day.'

When I returned to the bedroom, who knows how much later, the scene was as I had left it. Amanda sat bolt upright in bed, her arms folded like a shield against her chest. Kyle stood in the corner by the door waiting for I don't know what. But I felt remarkably calm. Maybe even relieved. I stood next to Amanda, looked down at her and simply asked, 'So?' She seemed not to understand. I said it again. 'So, Amanda? So? So what? Is that it?'

I'll never forget the look on her face. I swear that if she had had the strength, she would have killed me, literally killed me with her own bare hands. She spat out her words. 'Is that it, you're asking me? Is that it? What? Are you stupid? Do I have to spell it out for you? Okay. I was pregnant. Get it? The baby died. My husband died. Everybody died because of me and my selfishness. I didn't die, though I deserved to. But they did and it was my fault.'

Jesus, she was furious. She so much wanted a fight. She would have loved for me to yell and scream and call her all sorts of horrible names. Or maybe she wanted me to baby her and say, 'There, there.' But I didn't. I couldn't. I wasn't going to lie about my feelings. I wasn't going to pretend that this was the worst thing I had ever heard in my life, because it wasn't. Not by a long shot. And when I didn't fall apart, she looked as if she could have torn my eyes out. But I didn't care. Instead I said, 'Yes, Amanda. I get it. I get it. I'm sorry for your loss, okay? But I'll let you in on a secret. Not only didn't you die; you survived. You didn't kill any one and you survived. All that shit happened, okay. But look around you. Look where you've been living. Cambodia is all about this shit happening. Cambodians have millions of stories just like yours, and worse. But the ones who didn't die are getting on with it, are helping themselves and others. Shit, even though it's taken a generation to get here, now we even have this Tribunal happening. If a whole country can get on with it, so can you. So stop blaming yourself, get the hell out of that fucking bed, go out into the world and do some good.'

And that's when I really started to feel again. Up until that point I was as stony as Amanda herself, but now cracks were opening up in that stone and I couldn't keep my feelings back any longer. For a minute I thought I might even have been capable of grabbing her and hauling her out of that bed myself. But my hands felt as if they were already full, full of other dead children's bodies – a Khmer infant, an American college kid. All dead. All more worthy of my pity than that woman glaring at me there in that bed. 'Jesus Christ, you make me so fucking angry,' I said and stormed out of the room. I stood for a minute in the hallway. I was shaking all over, as if even a lifetime of deep breathing wouldn't calm me down. But then fatigue, overwhelming muscle-destroying weariness, overtook me. I searched for the hotel key in my pocket and decided all I wanted to be just then was alone, as alone as I had ever been. I looked at my watch. It was nearly 8:00 and I remember thinking that, at my age, I could legitimately almost call that bedtime.

My room was identical to the other. Same noisy air conditioner. Same concrete terrace, but the sun had already set and there was no reason to go out there. So I went into the bathroom, brushed my teeth, put on my pajamas and got into bed. I could hear intermittent crying coming from the other room, but eventually the crying stopped and it was just two murmuring voices. I remembered that I still had the sleeping pills that were meant for Amanda. Maybe she would need them, but I couldn't get myself to go back there and give them to her. All that mattered to me right then was that I knew what I had to do, and I had to get some sleep.

I slept the sleep of the righteous, or maybe it was the sleep of the dead. I must have slept nearly twelve hours, and when I woke the sun was seeping into the room from under the door. My first thought was that I was hungry. The second was that I had to call Sam. I fumbled around for my cigarettes and telephone. I had already called her the day before to tell her about The Baby. Now I was calling just to hear her voice. Everything was fine at home, she said, but when she started asking me questions about what was happening up here, I realized I had no answers. I had slept well into the morning without any disturbance so I assumed Kyle and Amanda had made it through the night. Whether they had stayed together in that room or not I didn't know, and, to be honest, I didn't really care. As I

183

began to dress I heard some movement coming from the other room. I didn't know what Kyle and Amanda were thinking, if they even had any plans at all. I did know, though, that I would be home that day, one way or another. And my life would get back to normal, or at least the newest version thereof.

I got myself ready to go as fast as I could. Before I went down to the breakfast room I knocked on Amanda's door. Kyle opened it.

'Still here?' I asked.

'Yeah, still here.' He shrugged. I peered into the room. 'She's taking a shower.'

'She okay?'

'Yeah, I guess. We talked. We slept. Now it's morning.'

'Well, I'm ravenous, so I'm going to get some breakfast, and then I gotta get home.'

'Okay. We just ordered some stuff up, so we'll see you later.'

Maybe it was just me, but the food in that hotel was incredibly good. I had two fried eggs, a grilled tomato, toast, coffee, even fried potatoes. By the time I was finished I felt raring to go. I knocked on their door again. This time Kyle let me in. I looked around the room for signs of trouble. A broken lamp on the floor. A picture hanging crooked on the wall. I don't know – maybe I've seen too many old movies. But everything seemed in order, except for the bed which was a tangle of twisted sheets and strewn pillows. I went over to Amanda who was sitting on the terrace eating and said, 'Hi.'

'Hi,' she said back without looking up at me.

'I called Mike for you,' Kyle interjected. 'He said he could be here by eleven. You can be home by 12:30 or so, okay?'

'Yeah, sure. That's great.' Then with hesitation I added, 'And will I be traveling alone?'

184

'Yeah. You don't mind, do you? I thought we'd take a day or two here. Get ourselves sorted. Maybe check out the temples, right Amanda?' he said, making a half-hearted stab at normality. When she didn't respond he whispered to me, 'We'll be back by the end of the week or so. I'm sorry. It just doesn't feel right leaving with her like this.'

'Sure. Fine,' I said. 'Of course. We'll all be waiting for you, whenever.'

As the taxi drove me away from the hotel and back to the airport, I knew I couldn't be certain that I would ever see either of them again. But somehow I believed that I would. I believed that I would live through Mike and his flying antics all in one piece. I believed that I would find my home and my kids healthy and happy to see me. I believed that I would watch the sun set tonight over Phnom Penh and it would rise tomorrow on schedule over us all. And it would even shine over The Baby and her ashes, those ashes that would now be starting their journey back into the earth, still infused with the love of those who had held her and the dreams of all our children everywhere.

I know that back in the States there are all sorts of books that help you talk to kids about death. There are support groups, psychologists, workshops even. I suppose that's a good thing, the fact that so many American children are so removed from death that their parents need professionals to help them fit the concept into their lives. But what a difference between there and here. Here we have nothing but the fact itself, and as I flew back to Phnom Penh I was thinking the whole time about what I would tell my kids when I got home. The Baby had gone away and now will never return. Too many of them have already experienced that nightmare. I hoped this would feel different, but how could I be sure?

185

My arrival home coincided with the kids coming back from morning lessons. We all met at the door, all at the same time. There were hugs and cuddles everywhere. I had only been gone one day, but it felt like forever.

Sam took my overnight bag, looked me up and down and started to laugh. 'I thought you would look not so good. Too tired. But you look fine, Mother. You do.'

'I know. I feel fine, too. What can I tell you? I slept. I ate. I'm fine. But I do want to talk to the kids right after lunch. I need to tell them what happened.'

'Okay, but they are fine, too. Everyone is. Really.'

'Yes, we are,' Srey piped in. I looked over to see her and Thom standing there like some teenage delegation. 'We all talked about it already,' she said.

'You did?'

'Yes,' Thom agreed. 'Some were asking questions and we could not lie.'

'No, of course not.'

'But do not worry,' he continued. 'They do understand.'

Thom was right. They did understand, each in their own way. Everyone talked about it, even before I could say anything. While Nita spooned out lunch, they all spoke as if they were explaining it all to me even before I could explain it to them. Little Sothy was the first to speak, I think.

'Mother, do not worry about The Baby,' he said. 'She was very sick.'

'Yes, she is at peace now,' Kiri then added, showing a thoughtfulness I never knew he had. That was Thom's influence, I knew, and I noticed him sitting beside Kiri, quietly nodding his head with pride. Seeing those boys like that, witnessing the kindness that ran all around the tables full of my kids, made my eyes well up with tears. I tried to hide it, but I guess Nary saw them. She stood up from the table and gave me a hug.

'This happens, Mother,' she whispered. 'Do not be sad.'

'I'm not sad,' I said to all of them. 'I'm not sad. I'm proud of each and every one of you. This has been a hard time for all of us, but you have all helped one another and that makes me very proud and very happy.'

'Happy tears!' Chak called out laughing.

'Yes. Happy tears.'

A little while later, Netra asked the one remaining question. 'Will Amanda be coming home soon?' As Thom had said before, I could not lie to them. I wasn't sure what to say, but Sam helped.

'Oh yes. Kyle and Amanda will come back, I am sure,' Sam assured her. 'And then we will see how long they can stay.' The perfect answer.

And so our lives went back to normal. The next day came and then the day after that. But now it felt like our Home was being run by committee. A year ago, everything was up to me, certainly with the strong support of Sam and the assistance of various neighborhood women, but it was all up to me nonetheless. Now there was a group, a supervising collective of sorts, consisting of me, Sam, Srey, Thom, and Nita who was around much more than ever before. Of course, I was still more equal than the others, but between the five of us everything got done. Yet, it did feel like something was missing, or rather someone. Everyone missed Amanda. We were all used to Kyle blowing in and out on his whirlwind of excitement. But the kids had gotten used to Amanda being there every day and they missed her. And surprisingly enough, so did I. I realized it the most during the next day's dance lesson.

I decided to sit in on the class this time and see how they were getting on. Srey said Madame had brought some new costumes and I had to discuss that with her anyway – who they came from, how we'd pay for them – that sort of thing. Sitting in there, watching the girls in their solemn, slow movements dancing like statues of goddesses come to life, I found myself thinking about Amanda, remembering that first time she decided to dance herself. I recalled the astonished giggles of the kids, the seriousness of Madame's instructions, the look of determination on Amanda's face. Yes, I had to admit, I missed her too. Sam commented on it that day just before bedtime. She had finished the last check of the night and came into my bedroom to give me a goodnight kiss. She sat for a moment on the bed next to me. As it happened, a letter from Pat was lying right there on the table.

'Mother, is Amanda really all right?' she asked.

'She wasn't. As it turns out, she had lost a baby of her own once,' I tried to explain. There was no reason any more not to tell Sam and she nodded in understanding. 'But I hope she will be alright now. I know Kyle is trying to help her. I just hope she's letting him.'

'Good. I am not surprised to hear what you are saying about her own baby. I thought such a thing might have been possible. And her husband, too…so horrible.' Then she began to smile, almost laugh. 'You know what is surprising, though? Kyle. He is good for her, I think. You know, he is actually very kind.'

'Yes, he is. He has been a very good friend to us all.'

Sam then leaned over me and picked up the letter. 'May I?' She only glanced at it. She didn't need to read it. 'Things happen quickly, don't they,' she said. It wasn't a question.

'Yes, they do.'

'Mother, if Amanda does not return…'

'Let's wait and see, okay? You are meant to go away to school. I know that now. We will work it out somehow.'

'I am meant to?' This made Sam really laugh. 'Is that my mother speaking?'

'Well, maybe even I can be taught. You know what they say about old dogs....no? You don't? Well, never mind. Let's just wait and see.'

'Alright. I will see you in the morning, Mother. I promise.'

There was such a quiet ease about Sam that night. I'm not sure what it was, but it filled me with such peace that I was nearly asleep myself as I breathed out my own nightly response of 'I promise'.

Amanda and Kyle did not come back later that week, as they had suggested. The kids stopped asking for them. Sam and I stopped looking towards the door and giving each other inquisitive shrugs. I worried that I had been too harsh with Amanda that night, after all. And now that my initial anger had subsided, my heart did ache for her, my arms did want to cuddle her close and tell her I was there to help. But I also understood that my reaction had been about self-preservation. If I broke down every time I felt sorry for someone around here, I would have been committed to a loony bin a long time ago. It wasn't my fault that those terrible things happened to her. God knows, I've already taken responsibility for enough terrible things that I never did. It wasn't her fault either, though. And I knew for damned sure that the people who actually did kill Amanda's husband and unborn child have never even given it a second thought. Murder? Responsibility? What does one thing have to do with another in this world, anyway?

Then one evening during dinner, about ten days later, there was a knock on the door. Nita left her post in the kitchen and went to see who it was. She let out a scream – she's got to stop doing that – but this time it was not one of horror like it had been when she first found The Baby lying there all those months ago. Now Amanda and Kyle

189

were standing there, and Nita was happier to see them than I ever would have guessed.

Amanda spoke first. 'Hello, everyone!' she called out. 'Sorry to interrupt.'

We all stopped what we were doing, talking, eating, wiping faces, and looked. Some of the kids held back long enough to shoot me a quick 'May I?' glance, but mostly everyone rushed to throw their arms around them: Kyle and Amanda, their long lost darlings. I just sat and watched greeting after greeting, some funny, some touching. I was certainly happy to see them, but more than anything else, I was relieved. Eventually everyone came back to the table, but before Amanda and Kyle could find chairs of their own, I stood up. I gave Kyle a bear hug first. That was easy. I was so happy to have him home I could barely believe it. I think I must have clapped him on his back five times, just to make sure it was really him. And it was really him. Really. It was Kyle there with us again, but Kyle as he actually was, now changed, less larger-than-life, less like our own action figure incarnate. Kyle-Mackenzie-the-man was now there with us. And although his back and arms felt just as strong as I hugged him, something had changed.

I wasn't sure, though, how Amanda would receive me. There were lifetimes of discussions waiting to be had between us, but would she let them happen? She approached me first, taking my hands into hers. 'Hi,' she said.

'Hi. I'm glad you're home,' I answered. And it was the truth.

Dinner turned into a party. Amanda was a bit quiet, but Kyle told stories about their adventures up north. 'One morning,' he told the kids who were sitting spellbound, 'we went to see sunrise over Angkor Wat. A lot of people go to watch the sun set, but we got up early to watch it rise. And, because I know the bloke who works security, we got to sit right up by the pool in front of the ruin. Right by the water. No one else was around. The gates weren't even open yet. It was absolutely quiet. There had been a monster rain shower the night before, and the ground was still muddy and frogs were jumping everywhere. But even the frogs were quiet. We watched the sun come up behind the temple...'

'Was it like magic?' Srey asked.

'Just about,' said Amanda.

'But then,' Kyle continued, 'just as my mate was going to open the café and get us cups of coffee, we saw something move up inside the temple. At first we thought maybe it was an animal, a tiger even. But then I thought, "No. Maybe it's one of the kids who work the tourists. Maybe some kid got locked in by mistake."'

'I know those kids,' said Kiri, making sure all eyes were on him while he showed off how tough an eight-year-old can be. 'They find a tourist, write a note they call an email, give it to them and then they sell them books. Only two dollahs, but many times. You can make good money. I did that once.'

'I bet you did,' Kyle laughed. 'So that's who we thought it was. My friend went up to investigate. We followed –but guess who it was after all? A tourist, from America.'

'For heaven's sake. Really?' I asked.

'Absolutely,' Kyle continued. 'There he was, complete with his camera around his neck and his little backpack and his brown socks and leather sandals. Some middle-aged guy from Nebraska or something. He'd been wandering around where you're not supposed to go,' Kyle explained, 'and he got locked in. Boy, was he scared.'

'Did he get in trouble?' Thom asked.

'Not really, though the guard hauled him out of there and said he could never come back. Americans, eh?' he teased, looking at Amanda.

I looked at her, too. She had been quiet throughout Kyle's little anecdote, smiling, nodding her head in agreement when he tried to elicit some response. But mostly she was quiet, somehow present and absent at the same time. Kyle was trying to hide his awareness of this, too, but it was obvious to me. He was working hard, laughing, teasing, oozing excitement as if trying to be present enough for the both of them, as if trying to deflect attention from the vacancy in Amanda's eyes. I was watching them closely, and I saw him give her a little nudge and a whisper in her ear. 'And now,' he said, hoisting their bags onto the table, 'we have some gifts. Amanda, will you do the honors?'

Amanda then reached into one of the bags and started pulling out presents for everybody. It looked like they had bought something off every single urchin they had met. There were postcards, caps, scarves, supposed gemstones, books about the history of the temples (one in Russian), beads. 'This one is for you,' Amanda told Sam, handing her a CD. 'If you find yourself far from home and lonely, play this. It will help.'

'It's made by a group of musicians I know,' Kyle told us. 'There are ten of them, all land mine victims. Some are missing a leg, some an arm, some are blind. But they play this most beautiful music together on traditional instruments. They've got a *sralai*, that oboe thing, a *sampho* drum, finger cymbals, gongs, the lot. It's amazing. And now they're selling CDs in aid of minesweeping. You know, like I used to do.'

'Used to do?' I thought, but Kyle was onto some other story even before I could say it out loud. What could that mean, I wondered? But I had to let the thought go because, suddenly, it was my turn for a gift. 'For me?' I asked, taking a box wrapped in gold foil. 'You shouldn't have…Wait, oh yes you should.' It was a box of chocolate, but not just any

192

chocolate. Godiva chocolate or, more likely, black market Godiva chocolate. 'Don't tell me,' I laughed. 'You know a guy.'

'Yeah, I know a lotta guys,' he said.

I thought I'd have a hard time getting the kids to bed that night. I thought they'd be too wound up from the excitement. But Amanda and Kyle helped us get them all ready and tucked in. If any of the kids had noticed a change in Amanda, they didn't show it. They were all just happy having them there, having them back. It was like everyone could now really relax, as if the kids felt that we were all now, finally, safe and home. Once everything was quiet, Sam, Amanda, Kyle and I sat down together in the kitchen. Kyle pulled two bottles of beer out of his sack. 'Here you go, old girl,' he said, handing one to me. I didn't hesitate. We were all quiet for a while. There was so much that needed to be said, but none of us could bear to be the first to say it. Eventually, Sam reached for Amanda's hand and simply stated, 'I am sorry about the baby.'

Amanda nodded her head and tried to smile. 'Thanks, Sam. Me, too.'

I didn't know what we were going to do when we went to the *wat* several days later. I had promised Amanda and Kyle that we would have some sort of ceremony, but what form, what shape, even what religion was beyond me. The old monk knew we would be coming, but who knew what he could do for us? We had no body to cremate, no ashes. We didn't even have a photo of The Baby. She had left nothing behind, poor child. And, because I wasn't sure what we would do once we got there, there was little I could do to prepare. All I could say to the kids was that nobody had to go. There would be no shaved heads. Nobody would be taking any vows of becoming a monk for a day or two, as was usually the case. After all, none of us was actually

193

related to the child. 'We are going to the *wat* to say some prayers with the monks and think about The Baby,' was all I could tell them. 'We are not really in mourning as if she was our sister. But if you would like to wear white, you may.' In the end, everyone decided to come, and together we led a solemn parade from the Home to the temple. Amanda and Kyle were up front. Sam and I walked with the youngest ones in the back, and all of us brought offerings of food and candles and flowers.

We might have had no idea what we would do at the *wat*, but it didn't seem to matter. Somehow, the monks knew not only exactly what to do, but also exactly what we needed. A group of them met us at the gate and led us to where the old monk himself was standing near a small outdoor shrine of Buddha surrounded by candles, already lit. Prayer rugs had been laid in front of the altar where we placed our offerings. The old monk motioned for us to sit. I stayed towards the back, and I remember feeling awkward and nervous. Cambodian Buddhist funeral rites are very specific and very severe. All of us had already seen too many of them, and that's not what I wanted here. A nice, pleasantly moving, Episcopalian sort of memorial service was more of what I had in mind, but, as we all sat around the altar, hands clasped in prayer position, I knew whatever was about to happen would be far from that.

The old monk struck the gong with a strong arm. It's impossible to ignore the shimmering, almost effervescent sound a gong makes. The pitch is both deep and high at the same time, and you can almost feel the ripples of the sound waves bouncing against your skin and lodging themselves into the base of your heart. Instinctively, we all bowed our heads. Two monks began to light the incense while the youngest monk handed out incense sticks and stems of yellow flowers for us to hold as we prayed. This may not have been an actual funeral, but there is nothing quite so heartbreaking as the scene of a crowd of children solemnly kneeling, bundles of saffron shedding light on their down-turned heads. As the monks began to chant, I looked at all of my children's faces. Each one, no matter how young, looked serene and serious, as if they had each retreated into their own private world. Some even seemed to be smiling, but not in an awkward, childishly giggling sort of way. Certainly not. The smiles I saw were more smiles of comprehension, maybe even contentment, and that's when I understood that this really was a funeral, after all. It might not have been a funeral for any one single soul moving forward into her new life-cycle. Rather, it was a funeral for all our lost souls, hundreds of them, and we were sending prayers to each of them to ensure that their next lives, and the lives after that, would be better than those we had shared with them here.

The old monk rang the gong once more. His voice rang out with it, picking up the pitch as the bell gradually fell silent. He prayed first in Cambodian but then, surprisingly to me, he chanted in English:

Even the gorgeous Royal chariots wear out, and indeed our bodies too wear out. But the teaching of goodness does not age; and so Goodness makes that known to the good ones.

As he finished, the younger monks took up the chant, and we seemed enveloped in the sound of their voices and the pervasive scent of incense.

Amanda then stood. I was shocked to see her do that. Although I, of course, had been watching her the whole time, I never really expected her to take an active part in all this. As far as I could tell, she hadn't really been taking an active part in anything since she'd been back. But the old monk nodded to her as if he had been expecting this, and motioned to a grass mat that had been set amidst a circle of candles. Amanda squatted beside it and placed a bundle of cloth in the middle. It was The Baby's sling, the one the

195

nurses at Dr Reith's clinic had given her months before. And that's when I understood that all that time I had not really been there at this ceremony at all. I thought I had been observing, but my sight had been selective. For everything I had seen, there was much more that I hadn't seen. I hadn't noticed that Amanda had been carrying that soft cotton sling all along. I hadn't even noticed that she was dressed in mourning whites. I also hadn't noticed that Dr Reith himself had joined us at some time and was now standing beside me. I was about to thank him for coming, but Amanda began to speak. Her voice was strong and loud, but also arid, like dust.

'I do not come from a Buddhist country. But there is a prayer that I have heard my family say that I would like to say now.' Then she took a piece of paper out of her pocket and began to read:

May God remember the souls who have entered the life of eternity. May they be at one with God in peace. May I always remember them with love, and honor their memory by showing kindness to others. Let their memory inspire me to live well so they may live on in me.

She stood up and nodded to the old monk, who then took his place beside Amanda's offering. As he struck a flame Amanda added, 'May God remember the souls of all our babies, and today may he remember the soul of the one we called The Baby, but who in my heart I have always called after my grandmother, by the name of Grace.'

We watched the sling burn. The old monk then covered the ashes with a banana leaf and gathered them all together. He presented the small package to me. Somehow, I knew exactly what to do, what to say. I stood up to accept his gift, this small parcel, and walked over to Amanda. Passing the ashes from my care into hers, I said out loud. 'Death is not the end of life, just the end of but one life-cycle. All the children who have gone before, who we have held in our arms and our hearts, live on, will live on, forever.'

AUGUST

A show at Playhouse Square. A rainforest in Metroparks Zoo. A world-renowned orchestra, or 6,000 years of art. All this and more awaits you in vibrant, surprising Cleveland.

Promotional Pamphlet: *Welcome to Cleveland,* **Cleveland Chamber of Commerce**

Sam had said that things happen quickly, but she had had no idea just what a whirlwind of efficiency her Aunt Pat could be. Before I realized what was happening our airline tickets were sitting on my desk. Phnom Penh to Seoul, Seoul to New York, New York to Cleveland. I had forgotten just how much of an ordeal it was to get there. I sat at my desk staring at the two envelopes and picked up the phone. I didn't even think about the time difference.

'Hello, Pat? It's me.'

'Deborah? What time is it?'

'Oh, Jesus, sorry. I didn't even think. It's 8pm here…oh that's not too bad….'

'Yes, it's nine in the morning here. You're lucky you caught me in. I'm usually out of the house by now. Everything alright?'

'Yes, everything's fine. I'm sorry. I don't even know why I'm calling. It's silly.'

'Deborah…? What?'

'Oh, it's just that I'm sitting here holding our plane tickets…'

'You got them? Great! What time do you arrive?'

'We'll get in late afternoon, but God, Pat. I can't believe it. I'm freaking out.' Pat started to laugh. 'It's not funny,' I complained.

'I know, I know. But it is funny.'

'What? That my daughter is about to go live thousands and thousands of miles away?'

'No, silly. Not that. But that you're surprised. Of course you're freaking out. We all do when our babies leave. Why should you be any different?'

'But it's ridiculous. Sam's leaving is a good thing, not a tragedy. With all that I've seen, how can I...' but Pat interrupted me before I could even settle onto my high horse.

'Deb, give me a break. "With all you've seen...." You know, not everything has to be the worst thing in the world for it to affect you. Face it, you're no different than the rest of us. Your kid goes to college and you get scared and sad and nostalgic and lonely and....but Jesus, you still have a couple of hundred other kids to take care of. Don't you? But anyway, listen. I was thinking. Are you going to be able to buy her a winter coat over there? I know things are less expensive where you are, but you might have to wait and buy that sort of stuff here.'

And so Pat brought me back down to earth and reminded me that what I really needed to be doing just then was not wallowing in nostalgic self-pity, but shopping. So I started to make a list.

> * electrical adaptors
> * underbed storage containers
> * lots of underwear
> * alarm clock
> * medicine kit

When Sam came in to say goodnight, she found me scribbling away like a mad woman.

'Mother, what are you doing?'

'Oh, good. You're here. Tomorrow morning, first thing, I want to take you shopping. I realize there's a lot we need to get you and soon.'

'We do? Like what?'

'Like more clothes, things for your dorm room, electrical stuff. A computer we'll need to get you over there, and I

198

think Pat made some arrangement with the school to help us pay for it, but there's a lot of other stuff.'

'Oh, I can't believe it. Okay, I will make a list too. There are so many things. So many. Oh, Mother!'

And that's when it finally happened. That's when Sam went from being reticent but accepting to downright excited. She threw her arms around my neck and gave me an even bigger goodnight hug than usual. 'Tomorrow, I promise,' she called over her shoulder as she rushed back to her room to start making her lists. It's amazing what the prospect of a shopping spree can do. When Srey heard what we were going to do, she went crazy. 'Oh please, Mom. Please. Can't I go? You won't have to buy anything for me. And I'll be a big help. I can carry things. I am good at shopping. Better than Sam. Oh, please, Mom.' And I did think about taking her along. We really could have used her help. But Sam said no. For all her excitement there was something else going on inside her as well. She pulled me aside.

'Mother, I know it is mean. But can it just be the two of us today? Just you and me without everyone else, anyone else? Is that horrible of me?'

'No, of course it's not horrible. Let's just have the two of us on our own little shopping trip.' I put my arm around Srey and took her aside. 'Thanks so much for offering to come, Srey. You would be a big help, I know. But I think your sister is nervous and wants to have as few people around as possible. Just me and her this time. Do you understand?' Reluctantly, she nodded her head yes. 'Good girl. I promise, you and I will have our own time, just the two of us together, soon. Okay?'

'Okay, Mother. We will do that then. I guess I should go do my homework anyway.' She began to slouch away but Sam stopped her and gave her a hug.

199

'Thank you, Srey. Thank you for understanding,' she said. That, more than anything, made Srey feel better.

And so off we went, leaving Amanda and Nita in charge of the kids at home, with Kyle heading off to play football with the others. We spent the whole day going from the Russian Market to the Central Market and back again, loading everything we bought into two new backpacks Sam found first thing. The backpacks were Amanda's idea.

'Every college kid in America has a backpack. They hold a lot and you can store it under your bed. But make sure you get one with a good hip-belt otherwise it will kill your shoulders, okay?'

'Yes, a hip-belt,' Sam noted as if she was learning astrophysics. 'Like you have on yours?'

'Yes, but try it on first and make sure the frame doesn't rub too much against your back.'

'Yes, the metal frame. I understand.'

Watching Sam maneuver her way through the markets was exhausting in itself. She looked, stopped, tried, wondered, worried. She went from insisting on only buying the least expensive items she could find, to rejecting things because of shoddy workmanship. One minute she was refusing to let me buy her a case full of pens and stationery because she could 'easily get it at school and it would be an unnecessary use of our money.' And then five minutes later she was begging me to let her buy new earphones 'in case' she decided to buy an iPod. I think she had more mood swings in the course of those few hours than she had had in her entire life. By the time we were ready for a late lunch, I could barely move.

'Mother, you sit here with the bags. I will go get our food. Is chicken curry good for you?'

'Yes, thanks. And a coke.'

'Coca Lite, Mother. Diet is better for you.'

'Yeah, okay. Coca Lite.'

I know we ate our lunch in silence at first because I can remember my brain churning out so many thoughts that I didn't know where to begin. In a funny way, it felt like this was the time for last-minute questions, but I wasn't sure what those questions could be. Pat had told me that when my nephew, Joey, went off to college she was scared to death that she hadn't taught him what he would need to know to be able to function on his own, like how to do laundry, how to put new sheets on a bed. Sam certainly knew how to do all that, and more. In some ways I thought she'd be better prepared than any other freshman in the world. But there were other issues about friends, and teachers, and safety, and boys that I knew she was way behind in. Should I bring those things up or not? Would that make her better prepared or just more frightened? And anyway, how frightened was she?

'So, I have to ask, honey: what do you think about all this? Just a couple of weeks and we'll be on our way. Are you excited?'

'Yes, very.' Then she hesitated. 'I am a little frightened, too. But I don't want you to worry.'

'Will you ever stop worrying about me?' She laughed. 'Well, here's the deal then. You stop worrying so much about me and I'll stop worrying so much about you. Okay?'

'Okay.'

'So, what are you frightened of? Not about us at the Home, I hope.'

'No, I am not frightened about that. Not any more. There are many hands now. And really, it is knowing that Kyle will be helping out that makes me the happiest. That I never expected, but I believe he does want to stay now.'

'Yes, so he says. But really, even if he decides some day he has to leave, we will still be alright... There's Srey, Nita, and Thom, and all the other kids are getting older all the time.'

'Yes, that is true. And there is Amanda, of course.' To that, I just smiled. Regardless of what anyone else might have thought, Amanda's presence in our lives seemed no more certain to me now than it had before. The difference now was that I had stopped worrying about it quite so much. Now, there were other things, like Sam's imminent departure, to think about instead.

'So then, what are your fears?' I asked.

'Well, America is a very different place to Cambodia.'

'It certainly is.'

'I think it is a place with expectations.'

'What do you mean?'

'It is a country that expects much, I think. The people I meet, the Americans, will also expect much.'

'Of you?'

'No, I do not think they will expect anything of me. They probably won't even expect me to speak English. But Americans expect much of the world. Of what they can have and do. I see the world in a different way. That may be hard for me.'

'But you will change to be more like that, don't you think?'

'No, and that is the fear. I do not think I can change. I do not think I want to. I am not sure that it is good to expect too much from the world, to expect that you can have whatever you want. Maybe it is better to do what you do because it is better for you now, not because it will get you more. To expect too much – that does not seem right to me.' And with that I, at least, started to feel much less frightened.

Sam's going-away party was an entire day full of surprises. I spent much of the time sitting under the banyan tree in our garden, watching. I think that's when I realized just how self-absorbed I had been. Of course I was dreading Sam's

202

departure, just as Pat had explained I would. My life might seem the same after she was gone. I still had kids to take care of, a house to run, a governmental bureaucracy to circumvent. But I knew in my heart that every day would feel different. As I sat there, the fact hit me square in the face that I wasn't the only one dreading her departure. Every single one of her brothers and sisters fought to find a way to spend their own few minutes alone with her. They couldn't do enough for her. They fought over who would bring her her next cup of mango juice, who would share their fried bananas with her, who would sit on her lap. That wasn't so surprising. After all, Sam was their oldest sister, the one who had always been a second mom. Plus, she was the first to leave. The first to venture out into the adult world beyond our Home. The first, and maybe the only one, to go to live in America.

There were others heartbroken, too. Nita, for one. Over the past few months, certainly since the day she found The Baby on our doorstep, Nita had been spending more and more time with us. She now came every day and stayed all day. I have no idea how she managed it. Whenever I asked about her own family, she just shook her head. Once I pushed her on the subject. 'But what about your own kids?'

'Old now. Fine,' she said with a shrug.

'And your husband?'

She answered that with a sharp spit on the ground. 'My place here.' I decided to let that bit of local color remain mysterious. She definitely did make her place here, specifically in the kitchen where she spent two full days leading up to Sam's party preparing all Sam's favorite foods. I tried to get some of the other kids to help but she wouldn't allow it. It was to be her gift to Sam. Mountains of fried bananas. Heaps of chopped coconut. Everything that she knew Sam would love and miss. The only help she accepted was from Netra, who began hanging around the kitchen months before as a way, I think, to avoid the judgmental glare of her older sister, Srey. Srey would do almost anything to avoid cooking, but Netra loved it. She was a natural and Nita knew it. Nita and Netra, chef and sous-chef, our own in-house caterers. And together they created a banquet for the family member that each quietly, in their own way, loved the most.

Another surprise in a party full of surprises was Madame. I had told her about the party, of course. And I had hoped she would drop by for a bite of birthday cake. But she did much more than that.

'Miss Deborah, please to have everyone in a circle in five minutes.'

I had just spied Dr Reith when Madame bid us to sit. Dr Reith was another surprise. Of course he had been invited, but I never dreamed he would be able to leave the clinic. 'Dr Reith,' I called, clasping his hands and even giving him a kiss on the cheek. 'I'm so glad you were able to come, but I never expected...'

'Nothing could keep me away. Sam is important to me too, as are all of you. You know that, do you not?' I think I actually blushed. For all that we have been through over the years, the worries, the traumas, the mended injuries and cured illnesses, we had never actually acknowledged the important place we held in each other's lives. I have often called Dr Reith my 'savior'. But just how important I was, how important we all were to him, I suppose I didn't really know for sure until Sam's party. 'It sounds like I have arrived just in time,' he said as he helped me corral everyone into a circle. I made sure Sam was sitting in a chair prominently positioned while everyone else sat in two long curves on either side of her. It was hard not to notice, though, that several key people had gone missing. Clearly, Madame had something up her sleeve.

'Dr Reith, you sit here next to Sam,' I said.

'Yes, thank you. And you, please, sit next to me?'

'With pleasure.'

I looked around to see who was missing. Srey, Nary, Kiri, Thom...

'Miss Deborah,' Dr Reith whispered. 'Where are Kyle and Amanda?'

'They've been playing with the toddlers.' But when I looked over to where the younger kids were all sitting, squashed between Sothy and Netra, I realized Amanda and Kyle were also among the missing. 'Where did they go?' I asked no one in particular. But I soon found out. A gong was sounded from somewhere back in the house and then, to the click of finger cymbals, into the center of the circle walked Madame in her most beautiful white satin and blue silk. She struck a pose and clicked her cymbals once again. Music started and then, into the circle, forming two lines behind her, came three pairs of dancers also in white satin shirts and silk trousers, but their trousers were pomegranate red to offset the depth of Madame's blue. Every one of us was quiet as Kiri and Nary approached first. I wasn't surprised to see Nary there. She loved to dance and always seemed to be able to bend her doll-like body into all sorts of positions. But Kiri? Dancing? And in front of everyone else? That, I couldn't believe, until I saw Srey and Thom approach. The serious and serene look on Srey's face made her look even more exquisite than usual. She took my breath away. I think Thom realized how beautiful she looked as well, because he stood slightly behind her and placed a quick, steadying hand on Kiri's shoulder as if to remind him to pay attention and behave himself. Finally, to everyone's delight and restrained hilarity, came Amanda and Kyle. And it certainly was hilarious to see Kyle there with them, without his Australian hat, his bare legs and feet sticking out of red silk trousers. God knows where they found a pair of trousers

205

his size. But nobody laughed, and not only because Madame would have killed us if we had. Nobody laughed because Kyle himself was serious, with a look of placid determination equal to that of the rest of the dance troupe.

'Oh, look at Kyle!' Sam whispered across to me.

'This I never thought I would see,' Dr Reith said quietly. I never would have believed I'd see this, either: Kyle taking a step back, humble, without bravado, without jumping into the limelight and absorbing it all into himself. This was a new Kyle, a Kyle who, I now realized, had been slowly emerging over the past few months. Love, clearly, had been the catalyst for this change. Up until the moment before this dance I would even have said it was his love for Amanda that had worked the miracle. But I now saw how wrong that would have been. Yes, it was love which was bringing about this change in Kyle, but it was his love for us, for our Home, for Sam, for the children, for who we were and who we were desperately trying to be; and yes, even if it was just a little bit, it was also his love for me.

The dance lasted perhaps ten minutes all together, and it felt as if we were all collectively holding our breaths throughout the whole thing. The dancers told a story with their bodies but it wasn't a story I had seen any of the kids perform before. The dance began with Madame slowly leading Kiri and Nary around the inside of the circle as if magically pulling them across space. Slowly they moved their arms like wings, or perhaps waves, as they followed her, turning from one direction to another. Next came Srey and Thom, their arms and legs bent like animals. Slowly they jumped back and forth menacingly, symbols of danger perhaps, or treacherous obstacles. They held a long silk scarf between them which they sometimes tossed, sometimes whipped. As the music grew louder, Madame and her four dancers began to make their movements not faster, but stronger, with heavier legs and more rigid arms.

Each face became even more intense. Yes, they were portraying danger and I instinctively put my hand on Sam's knee, more to comfort myself than to comfort her. But then with the crash of a gong came Kyle jumping into their midst with the stance of a warrior. Of course, Kyle comes to the rescue. And with a few sure, though not completely graceful movements, the dangers were defeated. Srey's and Thom's movements became softer as they slowly walked backwards in time to the quieting music. Then, with several more rings of her finger cymbals, Madame moved into the center of the circle, ushering Amanda before her. Together, like shadow puppets, they danced through their poses, Madame behind Amanda, each raising a leg with its outstretched foot, then an arm with its bent back fingers. Goddess poses, mesmerizing, strong and gentle at the same time, ending up with the appearance of the center of a wheel, the other dancers its spokes. Together their wheel made one deliberate revolution ending precisely with the music. As their final poses were struck and the final chimes were played, the dancers raised both hands to their chests in prayer and bowed, not to all of us, but specifically and deeply to Samnang, who rose from her chair, bowed back and then fell into Madame's embrace.

The party lasted into the evening. It seemed as if the entire neighborhood at one time or another came over to say goodbye to Sam. The owner of the corner shop brought her a pack of blank postcards. Her favorite *tuk tuk* driver came in with a swagger but left noticeably meeker. I had been so self-absorbed to think I would be the only one to feel Sam's absence. Everyone would miss her. Everyone dreaded having her leave, even though we all knew her leaving was the best thing that could happen to her. But Phnom Penh would be a much greyer place for all of us while she was away.

* * * *

When I first left home nearly forty years ago, my parents drove me to the airport and walked me as far as the police would allow. They would have walked me into the airplane if they could have, sat me down in my seat and made sure my tray table was up and my seatbelt fastened. Instead, they stood at the barrier and cried. Actually, it was my mother who did all the crying. My father just stood there, stoically patting my mother's back and shaking his head. I smiled and waved as I turned the corner into passport control, but I remember them crying for most of the flight that took me to the other end of the planet and a life my parents could never have imagined. Since then, I have always equated airplane flights with tears. A long, tearful, emotional scene at the airport is my idea of a nightmare.

'Kyle, you gotta help me with this,' I said, cornering him the day before Sam and I were due to leave for the States. 'This is going to be hard enough. No big scenes, please. Make sure everyone else stays home, okay?'

I shouldn't have worried, though. There was so much luggage there was barely room for me in the car. Besides my one old Samsonite bag, Sam had her two new backpacks full of clothes, one cardboard box tied with thick twine containing her sundries – electrical adaptors, medicines, God knows what else – plus a huge duffle bag borrowed from a teacher which I'd have to fold up and somehow bring back home with me. Sam had dismantled her corner of her room and packed it all away to bring to America. Her sheets, her blankets, photos of all the kids, even the silk wall-hanging the women AIDS victims had made for her after she wrote about them for the school newspaper. Everything that was important to her that could possibly be packed and carried, she took. I knew she wouldn't need any of it.

'You know, Sweetie, I'm not sure you'll have space in your dorm room for all this,' I tried to tell her.

'Well, maybe it is silly, but I would rather have it all with me just in case.'

Together, Kyle and Thom piled it all into an old station wagon borrowed from yet another guy Kyle knew. Too soon, it was time to leave.

'Okay, it's time to go, Sam,' I called out, unsure of where she was. I walked around the house looking for her, a trail of children growing behind me. I bet I looked like something out of the Pied Piper. We eventually found her in the toddlers' bedroom. 'Alright everyone. Don't be too sad now. You'll see me in a week and Sam will be back in just a few months. Before you even know it.'

Sam kissed each of the kids goodbye and went around the house making sure nobody was missed. You could almost hear her checking each one off in her head: Sothy, check. Nary, check. Kiri, check. Thom tried to get away with a simple bow, but Sam would have none of that. She pulled him to her and gave a hug which Thom, in the end, was reluctant to release.

'Srey, come here,' she said and then whispered, but loud enough so I could hear, 'I am relying on you. Remember.'

'I will remember,' Srey said and started to cry.

'No tears,' I then heard Amanda say. She had been so quiet all day that she startled me. 'No tears. This is not sad, everyone. This is happy. We are all happy for Sam. Right?' She looked around at all the kids gathered there and added, 'Right?'

'Yes…okay…right,' they all replied in their own fashion, some quietly looking at their feet, others loudly seeking approval.

'Thank you, Amanda,' I said.

'Yes, well it's true, and now it's time for you to go. Don't worry. We'll be fine. Everything is under control.' Just watching Amanda standing there, holding back the kids, waving goodbye with deliberate motion and an expressionless face left me with no doubt that everything, especially Amanda herself, was very much under control. If anything, too much under control.

Kyle cracked jokes the whole way to the airport. He was doing his best to keep the trip light, though Sam remained quiet. When we arrived, he loaded up a couple of trolleys and ushered us up to check-in. He even gave me money to pay for the excess bags. I had completely forgotten about that. 'Hey, don't you know a guy?'

'Not this time.' He then walked us up to the metal detectors and armed soldiers of security. 'Okay now. This is where I love you and leave you.' He gave me a quick kiss. 'Now don't you worry. Everything will be fine back here. You guys just have a great time. And Sam,' he said, giving her a hug, 'you, we'll see in just a couple of months. Behave yourself, but not too much. When you get back I want to hear at least one story that you can't tell your mother.' That finally made Sam laugh.

'I will try. But please write to me.'

'I will.'

'And take care of Mother when she returns.'

'Of course. I'll take care of everything. Stop worrying.'

'I will try. I promise. And I know you will help. But oh…' She threw her arms around his neck and then rushed away to place her carry-on bag onto the scanner, wiping away the tears she didn't want him to see. My own tears I didn't even try to hide. 'Here we go,' I called out to Kyle as I waved one last time.

I woke to sun streaming through an open window. I lay on my side for a while trying not to wake Sam who still slept soundly in the single bed by the door. A huge old elm tree cast its shadow against the side of the house and everything was quiet except for a solitary bird singing in the distance. It must be early, I thought. I reached for my glasses and looked at the clock. It was 6:20. The day had barely started, and I was waking to the hushed sounds of a very civilized suburb of Cleveland.

Now that I had my glasses on I gave myself a moment to look around. This room hadn't changed a bit since the last time I had slept in it, five years earlier. The same country-style curtains framed the window with green-and-yellow flowers stenciled on tan muslin. The bed I now sat up in had the same maple frame and light, waffle-woven blanket. The oval braided rug still lay between the two beds. The familiarity and strangeness of it all made me feel itchy, like I had to move around no matter how sleepy I was. I barely allowed myself to breathe as I grabbed my bathrobe and cigarettes and tiptoed downstairs to the kitchen.

'You're up early,' Pat said, standing by the coffee machine, filling up a glass jar and pushing buttons.

'Jet lag's my excuse. What's yours?'

'I'm always up at six. Can't help it.'

'You should have been a farmer's wife.'

'There are worse things.' I looked at her and couldn't tell if she was joking or not. I often couldn't tell with Pat. Either she had no sense of humour at all, or she found every moment of her life equally hilarious. 'Coffee will be ready in a minute.'

'Thanks. And what should I do with these?' I asked, pulling my packet of cigarettes out of my pocket.

'Throw them away? Flush them down the toilet?'

'How about I smoke one outside?' Pat poured us each a big mug full of coffee. Hers said 'World's Best Mom.' Mine said 'I've Been to the Biggest Mall on Earth'.

'Come on. We can sit on the back porch. Use this saucer as an ashtray.'

Sitting on that porch in my bathrobe, drinking weak American coffee and smoking a strong cigarette with my sister in the rocking chair beside me was one of the most peaceful moments I had had in a very long time. It was still early enough that the August sun wasn't scorching. There was just a hint of breeze sighing through the air which was, to me at least, noticeably dry. Amanda, Kyle, the kids, the whole cast of characters left behind felt a galaxy away. 'This is nice,' I said.

I knew there were a million things we needed to do before we had to move Sam into her dorm. Most of it, despite all the bags brought from home, was shopping. But there was also a dentist appointment, a haircut, and a meeting with the dean. But all that could wait. There was something I wanted to do first.

'Pat, do you think we could go to the cemetery?'

'Of course. I assumed you'd want to.'

'Yes, but how about we do it today? First thing?' That surprised her. 'I don't know. It just feels like I should go see them before I do anything else.'

'Sure. Whatever you want. But is this is eagerness or dread?'

It was a good question. I hadn't been back for five years, not since my mom's funeral. Seeing her and my dad both lying there after all this time was bound to be difficult. But I knew that the sense of loss around their deaths wouldn't be the worst part of it for me. Pat sensed what I was thinking, even without my saying it.

'You know, if it makes you feel any better, I haven't heard from our crazy brother in a couple of years either. Nobody has.'

'Really? I thought it was just me he hated.'

'I don't know if "hate" is the right word.'

'Well, he did accuse me of murdering our mother.'

'Insane…'

'I know, I know. And I don't want to make a big deal about it. What's done is done. But the last thing Derek said to me right after the funeral was that my life choices had broken Mom's heart and that I had killed her as much as the cancer had.'

'Well, for what it's worth, Mom worried about him way more than she ever worried about you.'

'Really?'

'Really. She missed you and was sad that you were so far away. But let's face it. Derek's crazy. He was never the same once he came out of the army. Could never keep a relationship. Never held down a job for long. Last I heard he was running a shooting club out in Montana somewhere. The idea of him surrounded by all those guns...'

'And he calls me a murderer.'

A noise from inside put an end to that conversation, and it was just as well. My brother was one subject I never wanted to think about. I knew he would never understand me and I sure as hell was never going to understand him. So I had cut him out of my life and left him lingering there back in my past, a shadowless phantom.

The door swung open and closed with a well-controlled click.

'Hey, you two. You're up early,' Greg said, giving Pat and I both a kiss on the tops of our heads. 'I'm off to work.'

'Dinner tonight at about seven?' Pat called after him.

'I'll be here. Have a good day.'

Pat and I smiled at each other. There really wasn't much to say about Greg. Pat and Greg had been together since they were sixteen. They would always be together. They made it look easy.

'Oh, here you are.' Then there was Sam standing behind us.

'Sam, it's not even seven o'clock. I thought you'd sleep in a bit,' I said. 'Did we wake you?'

'No. I just awoke. I think I am too excited to sleep now.'

'Come on, Sweetheart. I'll make you some breakfast,' Pat said, taking Sam by the arm with a hug.

'Oh, please do not go to any trouble. I can do it.'

'Don't be silly. I've been counting the days until I could wait on you.'

I sat on the porch, rocking and finishing my coffee for a few minutes more. It was quiet and there was nothing I had to do just then but sit and look at green trees, an acre of green grass, and nothing but sky in the background. A very strange, but wonderful feeling.

Why do people need to visit cemeteries? What's that all about, really? It can't possibly have anything to do with the person who died. Unless you believe in the sort of afterlife where all these bodiless dead people hover around in the atmosphere looking down and making judgments about the people left behind, then visiting someone's grave can have nothing to do with anyone else other than you. There are lots of places where you can pay your respects to those who have passed on, as they call it. If you carry someone in your heart then you can do it anywhere, everywhere. Right? But nonetheless there I was, in the passenger seat of Pat's car, having forced her to stop by the cemetery on the way to the mall for Sam's big American shopping spree. Force isn't really the right word: Pat was happy to do it. She said she was overdue for a visit herself. And, of course, Sam never objected.

'I have not been to a Christian cemetery since Grandmother's funeral,' said Sam. 'And I don't remember much about that. It is so different from what we do back home.'

'Are there no cemeteries in Cambodia?' Pat asked. 'Really?' I did have to laugh at how hard that was for her to understand.

'In Cambodia Buddhists cremate bodies,' I explained.

'Yes,' Sam added, 'and then some people have small shrines in their homes where they go to remember and pray. But not big parks likes this.'

We then turned into the gates of the big park, as Sam had called it, and stopped outside an old brick building that may have been used as the office, I suppose, but was now locked. Attached to the wall, though, was a plastic box full of maps.

'I always get lost in this place. It's so huge. Here, Deb – they're at Row 23 on Tranquility Road. Can you find it? I think it's towards the back left corner.'

'Tranquility Road? I laughed. 'Well, I guess that's better than Damnation Drive.'

'Very funny.' Pat was not amused.

'Sorry…Well, according to the map you take the fourth left on Serenity Avenue, then a quick right and then the second left.'

It was pretty tranquil once we got there. Lots of ancient trees with huge canopies. Acres and acres of grassy hills intersected by manicured drives and grids of tombstones. They almost looked like mini suburban housing developments. Mom and dad were lying in the shade of a sycamore, a few feet away from the road. Their graves were neatly trimmed, their headstones clean. Two separate graves lying side by side: two separate but identical marble stones with their names and dates. Precise. Unfussy. Like they had been.

'Sam, can you put the flowers on the graves? A bunch on each.'

'On the ground or on the stones?' She wanted to do it right.

'On the ground. Maybe leaning against the stone. Just like this.' I guided her hand and together we set the flowers down. They did look pretty lying there on the grass: lilacs and pink roses against the grey of the marble.

215

'Do we say something?' she asked.

'We don't have to say anything out loud,' Pat answered. 'You can say what you want to yourself. They'll know.'

It was a very hot day. I could hear a slight breeze meandering its way through the leaves, though I barely felt it on my skin. Nonetheless, the air was cool where we stood under that sycamore. Cool and protected.

'We don't need to stay long,' I said. 'Maybe, if I could have just a minute here by myself? Is that okay?'

'Of course. Come on, Sam. Let's wait for Mom in the car.'

Sam gave me a gentle rub on the back and then followed her aunt. I didn't know what I wanted to do there by myself. I didn't think there was anything I wanted to say. Certainly, no prayers came to mind; no formal ones, at least. At first I found myself thinking about the ceremony we held for The Baby. That was just a few short weeks ago, though it seemed much longer than that. The old monk knew what to say. More importantly, Amanda knew what to say. At the time I had hoped that her prayer would have brought her some peace, some closure. Isn't that what prayers and rituals are supposed to do? But from what I could see over the intervening weeks between that afternoon at the *wat* and this one here in the cemetery, Amanda hadn't found much peace at all. She still roamed around the house in silence, talking only when spoken to. Her laughter was rarely heard, and honestly, it was her laughter that had continued to endear her to me throughout all those tumultuous months. The prayers for The Baby had not brought her any peace. Why should I think any prayer spoken out loud now by me would do any better?

Nonetheless, I continued to feel the need to stand there in the shade, alone with my parents. I looked around at the hundreds of other stone markers dotting the landscape of that park of graves, and then I looked out further into the distance. I could see a steeple not too far off that I thought belonged to the chapel on the university campus. I remembered that church all too well. I remembered how crowded it was back in 1970, just after 'that day' known simply by everyone of my generation as 'Kent State'. I could almost hear once again the sobbing during the memorial service. It was so loud, so unrestrained. And so were the mutterings of anger and disbelief. Now standing at my mother's grave with that steeple so close by, I began to feel that fury and fear once again. A shudder went through me, a shudder like a gust of cold air, only I knew that the cold was coming from inside me. I crossed my arms for warmth and gave myself a quick hug. I understood then what I wanted to say and I spoke the words out loud, despite my sister's instructions.

'Mom, it's me. Deborah. I want you to know that I'm leaving Sam here. Ironic, isn't it? But I'm going to trust that it will be okay. Maybe the place is safer now. Maybe it will be safer for her than it was for me.' Then I stopped for a moment. I stood there shaking my head and trying to control my breathing which had gotten too full and too forced. It sounded like a roar inside my head. When I started to speak again, I wasn't so sure who I was speaking to. 'Who am I kidding? I know there's no place really safe. Not on a college campus in America. Not on the streets of Phnom Penh. But I can't be with her every minute of her life, can I, Mom? Just like you couldn't be with me. But I know this is the best thing I can do for her. So help me out here, okay? Look after her. Keep her safe.'

Two big fat tears rolled down my cheeks. I turned my back to the car and wiped my face so the others wouldn't see. It's not that I didn't want them to see me cry. It's just that I didn't want to have to explain what I was crying about, and what I wasn't.

217

It was the nightmares that had really forced me to leave Ohio. I had been plagued by them on and off throughout my childhood. Agonizing, sleepless hours filled with night terrors would crawl by for no apparent reason, and then just as inexplicably they would all go away. One night I'd be petrified to close my eyes for fear of another series of engulfing volcanoes or towering tidal waves. Then, the next night, exhaustion would force my eyes closed and the terrifying images would disappear. That was life for years, and it was awful. I suppose nowadays a child like that might be shipped off to some weekly counseling session. But not me. My mother reassured me it was 'all in my head' and that in time I'd grow out of it. And I did, sort of. I remember being fourteen years old and in the midst of another string of sleepless nights. I decided I had had enough. I sat up in bed in the dark, my little sister sleeping on the other side of the room, and said out loud, 'Enough. This is stupid. I don't believe any of this anymore. Deborah, cut it out.' And I did. That was the end of it. Sure, I had the occasional bad night after that, but nothing quite as frightening or so long-lasting.

But then came the murders at Kent State. By that time, though, the adult world was more evolved. Some adults still killed children, but at least others then took the survivors off to bereavement counseling. I expected the nightmares to return. They existed while I was awake, why wouldn't they persist at night? And they did at first, but those counseling sessions must have helped because I didn't have many of them and then, after a few months, everything fell back to normal. At least, we all pretended it was. We all went to classes, did our homework, even went to frat parties on weekends. I felt like I really had escaped. But then, shortly before I was due to graduate, the nightmares started again. I'd wake up screaming. I was being chased by faceless men. Or I was trapped against a statue that came to life and held me in place with its stony arms. I started to panic and took myself to the Health Services. I don't remember what the doctor called it, but it was the 1970s' version of post-traumatic stress syndrome. He gave me tranquilizers which I took long enough to get me through exams. Then I left. But leaving that campus, even the whole state of Ohio, wasn't enough. I believed the only real escape possible for me was to leave the entire crazy, violent, furious country that America had become. And it did work. The nightmares trailed off and became less frightening. Then they stopped altogether. And now, when I do have the occasional bad night, like I did back in May during our holiday on Rabbit Island, I understand it, face it, and move on.

I was apprehensive, though, the night after our visit to the cemetery, that night before I was due to move Sam into her dorm. Just the idea of walking back onto that campus, that place that I had avoided all this time even despite visits to my family living nearby…Well, let's just say that after thirty-seven years, the place still held too many ghosts. I thought, I hoped, I would be all right. Watching Sam sleep in the bed a few feet away would probably help. I did think about talking to Pat about it. But that infamous day and my presence at it was something I never talked about. Nobody did. And it just didn't seem fair to bring it all up now. So instead I took a strong antihistamine right before I got into bed and hoped for the best.

The drug worked because the next thing I knew Sam was up and dressed and heading for the bedroom door.

'Everything okay?' I croaked. 'What time is it?'

'Oh, Mother, I tried not to wake you. It is early. Go back to sleep.'

'No, I'm up. I'm up. What time is it?'

'About seven. I couldn't sleep anymore. I am so excited.'

219

'Yes, of course. Come here.' Sam sat down on the side of the bed and I gave her a big hug. She seemed to sink into me. 'The dorms open at nine, right?'

'Yes. And remember my appointment with the Dean is at 11:30.'

'Got it. We'll be ready by then, don't you worry.'

Over the years, Pat has become my lifeline to the West – more than my other sister who was much too involved with her own life out in California, and of course more than my angry, reactionary brother. On the day we moved Sam onto campus, Pat was a lifesaver, organizing everything, carrying boxes, cracking jokes. By the time I was showered and dressed and making my way towards the kitchen, Pat and Sam were already finished with breakfast.

'Come on, sleepyhead,' she teased, handing me a cup of coffee.

'Sleepyhead? It's only 7:30.'

'It's 7:45, and we want Sam to be the first one in her dorm room.'

'We do?'

'Yes, we do. That way she can get the best bed.'

'Yes, Amanda told me we should do that, too.' Sam said. 'But why? Are the beds different?'

'No, the beds themselves aren't different,' Pat explained. 'But you want to be able to choose which one you want. Near the door or near the window. Or if it's a bunk bed, do you want the top or the bottom?'

'Oh, the bottom, definitely,' Sam said.

'Okay then.'

I was lifted up and carried off by these racing waters of industry and good humor. And I was thankful for it. Between loading the car, getting the room key, finding the building, unloading the car, meeting other families doing the same thing, there was no time for me to notice the old building where I had taken my nursing classes, or the bed of lilies blooming around the base of the quad's equestrian statue, or the bells ringing in the church steeple. At 11:00 we were finished readying the room. Pat had set up Sam's new computer. I had hung the gift from the AIDS women on the wall beside Sam's bed.

'I think everything is perfect, don't you?' asked Sam.

'Yes, it's all perfect,' I agreed.

'You'll be very happy here. I know it,' Pat added giving Sam a squeeze.

'We should go to my appointment then. I must not be late.'

I knew the dean's office was a three-minute walk away, but I could see Sam was getting anxious. She would have much rather sat waiting outside his office for twenty minutes than linger there in her perfect room.

If anything made me feel comfortable that day it was the fact that the Dean was taking a special interest in Sam. Maybe he did that with all the foreign students. Maybe it was just his job. But he wanted to meet her right away, make her feel welcome and let her know that he was always there to help her if she needed. Actually, he was waiting for her when we got there, and had done his homework.

'Miss Youngman. Lovely to meet you.' I was so glad not to be called Mrs Youngman. 'And Samnang. *Sua s'dey.*'

Sam laughed and then both bowed and reached out their hands. '*Sua s'dey.*'

I was impressed. He looked hardly older than Sam herself, but when he nodded goodbye to me and ushered her into his office, I felt confident enough to leave her there.

And that's when it hit me. Walking down the familiar steps of that brick building and into the newly mown lawn crisscrossed by paved walkways full of young students, I finally focused on where in the world I was. My life had brought me full circle. Time had somehow deposited me

221

smack in the middle of my worst nightmare. From my perch on the base of a statue, I could see where the grass had once been clumped with blood from my friends' wounds. I could see a row of trees that now lined the space where the state troopers had stood shoulder to shoulder, riot gear and rifles glistening in the sunlight. I remembered tripping over the flagstones as I dodged running teenagers and streaming bullets. And, turning my head to the right, I could see the path leading up towards the infirmary and once again I felt the weight of that boy in my arms as I helped drag his lifeless body towards it. And yet today the sun was shining. I was fully awake and my heart was not pounding with fear. My eyes were open but they were not clouded. When Sam and Pat found me there, maybe thirty minutes later, I was able to meet their smiles with a smile of my own and really mean it.

When I finally said goodbye to Sam later that day, of course I cried. All mothers cry when we release our children into the adult world. It's a big moment, and a bittersweet one. For me, that moment may actually be the definition of the word bittersweet. Though Sam cried too when she gave me what we both knew would be her last hug for a long time, her arms felt loose around my shoulders. Her palms were open and relaxed.

'I will be fine, Mother. You will see.'

'You're already fine, Sam. I know that. And I will be too, okay?'

'Yes, I know. And I will call you every Sunday.'

'If you can, that would be great. Just call whenever. Don't worry about the time difference. I'll always be ready to talk.'

'And don't forget to send me news about the Tribunal. I might not be able to get the same news here.'

'Absolutely. I'll keep you well informed.'

'And tell Srey…'

'Don't you worry about Srey. She's fine, too. They all are.'

With that Pat took me by the arm and started to lead me back to the car. 'Okay girls, time to go. Bye, Sam. Have fun.' Then turning to me she whispered, 'She'll be fine, really. And remember, I'm just a few miles down the road, anyway.'

'I know. Believe me, I do.' I said.

Airplanes do more than just take you from one part of the globe to another. If you let them, if you need them to, they can also provide transitions, real, physical transitions through both space and time. Suspended over the earth in a large metal tube for hours and hours, a person can do more than just get from one place to another. You can move from one need to another, one purpose, one dream, one reality to another. At least that was what the flight back to Phnom Penh did for me.

I slept through most of the first leg. I wrapped those uncomfortable black plastic headphones around my skull, listened to whatever the classical music channel had to offer and closed my eyes. I say I slept, but airplane sleep is not the same as real sleep. I don't dream and I'm aware of every little jolt. But my eyes do stay closed and time passes without awareness. It's enough to stave off exhaustion and that's worth something because I was very, very tired. It had been a week full of shopping, moving, packing, repacking, visiting, talking. Too many late nights. Too many rushed days. I had thought as much as I could think, feel as much as I could feel. I may not have been ready to say goodbye to Sam, but when the time came, I was ready to go home.

Home would be a different place, though. I did realize that. Not just for The Khmer Home for Blessed Children, but now with the Tribunal a reality, for the whole country.

As I sat there strapped in and hurtling through the clouds at five-hundred-miles-per-hour, I made a semi-conscious decision not to try to anticipate how that place might have changed for me. I would just let it be. I started to think about how for the last few months especially, all my thoughts were focused on other people. There had been the mystery of Amanda, The Baby's desperate needs, Samnang's worries. Children were growing up. The entire country was growing up, and each one had its own growing pains to contend with. Now, at long last, with the hint of clouds visible through my lightly closed eyelids and the crackling transmission of Vivaldi's *Four Seasons* playing in my ears, I decided I would focus my thoughts on myself. Amidst all this change, all this turbulence, what would I need? I didn't know for sure, but I promised myself that whatever those needs might turn out to be, I would make sure that fulfilling them would be towards the top of my to-do list. Number 2: Do what I need to do; right below Number 1: Keep everyone safe.

It surprised me when the captain's voice came over the speaker to announce thirty minutes to landing. Suddenly everyone got busy. The stewardesses began to march up and down the aisles collecting and checking, closing and fastening. I lifted up the window-shade and looked outside. The green of Cambodia was coming into view and I began to smile. There was so much down there waiting for me. Srey undoubtedly would be full of stories about who did what and how she fixed it. The smallest kids would throw their arms around my waist and attach themselves to my legs. Kyle would be waiting at the airport to meet me, an eye winking beneath the upturned brim of his Australian hat. And Amanda? I didn't know what kind of reception she would give me. At least I knew she was still there. She was the one who had answered the phone when I called just before Pat drove me to the airport. I don't know why that surprised me but it did. She heard it in my voice, too, and said as much.

'I told you I would stay. I promised Sam I would,' she said, sounding not defensive but rather cool and detached.

'Of course. I knew you'd be there. I just didn't expect you to pick up the phone, that's all. Silly of me. But never mind. What's new?'

'Nothing's new. Everyone here is fine. Nobody's sick. Kyle is at the swimming pool with Thom and a bunch of kids. There's a group in the library putting together a file system for the books.'

'Really? That's a good idea.'

'Yes. It's not exactly the Dewey Decimal System but it's a start. Srey and I thought we should set up a system so we know who has what. Lots of books seem to go missing otherwise.'

'Great. Thanks. We've needed that for a long time.'

'Otherwise, nothing new. Oh, but wait a minute. Kiri wants to talk to you.'

Kiri? That really did surprise me. What would Kiri want? Had he gotten into trouble again? But if he had, why would he be telling me himself? And why wasn't he swimming with the others?

'Hello, Kiri. Is everything all right? You know I'll be home very soon.'

'Yes, Mom. I know. But I knew you would call now and I want to tell you what is happening here.' Oh boy. Here it comes, I thought. What has he done now?

'Go ahead. Tell me.' What he told me really did amaze me, both for what it was and for what it wasn't. Kiri's news had nothing to do with himself or any of his brothers and sisters. There had been no quarrels, no slights, imagined or otherwise.

'I was reading the newspaper,' he started.

'You read the newspaper? Really?'

'Yes. Well, Kyle helps me. And I am now cutting out things that I think Sam would like to know. Then I will send them to her.'

'That's wonderful, Kiri. She'll love that. You can tell me all about it when I get home. But I need to go to the airport now.'

'Okay. Then I will tell you about Duch later.'

Pat was already standing in the doorway holding the car keys but this stopped me. I couldn't imagine what Kiri was talking about. Duch? I don't know any Duch, except for...I motioned to Pat that I needed one more minute. She pointed to her watch and scowled, but I didn't care.

'Kiri, which Duch do you mean?'

'Duch. You know. The big horrible killer from before. The Tribunal arrested him. He will go on trial now. Kyle said it was important and that Sam would want to know.'

I couldn't believe it. Duch, the head of Phnom Penh's notorious S-21 Prison, that one-way gate to the Killing Fields? Duch, Pol Pot's Chief Executioner? Arrested, after all these years? Sam had said they had hoped to do that. She had heard as much back when she went to the Tribunal's swearing-in session. But this was more than I had ever thought possible. 'Yes, Kiri,' I said. 'Well done. It is very important. We'll talk all about it when I get home.'

And then I wanted to get home, desperately. I rushed to the airport, rushed onto the plane, and even as I slept and pretended to relax, I knew I was silently willing the plane to rush me home. I had been gone for a week but in those few days two things had happened. I had, in effect, traveled back in time, faced an old nightmare and the fear of an uncertain future. But at the same time Cambodia had moved forward, facing the unfathomable depths of its past and driving forward towards a less insane tomorrow. I couldn't get there fast enough.

226

DECEMBER

Our Cool Season brings clear skies and chilly nights: an excellent time to experience Cambodia's beauty in comfort. Come see our new country of prosperity and freedom. We welcome you all — those who come for the first time, and those who return again and again.

A Touristic Handbook, p. 30

If you like holidays you'll love Cambodia. We can't get enough of them. Every month presents its own reasons to close up offices and schools. Everyone stays home. Some sleep. Some drink. Many stare off into space thinking about nothing much more than, perhaps, their next opportunity to sleep and drink and stare off into space. But I don't mind these one-day disruptions to our schedule, especially when we're stopping the rituals of our daily lives to acknowledge something like UN Human Rights Day. This is a funny sort of holiday to plunk down at the beginning of what most Westerners think of as the most religious month of the year. But December is a month to remember miracles. Christ is born. The Jews rededicate the Holy Temple. The United Nations adopt the Universal Declaration of Human Rights.

December 10th was a beautiful day to have a holiday. The air was so crisp, the sky so blue that I could almost hear the unmistakable crunch of a newly ripened, newly picked tart red apple. December in Cambodia felt like autumn in Ohio. It was enough to make me leave the house and head off to the park with the kids.

'Come on, guys, you want to come, too?' I called out. 'Let's go meet Kyle and the big kids in the park. Srey, do you minding staying back?'

'No, of course not, Mother. Some of the girls and I will practice our dancing.'

'Khmer or rock'n'roll?' I joked just to get that wonderful Srey look of disdain. 'But Amanda, where's she?' Actually, I knew where she was. In the library. Unless she was asked to do something specific, like help Nita and Netra in the kitchen, Amanda was always in the library these days. Sometimes she would hold story-time with the toddlers. Every afternoon she met with the older kids to supervise their homework. But in between she filed, reshelved stray books and sat alone in the quiet. Plus, I noticed that she had begun to bring a backpack to work. It was full of something, but I didn't know what. And I didn't ask. The kids even had a new nickname for her. It began as 'Amanda-librarian' and soon slipped into 'Amandabrarian.' Clever, I must admit, and it suited her now.

We reached the park in less than ten minutes, me at the end of our thick, knotted rope which was punctuated by the clenched little hands of my straggling parade of kids. They were well trained. Holiday afternoons on the streets of Phnom Penh are always busy. Plus there were tourists everywhere. But my kids knew to hold onto their bit of rope and so we all stayed attached as we marched down the side streets to the park behind the school. Once there, they spotted Kyle and the big kids in a nanosecond and I was left trailing the rope behind me.

'Well, look who it is. Come to play goalie?' Kyle teased.

'What a day. I couldn't stay inside. But cheering from the sidelines was more what I had in mind.'

Kyle clapped his hands and all the kids gathered around. It was quite amazing to see, and to think about. When I first met Kyle a few years back he seemed hardly more than a kid himself. Maybe not in age, but certainly in demeanor. Like an overgrown puppy, he was exuberant, all over the place. And he was still that way. But now it was as if he had been cooled with a dose of temperance, like when Nita

228

adds a little more coconut milk to the soup. All that good spice is still there. It just doesn't burn so much.

'Now kids, let's see you take all these skills you've learned and teach them to the younger ones,' he explained in good coach fashion. 'You know, they say if you can't teach something then you don't really know it yourself. Thom, why don't you split them up into teams.'

'Yes, Kyle. I will. Come everyone. Come with me,' and Thom moved them all back onto the field.

'You've really got them organized here, haven't you?' I said to Kyle. 'Very impressive.'

'Well, you know we strive for order. Yes, order and discipline have always been my watchwords.'

'Right. That's just what I think of when I think of you,' I teased, and my teasing produced the desired effect – a big, openhearted Kyle Mackenzie smile.

'Did you speak with Sam last night?'

'Yeah, she's great. Heading into finals.'

'Already? Jesus, the time has flown by.'

'It really has, hasn't it? I never would have expected that. She'll be home for her holiday in just ten days. Ten days. I can't wait.'

'The kids can't either, you know? They're already talking about a coming home party.'

'Coming Home Party. I like the sound of that.'

'Yeah, something very stabilizing about it.' Stabilizing? A funny word, I thought, and then the expression on Kyle's face confirmed it. I must have given him a questioning look back because he then started a conversation which was much more serious than I would have expected for an afternoon playing football in the park.

'Listen, Deborah, I've been thinking. Well, actually, I've done more than that. I've acted on what I've been thinking.' My stomach flipped.

'Is this bad news? Should I be sitting down?'

'Sure, let's sit down. Over there. But don't worry…' He put his arm around me and led me to a bench. 'It's good news, unless you don't like having me around.' As I sat down I kept my hand on his arm, my eyes on his face, for support. It's embarrassing to admit the crazy things I was thinking in those few seconds before he continued. Kyle was staying. He was going to do something to ensure he would stay, always stay, with me. Finally, Kyle and me together. An old woman's fantasy, ridiculous, and not very long-lived.

'Amanda seem okay to you?' he asked.

'Okay. Just. But she's never really seemed more than just okay to me, you know.'

'Yeah, well, I think she's settled down now. She's better since…'

'I suppose. She's certainly quieter. But you would know better than anyone, right?'

'Yes. Yes. We're still – close, I guess you'd say. But she holds so much back. Even with the kids. I think she's still afraid.'

'Makes sense.'

'But she can't always stay afraid. I began to think there must be something I could do to make her less scared. More secure.'

'More stable?'

'I suppose. So, I've decided to make it official.'

I couldn't believe what he was saying. No way could he mean what I thought he meant. Please, not that. 'What?' I gasped. 'Official? As in getting married?' But Kyle laughed.

'Don't be so horrified. No, not yet, at least. But I don't think she'll ever let me get any closer as long as she thinks I might still be minesweeping. It never seemed to bother you, but it scares her too much, I think.'

I was listening to what Kyle was saying but I couldn't hear it anymore. What could he be thinking? How could he

230

possibly know what bothered me and what didn't? 'Kyle, I just never presumed…'

'I know. I know. You're a lot stronger than she is. Anyway, I don't know – maybe I just have this need to save her or something. But never mind. The point is, I wanted to tell you I've officially quit.'

I wasn't at all sure what he was talking about. 'Quit what? Minesweeping? The agency in general?'

'Yes. The whole thing. No more minesweeping and I resigned from the agency, too. I've got a better offer. I'm going freelance.'

Suddenly, I had an overwhelming desire to watch the kids play football. This was all too much to take in. 'Freelance? What, in like you-know-a-guy?'

'I know lots of guys.' Then he laughed. 'Jesus, Deb. What do you think I am? I'm not going into the racket. I'm not a criminal.'

'Well, I mean…'

'Look. With the Tribunal and all, more and more companies want to come over. I'll help set them up. Introduce them to the right people. That sort of thing. I've already lined up a couple of clients. Get it?' Obviously, he could see from my face that I didn't get it, so he spelled it out. 'This way, first of all: I can stay in Phnom Penh. Second: I can make some real money, which, I might add, I'll funnel in your direction if you play your cards right. Third: I can make my own hours and be with you guys on a regular basis. And four: I won't be in danger of blowing myself up all the time.'

'No more death wish?'

'No. Too much to live for, I guess.' Then I got it. I saw it all: everything as it was playing itself out in Kyle's brain. Kyle the Fixer, forever. But whether this new fix could really do what he wanted, namely number five: make Amanda love him, was, at least to me, a huge, overhanging, vulture-like question mark. 'What? I thought you'd be happy,' he said. 'I'll be around all the time now. I might even move in.'

'Happy? Of course I'm happy,' I said. 'Can't you see? This is my happy face.'

If Sam had been home that night, I would have had her sit on the side of my bed and chat to me about nothing, just to settle me down. I needed settling after that talk with Kyle. It was already past midnight; I had to get some sleep, but sleep just wouldn't come. I had been lying there for at least an hour with my eyes closed, then open, then closed again. I needed Sam, or at least I thought I did.

But then I sat up, plumped the pillows behind me and started to talk to myself, calmly at first, but then louder and more angrily into the dark, empty space:

'Enough, Deborah. Stop it. You don't need Sam to calm you down. You yell at her for feeling too responsible for you, but here you are tossing and turning, unable to settle yourself down without her. And why? What are you afraid of? Are you afraid of being alone?

Yes. Okay. I'm afraid of being alone.

How can you say you're alone with a house full of kids down the hall?

But that's different.

What's so different about it? You're surrounded by people who love you. Your world is full of such people, whether they are down the hall or across the planet. Your life is full.

Full of children.

Yes.

And I love them all.

Of course you do. So what's the problem?

232

It's not enough. There, I said it. Am I asking too much? Am I too selfish to want more, at my age? To want more than just the love of children?

But you have friends who also love you.

Yes, I know. Friends....

Kyle? Don't be ridiculous. He's in love with someone else. But face it. You took yourself out of that game years ago. Maybe if you stopped acting like an old woman – an old, worn out, finished woman ready to let the world march by while you stand on the sidelines waving some flag of Saint Deborah... It's not too late, you know. There isn't much time left, but Goddamnit, it's not too late. Not too...'

I lay back down and turned towards the window. A slight breeze crept in through the window frame and moved the curtains ever so lightly, like a hand gently screening out the blackness. I watched the movement of the air against the cotton and felt it from far away against my cheek, across my closed eyelids. Cool, soft, loving, it carried me into sleep.

Leave it to Srey to realize that there was shopping to do. I was standing at the doorway waiting to wave goodbye as she marched the kids off to school, when she stopped and said, 'Mother, Sam comes home in less than one week. We must go shopping.'

'Shopping? For what? Nita will get all her favorite foods.'

'No, not that. Her part of the bedroom. She took so much with her, it looks empty.'

'Really? You think so?'

'Oh, Mother, please. Go see for yourself. Today after school we must go.' She started to head the troop down the road in the usual two straight lines, but then called back. 'The Russian Market has the best things. We will go there.'

So, of course, we did. You don't mess with Srey. Every day she becomes more and more forceful, but with a determination and clarity that I find, honestly, humbling. She is so often right these days, and she was right again about Sam's room. I went to look at it – really look at it – as Srey had bade me to do. The walls around Srey's own corner were covered with photographs torn out of magazines, drawings she had done herself, and postcards she had been collecting from who-knows-where. Her bed was covered with the sunburst-yellow duvet and pillows I had bought her for her sixteenth birthday. Her corner was full of color, sparkly, busy, but purposefully so. It was Srey. But where was Sam? Her bed was stripped. Her walls, bare. Srey was right. Sam was completely gone from that space. Something must be done.

Later that afternoon I left Amanda and Kyle in charge and took Srey to the Russian Market. Rather, Srey took me. I hadn't been there since Sam's pre-college shopping spree. I usually avoid the place. All those stalls. Shelves and shelves of everything from marble Buddhas to knock-off Fendi bags. Saris and blouses and dresses, embroidered skirts and hand-painted t-shirts hanging from railings, pipes and ceiling fixtures. It overwhelms me. But not Srey. She guided me around with the confidence of a CEO showing off his company. She may still have a teenage heart fluttering in that chest of hers, but her eyes have the focus of a business mogul.

'Mother, I made a list of what we need to buy.' She pulled a long sheet of lined paper out of her bag.

'And when did you do this?'

'Today. In school.' She saw the look on my face. 'During science. I had already finished the experiment. Really, Mother.'

'Okay, okay. But look at all this. We can't…'

'Don't worry. It won't be too expensive. I will make sure. Anyway, Kyle gave me some money.'

'He did? What for?'

'For this. To help buy what we need for Sam. He said you would take it.'

Sure, I took it. I was happy to take whatever Kyle could give me. But I didn't really have a choice anyway because there was no stopping Srey. She led me from booth to booth. First, a new bedspread and matching pillowcases. Then, a wall-hanging to hide the sheetrock of the wall besides Sam's head.

'These colors remind me of Sam, don't you think? For me, I would like more oranges and reds. But for Sam, blues and greens are better. Do you see?'

And, quite amazingly to me, I did see. In the past, I never took the time to pay attention to such things. I guess you could say I was a function-over-form kind of a person. There was always too much to do and too little time to do it. But, standing there with Srey, watching her finger fabrics and compare color dyes, I began to see everything the way she did. Colors had meanings. Textures had purpose. There was great beauty to be found in that market. And what could be more important than finding beauty?

When we finished buying everything Srey believed we needed, I checked my watch, saw that there was still plenty of time before dinner, and gave in to an impulse. 'Srey, could you help me with one more thing now?' I asked. 'I think I'd like to buy a bracelet.'

'Ooh, wonderful! A bracelet!' Srey nearly jumped with excitement. 'For Sam?'

'No, for me.'

'For you? Really?'

'Yes, I know it's funny, but I think I deserve it. What do you think?'

'Oh, Mother. Yes!' and she threw her arms around my neck. 'I know exactly the right stall. Lavender beads, I think. With some silver. Yes, follow me.'

Later that night, Srey and I had a wonderful time decorating Sam's room. We placed the wall hanging right where the AIDS victims' piece had hung. We made up the bed with the new sheets and cover. We dusted the shelf besides her bed, but there was nothing on it except one old computer textbook.

'Oh, Srey. This is terrible. She took everything. It looks so empty.'

'Yes, I thought of that. Look.' Srey pulled out the box of treasures she always kept under her bed and looked inside. 'Here. We will use these.' She chose six ceramic figurines from the box and arranged them neatly on the shelf.

'Your animal collection. I remember these,' I said.

'These elephants are from different New Year's Festivals. And remember when those children from London came and brought this bear?'

'Right. The Harrods Bear.'

'We called him Harry. Remember? I always loved these things.' Srey turned them around from side to side, each one getting its most flattering position. 'But this one here…the kangaroo. This actually belongs to Sam. Kyle gave it to her many years ago. Don't tell her, but I secretly took it before she left. It reminds me of her and I was afraid I would be too lonely without her, so I hid it away. But I have been okay and now she's coming home, so I will give it back to her.'

'Perfect, Srey. Yes, everything looks perfect. And I could never have done it without you.' I gave her my biggest hug. 'And don't worry. I won't tell Sam that you borrowed her kangaroo. It will be our secret. But look. It's getting late. I want to check on everyone else and you should be getting to bed yourself. School tomorrow.'

'Are you sure you don't need help with the others?'

'I'm sure. Sleep well, love, and thank you.'

'You are welcome. It was fun. Oh, and Mother,' she called after me as I turned to leave. 'Your bracelet looks beautiful on you.'

It did look beautiful, and I was staring at it on my wrist as I walked down the hall to the boys' rooms. Everything was quiet. The younger ones were mostly asleep. The older ones already in bed. Chak's light was still on, though.

'Everything alright?' I whispered.

'Yes, Mother.'

'Let's put out your light then. We don't want to wake your brothers.'

'Okay. Can I have another kiss, please?'

'With pleasure.' I sat down on the bed, gave him a kiss and stroked his hair. 'You have grown up so much over the past months.' He smiled and placed my hand on his cheek.

'Yes, I have,' he whispered and closed his eyes.

Finishing my rounds, I stood for a moment in the entryway and listened. Everything was hushed and peaceful. It was wonderful, and I felt enveloped by the quiet, ready for the solitude of my bedroom, ready for sleep. I assumed I was alone with the kids, but as I passed by the library I heard Kyle and Amanda's voices. It was after ten o'clock. They were usually gone by this time. But although I could hear they were talking, I couldn't make out what they were saying. The anger in their voices was unmistakable, though. At least, the anger in Kyle's. I didn't want to be a part of whatever drama was unfolding in there. I figured I'd be sucked into it soon enough, anyway. But before I could turn the corner into the hallway leading to my room, Kyle came out of the library, walking fast. He saw me and shook his head.

'I'll see you tomorrow,' he said with the quick decisiveness of a guillotine.

I started towards my room but I stopped myself and turned back into the library. I was already sucked in.

'Amanda?' She was picking up a last pile of books from the table. She looked impenetrable. 'Everything alright?'

'Fine. I'm just finishing up. I'll be gone soon.'

'I just saw Kyle…'

'Yes, well. He'll be fine.'

I walked over to her and even took the books out of her hands. I expected, hoped, to see tears in her eyes, to see anything at all, but there was nothing. 'But he isn't fine now,' I said. 'Maybe it's none of my business, but…' She laughed at that, and didn't even try to hide it.

'Well, really. It's silly. He should know better.'

And then I saw it. The whole thing. The offer. The refusal. The broken heart. 'I know about his resignation, the new job, all of it,' I said. 'He did it for you, you know.'

'I never asked him to.'

'He did it anyway.'

'But, like I said, it has nothing to do with me.' Then she took the books back out of my hands and glared into my eyes. 'I don't know what you were imagining, Deborah. But really, the idea of anything permanent happening between me and Kyle? Well, it's preposterous.'

'Preposterous? How can you say that?'

'Why wouldn't I? It's the truth.'

'Yes. I see now that it is. But to be so cold…' Amanda shook her head, finished shelving the books and walked towards the door. I could almost feel the empty space around her, airless, without light or life except for what little she left behind as she passed by. I almost hated her for what she was doing to Kyle. I hoped she would leave and not say anything else. I hoped she would just leave.

But instead she said, 'Don't worry. He'll survive. We all do, right?' And walked towards the door.

Tonight would be another sleepless night.

* * * *

The day had finally arrived. Sam was coming home! Three whole weeks she would be here, well into the next month. On into the next year. Nita and Netra had been cooking all day. There would be a party tonight.

'All of Sam's favorite foods,' Netra said. 'Just like we did before she left.'

'Like Samnang never not here,' agreed Nita in a rare dive into English.

Kyle borrowed a car and drove me to the airport. I was so excited, I was talking non-stop. 'She already sounded tired when I spoke to her before she left. She had just handed in her history paper. She wrote about the Dred-Scott Act, of all things. She said she had one French exam to finish and then she was done. God, she's been working hard. And she did sound tired. I hope she gets some rest on the flight. The kids are so excited. They won't be able to leave her alone for a minute.' Kyle smiled but didn't say anything. 'And how about Kiri's scrapbook? He can't wait to show it to her. What a great idea that was you had. Don't you think? Don't you?' Still, he said nothing.

I had never mentioned to him my talk with Amanda. If you could call it a talk. He never mentioned to me what had happened that night in the library. We were all clearly pretending that nothing had happened, nothing had changed. They both still showed up at the Home every day. The children were taken care of. The place functioned as it always had. But some sort of life had gone out of it. I'm not sure if the kids noticed, but I did. Amanda had already withdrawn into herself months before, but now it felt like Kyle had given up, too. He had stopped fooling around, and his sobriety was killing me. In less than an hour, Sam would be sitting in this car beside us. If he didn't snap out of it, she would notice it in a second. And then what? I couldn't stay quiet any longer. I had to say something.

239

'So, are you going to keep this up while Sam's here, or what?' I finally challenged him.

'What do you mean?'

'This silence. This, I don't know, depression. Are we going to talk about it or are you going to pretend it's not happening?' He looked at me and then back at the road.

'I was going to pretend it's not happening, but clearly you're not going to let me do that.'

'No, I'm not. I just can't stand it anymore, Kyle, and to be honest, it will only get worse once Sam's here because she'll notice it, too. Then she'll start worrying again. She'll start making a fuss. Hell, maybe she'll even start saying she can't go back to school. And, anyway, I love you too much to see you like this.' I stared at him, but his eyes never left the road. I know he heard what I said. I could hear it in the way his breathing changed. I could see it in the rising of his chest. I had told him I loved him, but whatever anger or frustration had forced me to blurt it out had now turned to disappointment and resignation. 'Believe me, Kyle, I'm doing you a favour by making you talk about this.'

Kyle's head began to bob up and down slowly, seemingly without his knowing it. 'You women,' he said, without any sarcasm or humor. 'How did I get stuck with such a group of women?'

'I don't know – a man's man like you...'

Kyle let out a very long sigh. 'Well, I guess you know she dumped me.'

'I figured as much.'

'It's not really a dump, I guess. If I'm honest with myself I'd have to admit that the whole thing barely got off the ground. Even after Siem Reap. Even after The Baby. So let's just say that all my big plans for us are over.' He kept driving and staring straight ahead. I put my hand on his leg.

'You couldn't save her, Kyle. She'll have to do that for herself somehow, sometime. She's just not ready yet,' I tried to explain. 'Look. She's been wounded, badly, and she's grown a scab over that wound so that it doesn't turn septic and kill her. For a while that scab will be impenetrable. It has to be. But, hopefully, in time...'

Kyle started to laugh, an angry sort of laugh that I had never heard from him before. 'Oh, you think so? That's your professional opinion? Well, she fooled us both, then. She's not so wounded, so helpless. She's just fine.'

'Fine? What are you talking about?'

'She used us. Don't you see? For the past few months she's been making all kinds of plans, figuring things out for herself. For herself alone. And she never said a word.'

'What are you talking about? What plans?'

'She's going back to the States. She's going to be a psychologist or some such thing. A head case like her – can you imagine? That's what she's been doing all that time in the library. Reading, observing, filling out forms. She's applied to go back to school.'

'What? Just like that?'

'Just like that. What an idiot I've been. What a chump.'

I couldn't believe it. I mean, I could believe that Amanda was leaving. I always knew she would. She'd have to, one way or another. But so secretly? With such detachment? Had she come to hate us so much? Kyle and I sat in silence for the last mile or so up to the airport. But when we turned into the parking lot, I asked like some little girl, 'Now what?'

'Now what? Well, now we pick up Sam. Then we go home. Then we wait.'

'Until?'

'Tomorrow and the next day and the future.' We had arrived at the airport. Kyle pulled the car into short term parking, turned off the motor and looked at me. 'I don't know what's going to happen, old girl, and I've been thinking about it a lot. But I've made one decision. I won't

241

leave you and the kids. Regardless of what Amanda does and when. For my own sanity's sake, I don't dare. So cheer up. Let's go get Sam. And bloody hell, will you stop crying?'

I hadn't even realized I had begun. 'Okay. Okay. But I'll tell you one thing. No matter what happens, you damned well better stop calling me old girl.'

From the depths to the heights. In one minute we were staring at each other outside the car. In the next, we were staring at Sam. Of course, she looked beautiful. She looked tall and strong and healthy and happy. Sure, she always looked that way to me, but now there was something else, too. You could see it from a mile away. Kyle and I both saw it as we watched her push her luggage trolley past the barricades and down the long corridor to where we waited.

'Look at her,' Kyle said first. 'She looks like a woman.'

And she did. There was a new easy confidence in her walk, in the way she held her shoulders back and her head lifted. 'She's perfect,' I said. 'Sam…Sam!' I started to wave, and before we knew it we were holding each other, laughing and crying.

'I thought you hated tearful airport scenes,' Kyle joked as he ushered us out of the building.

'I changed my mind. This kind of scene I like.'

As we drove back home, Sam was the one talking a mile a minute. 'Oh, it is so good to see you,' she started. 'So good to be home. I love it at school, but oh…this air. How I missed these smells. Fried bananas? Will there be fried bananas at home?'

'Yes. And coconut and papaya salad. Netra and Nita have been cooking all day.'

'And is everyone fine? Srey?'

'Wonderful. Wait 'til you see her. In a few short months she's grown up a lot.'

'And Thom?'

242

'Yes, Thom's great. Mr Responsibility.'

'Oh, I can't wait to see everybody. And Amanda?'

Kyle answered that question. 'Yes, they'll all be waiting.'

And they all were, right at the door as we pulled up. Sam could barely walk into the house for all the kissing and hugging. Our brightest star had returned.

There was so much excitement around Sam's arrival home that I never questioned Amanda about her plans. I was going to. At least I thought I would. But once Sam was beside me all my attention turned to her and my desire to confront Amanda dissolved. If there had been a change in the atmosphere at home, Sam didn't seem to notice. And anyway, she was too busy talking and playing and giving out little gifts. Right after her first dinner at home, she reached for a bag stashed deep inside her backpack which was still lying dropped in the hallway.

'Everyone, there is a special treat to all of you from Aunt Pat and Uncle Greg. They send love to each one of you.' The bag was full of Pez dispensers, small plastic models of Bugs Bunny, Cinderella, Teenage Mutant Ninja Turtles, all with bodies full of candy and heads that jerked back to offer up the sweets.

'My God, leave it to Pat. I had no idea they still made these things,' I said. 'Kyle, Amanda – can you help load them up? I could never do it.'

'And for the little kids, look,' Sam said, walking around to the row of high chairs. 'Finger-puppets. You put one on your finger like this and make it dance.'

Pat's gifts kept the kids happy long enough for me to help Sam bring her bags into her room. Funny, but I was nervous about what she would think of the changes we had made.

'You took so much to school with you, your bed looked bare. We hope you like it.'

Sam sat down on her bed, ran her fingers along the coverlet and then stretched out. 'It is all wonderful. Thank you, Mother. I love the colors.'

'Well, you can thank Srey. It was all her idea. And she chose everything just for you.'

'Oh, and these are her animals on my shelf? And my kangaroo? She found that, too?'

'Yes, she did.'

'I must go thank her right now,' and she ran back into the dining room to find her sister. They had missed each other much more than I had ever guessed, and I remember allowing myself a little pat on the back for that.

It was a couple of nights later that I learned that Sam had felt something different at home, after all. She came into my room to say goodnight, just as she always had. She sat on the edge of my bed and took my hand.

'So Sam, how does it feel to be home?' I asked. It really was an innocent question.

'It feels wonderful, Mother. You know, I do love school. I have good friends now. A life I never thought possible. And to be honest, I really don't think about home so much.'

'Good. I wouldn't want you to be thinking about us all the time.'

'But now that I am here, I am so happy.'

'Well, that's what home means, isn't it? The place you can always come back to and always feel...'

'... at home?' she said, laughing.

'Yes.' I laughed, too. 'Even when things change, home is still the place you can come to and feel good. At least, that's the idea.'

Sam then got that look on her face that meant she was balancing her words and her thoughts. She began to play with the bracelet on my wrist.

'Mother, when did you get this?'

'Oh, I bought it for myself. Surprised? Yes, I know. It's not like me.'

'But it is beautiful. And it looks beautiful on you.'

'Thanks. I love it. I seem to wear it every day. I guess I decided I wanted to do something just for me. Silly...'

'No. Not silly. It is the sort of thing you would tell me to do for myself. You are learning your own lessons,' she smiled as she chatted, as if she was saying nothing of consequence. 'You know, I have not been away that long, but all the children look like they have grown.'

'Kids do that. They can change in a minute.'

'Netra and Chak and...what about Kiri? Did you see the scrapbook he is making for me?'

'Kyle started it with him when you first went to school. Kyle thinks the reason Kiri acts up so often is because he's so damn smart. Reading newspapers, putting that book together, gives him a way to use that brain of his.'

'He is like my own private journalist now. It is so funny. Oh, and he told me about the big march in a few days. Do you know about it?'

'The one with the monks?'

'Yes, and nuns and anyone who wants to join so they can support the Tribunal. I think I might go.'

'Really? Gee, I don't know. But I guess if you want to...'

'Oh, Mother. Do not worry. I will think about it. We will see. But anyway, Kyle is very sweet to help Kiri like this, don't you think?'

'I do. I think it's been good for both of them, actually.'

'But Mother, I must ask. Is Kyle alright? He seems less...less...I don't know.'

And there it was: the awareness, the concern. I took a moment to answer. 'Kyle is, well, okay. Just okay. He's had a disappointment.'

'Amanda?'

'Yes.'

'She is not okay then?'

'I don't know. I don't think anybody does. But she's not ready for Kyle. Not now. Probably not ever.' Without thinking about it, I had decided not to tell Sam about Amanda's plans. With each passing hour, those so-called plans seemed less and less real, as if, perhaps, they were just something she had said to Kyle to push him away. Really, from the first wintry day Amanda had arrived unannounced, nothing had ever made sense to me about her. For nearly a year I had gone from angry to enchanted to befuddled and back again. Now nothing or anything would surprise me. Like Mary Poppins, she had blown in on a cold wind. God knows what she would do next. It certainly wasn't for me to say.

Sam was quiet for a long time, so long that I was about to give her my goodnight kiss and start to get ready for bed. But then she voiced one more last thought for the night. 'Home is a funny thing, isn't it Mother? It should be so easy, but I think for many people it is not. I am lucky to have a home that I love so much. Not to feel at home anywhere – how painful that must be.'

Our hug that night was long and still. I could feel our chests rising and falling with the combined beatings of our hearts. 'In the morning, I promise,' we both said.

We don't celebrate Christmas at the Khmer Home for Blessed Children. But out of respect for the wishes of the nuns who founded the place so many years ago, I do put up a Christmas tree. Of sorts. It's an old plastic tree that the nuns left for us in an upstairs cupboard. Every year I send a bunch of kids up into that closet to retrieve the tree and the box of haphazard ornaments we use to decorate it. It's a bigger job than it sounds: the thing's got to be nearly six feet tall. Plus, it's inevitably full of dust with a couple of branches that need fixing, not to mention the plastic stand that requires assembly and the lights that need untangling. But, like so much around here, getting it out and setting it up has become a tradition. We do it on the afternoon of December 24th, and the kids love it.

This year, Thom was in charge. 'There are five of us ready. Should we go now?'

'Okay, but be careful. Do you want Kyle to help?'

'Oh no, Mother. That is not necessary. We can do it.' Silly me.

We were all busier than usual, it's true, but that's no excuse for the fact that for a long time that day none of us was aware of Amanda's absence. Surprisingly, it was Nita who first mentioned it. She was beginning to prepare dinner. Netra was with the other kids working on the tree and so, I suppose, Nita went looking for Amanda to help chop some vegetables.

'Miss Deborah? No Amanda today?'

'Really? Jeez, you're right. I haven't seen her all day. I'll go look.' I went directly to the library. The lights were off. I flicked them on to find the room all neat and tidy, every book in its position, every chair in its place. But nobody was there. I looked for Sam and Srey to ask them if they had seen her, but I already knew what their answer would be. I could feel panic rising up into my throat. My mind began to race. Had something happened to her? Was she sick, or worse? Had somebody done something to her, or had she done something to herself? I forced myself to be calm when I went over to Kyle who was sitting on the floor in the midst of meters-worth of tangled wires.

'I tell you, this year I'm getting this all organized. I'll find something to wrap these wires around. It's an accident waiting to happen…What?'

I motioned him off to the side. 'Kyle. Amanda?'

'She said she'd be late today.'

'Well, it's almost five o'clock.'

247

Kyle's face turned white. It was as if all the unspeakable things I had been thinking were automatically transferred into his head. He thrust the tangle of lights into my hands. 'Here. Don't say anything to anyone. I'll be back.'

I looked at the mess I was holding, and then looked up to see Nita still standing in the kitchen doorway. I slowly shook my head. She nodded and turned back to her vegetables.

It was hard to keep my fears to myself as I sat there in the middle of all that activity. Clearly, despite the mixed emotions throughout all those months, I still cared about Amanda. I cared more than I had ever realized. I placed myself in a chair with little Arun in my lap. There's nothing like holding a squirming four-year-old boy to keep you rooted in the present and away from all your imagined terrors. Hiding behind his bobbing head, I watched Sam take over the job of untangling the wires while Srey and Nary unwrapped the ornaments.

'Oh, remember this?' Srey would say with each one.

'Did that come from those people from Canada?' someone would say.

'How about this one? I love this one!'

'Yes, Dr Reith brought that back from his trip to France. That was a long time ago.'

Each ornament brought a new memory, a new connection, now severed but still, somehow, there.

It wasn't until all the lights were strung and all the ornaments hung that anyone asked for Kyle and Amanda.

'Mother, is Amanda still not here?' Sam finally said to me in a whisper.

Then Thom came over and asked, 'Should we wait for Kyle to turn on the lights, just in case?'

I didn't know what to do. How long could I stall? Kyle had been gone nearly an hour and it was getting close to dinnertime. Chak came over and raised his arms to be picked up. He needed comforting for some reason or other. But then again, so did I.

I was just about to make up some sort of excuse when I heard the door open and then close. Kyle was back. He was alone and holding something in his hands, something I couldn't see. But I wasn't looking too closely. I was too focused on his eyes. They were as dark as if all the light had gone out of them. But there was no sign of tears. Actually, they looked empty. There was no sign of anything. He came over and rested one hand on my shoulder. Suddenly, all went quiet. Everyone was looking at him.

'So, it's all finished, eh?' he said, pointing to the tree. 'Thom, are we ready to try out those lights?' His voice was solid and even. Thom's questioning look could have meant so many things, but Kyle softly urged him on. 'Go ahead.' Kyle shut off the ceiling lights and Thom plugged the tree lights into the wall socket. Without a pop or a fizzle or anything frightening at all, the tree lit up from the star perched on its top to the bells jangling off the bottom. Instinctively, we all turned to look at it and we all, of course, said 'Ahh…'

Kyle stared at the tree for a few minutes before he spoke. 'Everyone, come here,' he said. 'I have something to tell you.' He waited a moment for the whole room to gather around him, every eye was focused on his face. Even the smallest ones were quiet with expectation. 'I've just been to Amanda's apartment and I talked to her landlord,' he began. I could tell he was struggling not to show too much emotion. 'Amanda left Cambodia this morning on a flight back to the States. Mr Chea said she told him that her uncle is getting married and that she is flying off to Boston for the wedding.'

At first, I honestly didn't know if I believed him. Despite what Kyle had told me about Amanda's plans, she had never said anything about them to me. To be honest, Kyle could have found anything over at that apartment. Seen anything. I willed him to look at me, eye to eye, to somehow let me know if what Mr Chea had said was, indeed, the truth. The sadness in his face convinced me. It was a sadness born not of horror or tragedy, but of loss, quiet and long-dreaded.

'Will she be coming back?' asked Netra. I looked at Nita and she put her arm around the young girl's shoulders.

Kyle cleared his throat and took a breath. 'No, darling. She will not be coming back.'

And then Srey: 'She didn't even say goodbye?' That's when my eyes filled with tears. I closed my eyelids once, twice, to try to clear the tears away, but I couldn't. I felt Kyle's hand press more firmly on my shoulder.

'Actually, she did say goodbye. She left this note.' He pulled an envelope out of his back pocket. 'It is addressed to All the Blessed Children.' He took out a folded sheet of paper and handed the empty envelope to Sam. 'She says: "Please forgive me for leaving so suddenly. I have loved being with you and hope I have helped you as much as you have helped me. But it is now time for me to go. I will hold all of you in my heart always. Love, Amanda."'

No-one said anything for a long time. I knew they were waiting for me to speak first. Whatever sorrow, anger, frustration or fear I might have been feeling myself, I had to hide it all and find the words that would best help my children. I don't know if I said the right thing. I don't know if there even was a right thing to say. All I could do was start. 'This is very sad for all of us. I cannot pretend that it isn't. But you know, isn't it kind of her to have left just at a time of celebration? Just at a time when we are all together as a family, having such fun around the tree with our memories, just like we do every year? Amanda has been our friend. A good and important friend. And she always will be, whether she is actually here with us or not. Right?' I looked around the room. It was full of little, sad faces and I thought my heart would turn to powder and blow away. I wished I could take all their pain and feel it for them. But, of course, I couldn't, and I knew, I really did, that it wouldn't help them any if I could. 'Right?' I repeated.

'Right!' Sam said, with a forceful exclamation point afterwards.

'Right, Mom,' Srey echoed.

'Right,' everyone repeated in their own way, their own voice, as best they could.

I switched the lights back on in the room, and Nita began to bring dinner to the table. As the kids settled themselves and each other in their chairs, Kyle took Sam and me aside.

'When I got there, the place was empty. But she left these messages for you.' He handed an envelope to Sam and one to me. 'I got one, too.' He shoved the folded piece of paper meant for him into my hand. I read it to myself: 'Believe me, this is better for us both.' I went to hand it back to him, but he just smirked, shook his head, pushed it away and then went off to help with dinner. I watched Sam open her envelope and read its contents. I never intended to ask what it said. Sam didn't offer to show it to me, either, but she did tell me what was in it.

'Amanda just said that she left because she knew she could. That we would all be fine just as we were, without her.'

'She's right, you know.'

'Yes, I know. And she asked that I forgive her. But that is silly. There is nothing to forgive.'

My own envelope I didn't open until later that night in my room. There was dinner to finish, homework to oversee, bedtime to enforce. Those were my excuses, at least. Really, I didn't think there could be much that Amanda would have wanted to say to me. So imagine my surprise when later that night, in bed, I read the message which simply said: 'Thank you for saving my life.'

I was nervous. Of course I was. Even Kyle was a bit unsure about letting Sam join the march. Certainly, these sorts of demonstrations are becoming more frequent in Cambodia nowadays. And it's a real sign of progress that they are. That doesn't mean they're not dangerous, though. Anything can happen in Phnom Penh. Politics can still be a very violent game here, and although I'm thrilled to see people taking to the streets and standing up for what they believe in, it doesn't mean I want my own child there in the fray.

'You're a mature woman now,' I told Sam. 'I can't stop you from doing this if you think it's important. But you can't stop me from worrying.'

'If it looks dangerous I will come home.'

'If it looks dangerous? How will you know?'

'Yes, Sam. I think maybe Mother is right. This is exciting. But maybe it is dangerous, too.' Srey was eavesdropping on our conversation. 'You are very important and are only here for a few weeks. You must not take chances. There is still more fun to have before you go back and I do not want you to miss it.'

'Oh Srey, thank you. But I won't miss anything, and I promise, I will be fine. But thank you for saying I am important. It is not really true, though.'

'Oh no, Sam. You are wrong.' Srey's voice became extraordinarily tempered and unusually serious. 'You are very important. To all of us. To the whole country. You must keep yourself safe so you can come back and make things better.'

What could any of us say to that? Srey had uttered something beautiful, and the three of us stood there staring at each other for a time, letting the thought lower itself and anchor between us.

'I have an idea, then,' Sam said at last. 'Srey, if you are happy to take charge here, then Mother – why don't you come with me? We will march together. We will keep each other safe.'

'Really? Me march with you?'

'Yes. The Tribunal is important to you, too. Isn't it?'

'Of course.'

'Then come with me. We will march to the courthouse.'

'Yes, Mother. That is a great idea,' said Srey. 'But wear your sneakers.'

And so, at noon on Christmas Day 2007, Samnang and I waved goodbye to our Home full of loved ones and strode off to join hundreds of others in our march for justice. A huge group of people was congregating outside the Royal Palace. It was frightening to be swamped by such a crowd. I felt lost at first and unsure of what to do or where to go. Sam took me by the hand and we pushed our way through the throng of saffron robes, white habits, tie-died t-shirts and blue silk sarongs. Out of the crowd, though, came a distant voice that grew closer and more insistent with each of our steps.

'Miss Deborah. Miss Deborah! Over here. Come!' It was Dr Reith, calling out above the noisy crowd. One hand held a sign reading *Reconciliation*, and the other was reaching out to us.

'Doctor, you're here, too? I'm so glad.'

'Yes. Yes. I couldn't miss this. Not after all I have been through…we have been through.' In a rush of unfiltered emotion, he took my hand and kissed it. 'I am so glad you are here. I knew in my heart you would be. And Sam?' He reached across me to touch her face. 'How wonderful to see you here, too. Now come. Come with me. We will stay together.'

He placed his arm around me and shepherded us through the growing mass of people. All around us demonstrators held small chimes and tambourines, flutes and bouquets of lilies, signs proclaiming *Make Justice Swift*, and *End Torture Forever*. Amidst it all, I could feel Dr Reith's energy beside me, helping me feel safe, making all of us safe there on the streets of Phnom Penh.

Within a few minutes a rumbling sound started from the front and moved like a hum throughout the crowd as together thousands of feet hit the tarmac. We were marching.

'Oh my God, Sam. Look,' I said clasping her hand. 'It's begun.' I could feel my heart pulsing in my chest, moving up into my throat with the excitement. My legs felt light. I was weightless, carried away by the determination of all these new friends around me, by the dedication of the partner I had always found in Dr Reith, and by the love of my daughter standing by my side. We were moving further and further forward with every step. Each footfall brought us closer to the courthouse and closer to a dream of justice that so many of us still held tight to our hearts. I looked up to see that we were now standing under a huge banner that spanned the entire breadth of the mass of demonstrators. It read: *The Tribunal is the Remedy for the Cycle of Vengeance*. A remedy for vengeance. What an amazing idea, I thought. And isn't that just what we need? Isn't that what all of us have always needed, from the Kent State and Phnom Penh of the 1970s to the America and Cambodia of the future? A remedy for vengeance. A promise for the morning.

I was crying, I was so happy. But Sam was laughing. 'Okay, Mother. Hold on. Here we go,' she said.

ACKNOWLEDGEMENTS

A Clash of Innocents began with a trip. In 2006, I traveled to Cambodia to volunteer in the house-building efforts of the charity Tabitha, and to work with the children of the shelter Sok Sobay. This was my first foray into Asia and I think it is truthful to say the trip changed my life. There is now a novel to prove it. But more importantly, there are friends and colleagues.

I would first like to thank the adults and teenagers who accompanied me on that trip and helped open my eyes to a new part of the world I have come to love. Although I can't name you all here, I will especially thank Yolanda Henry, our trip leader, a Tabitha Board Member, and a friend who continued to help me with my research and encourage my enthusiasm for this project.

During the writing process, I was greatly helped and sympathetically guided by my writing group, Kate Beswick, Liz Rutherford-Johnson and Sarah Tyrer, talented writers all. I know I am a better writer because of their efforts.

Much of this book was written under the sheltering care of Sue Booth-Forbes and her great creation, Anam Cara Writers' and Artists' Retreat. West Cork, Ireland is a magical place, but Sue has worked her own magic to turn my enthusiastic ramblings into a novel. I thank her for her love, her friendship, and her insistence on authenticity.

My friends, Verity Langley and Sonja Rein, have continued to be tireless supporters of my efforts, always believing in my abilities and working hard in their own lives to ensure that my artistic fancies become reality.

Heartfelt thanks go to my publishers, Adele Ward and Mike Fortune-Wood. Their fearlessness and determination in establishing Ward Wood Publishing during the present economic conditions is an inspiration and a lesson to us all that as long as you keep your heart open and your wits clear, any dream can come true. I am honoured to have *A Clash of Innocents* chosen to be their first publishing effort.

And of course, last but never least, my husband, Don, and my sons, Alex and Noah, who continue to believe in my dreams, love me despite them all, and still laugh at my jokes.

BOOK CLUB QUESTIONS

Historic events continue to have an impact on the lives of the characters. What is the role of history in the novel? In what ways does history continue into the present?

Deborah reacts strongly to Amanda's response to The Baby's death. Why does she treat Amanda the way that she does, and is her response to Amanda's grief cruel or kind?

How does Kyle change over the course of the story? What causes these changes?

What is the meaning of family as portrayed in the novel?

Why did Amanda decide to leave Cambodia?